T0105697

Very Truly Yours

MAXINE THOMAS

WESTBOW
PRESS
A DIVISION OF THOMAS NELSON

Cover artwork by Joanne Meller Lamson, Designs by Meller, Mount Holly, NJ.

WestBow Press books may be ordered through booksellers or by contacting:

WestBow Press
A Division of Thomas Nelson
1663 Liberty Drive
Bloomington, IN 47403
www.westbowpress.com
1-(866) 928-1240

ISBN: 978-1-4497-7145-4 (sc)
ISBN: 978-1-4497-7144-7 (hc)
ISBN: 978-1-4497-7146-1 (e)

Library of Congress Control Number: 2012919226

Printed in the United States of America

WestBow Press rev. date: 10/18/2012

To Errol, for now and always.

" For I know the plans I have for you," declares the Lord, "plans to prosper you and not to harm you, plans to give you hope and a future"—Jeremiah 29:11 (NIV)

Chapter 1

*I*t was the perfect day for a wedding. The brisk morning air had given way to a comfortably cool afternoon. Puffy white clouds meandered nonchalantly across a backdrop of blue sky, playing hide and seek with rays of sunshine.

Leaning casually against the deck rail at the rear of his townhouse, David Willoughby squinted against a sudden burst of brightness and turned his head to avoid the piercing rays. On this, his wedding day, he could hardly summon appreciation for sunshine.

His chin brushed against the starched collar of his tuxedo shirt, reminding him that he really needed to finish dressing and get on his way. Reaching for the ends of his black bowtie, he folded one over the other and then let them fall back, still untied, against his shirt.

What had caused his sullen mood? It had been present for the last few days, and he couldn't seem to snap out of it. Still, he could fake happiness if that was the only way to get through the ceremony and the party afterward. It wasn't that he was having second thoughts about getting married. Although he wasn't quite ready for kids or a house in the suburbs, he was looking forward to the connections this liaison would produce for him: the best clubs and the most influential business contacts.

David slid back the cuff of his crisp, white shirt and glanced at his watch. Less than one hour to go. Unperturbed, he settled back against the deck post. Leila, his bride-to-be, would be furious if he showed up late. Actually, it was her mother who would be livid, although she would disguise it well behind a steely mask and then confront Leila about it later. Unlike her mother, Leila's anger would peak and fall in as many seconds as it took to inhale and exhale.

Or she might not bother to show her anger at all.

Either way, he cared little. By marrying, they both would get what they wanted: he the social connections that would give his career a good head start, and she the freedom from her parents' restraints she craved and the stability of a husband who could provide for her financial and emotional needs.

"Ready, son?" his father called through screen doors.

"We've still got a few minutes, Dad." Without turning his head, David waved in the general direction of his father. But his thoughts remained on Leila.

Leila was not the kind of girl he thought he would marry. She was free-spirited and sprightly and devil-may-care. He'd been surprised at their instant attraction. He'd been caught by the way she threw back her head and laughed with her whole body, uncaring of what others might think. He liked her capricious nature, her willingness to thumb her nose at convention and take on any circumstance in her own way. There was no new adventure she wasn't willing to try, no dare she wouldn't go after.

And she was gorgeous.

She's not right for you.

His mother's words slipped into the forefront of his consciousness before he was able to harness them and cast them away. His mother disliked her from their first meeting. His dad also expressed disapproval that first time but held back any further negative comments, unlike his mother who repeated her warning at every opportunity until David firmly let her know that the subject was off limits. It wasn't that he didn't care for his parents. He loved them dearly and valued their opinions. Except when their remarks were about Leila.

Unlike his own parents, Leila's folks had embraced him from the first time they met. It didn't seem to matter that their daughter had known David for only a few weeks when they announced their intention to marry. They were satisfied that he had a bright future ahead of him and could provide for their daughter.

"It's showtime, son." The voice at his elbow startled him. "You don't want to be late. That's the bride's prerogative."

"Hi, Dad. I didn't hear you come outside."

Making an effort to dispel his gloominess, David grasped the ends of his bowtie and twisted and knotted them until he was satisfied he had the perfect bow. Then he turned to follow his father through the door. It was his wedding day. In a little while, he and Leila would exchange vows and be united as one, as securely bound as the knot around his neck.

At precisely five o'clock in the evening, the notes of the "Wedding March" swelled from the pipe organ. Leila Amherst began the long walk down the aisle of the very old, ornate sanctuary of the First Presbyterian Church on the arm of her father. Her heavily beaded skirts swayed with each step.

Leila's grasp slipped from her father's arm.

"Don't dawdle," she heard her father whisper from between lips that remained fixed in a smile. She tightened her grip on his arm again and tried to ignore the reprimand.

If there was one day she and her folks should have felt some real warmth toward each other, this should have been it. But their relationship was as distant today as it had ever been.

So she'd never been the perfect daughter. She'd never been able to gain their approval. Maybe that was the real reason she craved attention, even negative attention, from anywhere and anyone.

She flashed back to the seventh grade where she had spent what seemed like every other day in detention for one reason or another. Her mind leapt to the very expensive, rigidly strict Connecticut boarding school where they were probably still talking about the girl who'd put live goldfish in the headmistress's water cooler. Certainly she had not gained her parents' approval at her high school graduation party held at the exclusive country club where the Amhersts were third-generation members. A couple of her friends had spiked the punch, and within an hour the party had become so raucous they were asked to leave. She snickered at the memory and disguised it with a fake cough. Any other club member would have been asked to resign, but her father's money and circle of influence prevailed.

And now she was doing what they wanted.

They wanted her gone, off their hands, somebody else's responsibility. And since David-the-architect was acceptable, she was marrying him.

And still they were not pleased.

Leila tossed a careless smile at her father as he handed her off to her bridegroom. As he released her fingers, he leaned toward her but kissed the air near her cheek.

She heard the sound.

She never felt his touch.

Sighing at still another rejection, she followed David's lead as he guided her up three carpeted steps where the minister waited for them. She wished she could see his face, but he stared straight ahead, apparently intent on every word the minister spoke. Was he as uncomfortable as she? She glanced up at two spotlights trained on them and couldn't help fidgeting from the heat emanating from them. *Somebody turn on the fans, for goodness' sake.*

Leila took a small sidestep away from her bridegroom and hoped the increased space would encourage some air to pass between them. While David repeated the vows spoken by the minister, she slid one finger under the shoulder straps of her wedding dress, rotated her shoulders, and tried to dispel the clamminess that was seeping through the satin slip.

What's with this heat?

She barely resisted fanning her fingers under her chin in an effort to move the air around. She shifted her weight from one leg to the other. A curious restlessness settled around her, and the lack of air movement in the church only increased her distress.

It was her turn to recite the vows. She repeated the words without emotion, received her ring and the obligatory kiss, and smothered a deep sigh.

She'd been sighing a lot lately, but this wedding was the last demand her parents would make of her. David was easy. He'd let her have her way whatever the circumstances. This marriage would be convenient for both of them. She had an inkling that he really didn't want to marry her. He'd never said that, of course. Still, they would both get what they wanted. David would have her father's connections, and she would gain her freedom.

She ran her tongue across her lips in a frantic effort to quench her dry mouth. What she needed was a cool drink, preferably something in a tall glass with a slice of lemon. And lots of ice. And friendly faces.

A glance around the church reminded her that most of the guests in attendance were her parents' friends, not hers. Her friends weren't good enough for this crowd. Walking down the aisle with her father, she'd recognized a couple of executives from his bank, one state senator, her uncle (the judge), and a representative from the governor's office whom she'd met several times but whose name she was happy to forget. These were people who could further her father's business deals and community standing.

Not *her* friends.

Not even one!

Leila quickly swiped the back of her hand across her brow. She was beginning to feel a little cooler. But the coolness was coming from inside her, not from the obviously defective air conditioning system. The coolness was like the sappy clamminess that comes one step ahead of a fainting spell.

The ceremony was over. Without consciously doing so she accepted her bouquet from the maid of honor, turned toward the congregation, and slipped her free arm into David's. Now if she could just get outside without making a complete spectacle of herself.

"Friends," the minister began, "I present to you for the first time ...'"

Leila nudged David with her elbow and raised pleading eyes to his. Surely he would help her. "I'm going to be sick."

She dabbed her fingers across tiny droplets of sweat that dotted her brow and upper lip.

David tilted his head toward her. "Can you hold on for another few minutes?"

"No, I have to go now," she whispered through the fake smile that remained pasted on her lips even as her eyes glistened with unshed tears. "I'm getting a woozy feeling."

"Okay, let's go outside. Don't stop to greet the family like we rehearsed," he whispered. "Just hold on to me. Keep smiling. That's my girl."

Leila relaxed, happy to leave the outcome of the unrehearsed retreat to her new husband. He must have signaled the bridal party because three pairs of bridesmaids and groomsmen, the flower girl, and the ring bearer fell in line behind them with the precision of a military color guard. With her hand secure in David's grasp, she kept pace with him as he led the wedding party through the arched doorway into the courtyard.

In the cooler outdoors, Leila took several gulps of fresh air as David watched attentively. Someone handed her a paper cup of water. She gulped half its contents, took several deep breaths, and passed the cup to David. She swiped the back of her hand across her forehead again and finger-combed her bangs back into place. She was beginning to feel better. One more deep breath and the warmth returned to her cheeks.

"Better?" David asked, searching her face.

"Yeah," she said as she nodded.

Leila felt rather than saw her mother take her place beside her. Faces came into focus and then faded away as the guests moved along the receiving line. One overzealous little boy tossed a handful of birdseed directly at her. She casually dusted away the pellets from her face. She smiled lazily in response to the guests' sentiments. She really wanted this to be over. Although she no longer felt faint, she was finding it difficult to express any enthusiasm toward her guests—quite unlike David who was effusive, hugging and kissing acquaintances and strangers and introducing his parents, who stood beside him.

She was amazed at his ability to take charge in a tense situation and his ability to win over strangers. No wonder her parents loved him. He certainly would not be a disappointment to her father. She imagined her father's conversation with the governor would include words such as *good match* and *social asset*.

She, on the other hand, was glad the ceremony was over. This charade was taking more out of her than she'd anticipated.

Suddenly, like a clap of thunder, a motorcycle roared into the driveway, scattered fallen leaves out of its way, and screeched to a halt. The rider, dressed completely in black, lifted the visor of his helmet with one hand while the other hand flexed sporadically, revving the engine to punctuate his words.

"It's your last chance, darlin'." *Vroom, vroom.* "You don't have to play by their rules." *Vroom, vroom.* "Come away with me. Come with me *now.*"

Leila's eyes widened in heady anticipation. She took several quick breaths through parted lips. Two bright spots of color heated her cheeks and she covered one with her free hand.

After only a moment's hesitation, she spun on the ball of her satin slippers to face her groom. Her coal-black eyes darted left and right. She spun toward the cyclist but encountered her father's angry stare across the path.

No. She read her father's silent command. "No," he said aloud.

Leila pivoted to face David again, the tulle of her headdress twisting on her shoulders in response to her frenzied movement. For the space of two heartbeats, neither moved. Neither spoke. Only the impatient *vroom, vroom* of the motorcycle measured off the passing seconds.

She sprang into action. "Sorry," she whispered to David as she backed away from his protective warmth. "Sorry," she cried again. "I'm sorry," she shouted to the gaping group as she ran backward toward the cyclist.

Lifting the voluminous skirts of her gown, she turned, sped toward the motorcycle, and leaped onto the pillion seat. "I'm sorry," she shouted one last time as the rider gunned the motor two, three times in rapid succession.

In a single motion made perfect with practice, she placed her feet on the footrests and threw her arms around the rider's waist.

"Go. Go!" she shouted at his back. The rider needed no further encouragement. Releasing the clutch, he gunned the motor and escaped with his prize, a bubble of white tulle and embossed satin billowing out behind them.

Chapter 2

The main dining room of the Whistle Stop Diner was almost deserted, but a weary Buddy Madsen still had a full hour of work ahead of her. She placed a carefully folded napkin between each setting of flatware on the table in front of her and wished for the umpteenth time that she had a job she could perform from a seat. Not a plush seat, not even one with armrests. Right now she would settle for anything soft that would allow her to take the weight off her aching feet. Oh, how her feet hurt.

Balancing on one leg, she slowly rotated the other foot, wincing from the pain as feeling returned to her toes. A muffled sigh of relief escaped her lips, and she began applying the same treatment to the other foot. *Just a few more tables,* she consoled herself as she gathered up the dwindling pile of napkins.

As she moved on, she tuned half-heartedly toward the droning voice of another waitress who kept up a running commentary about nothing in particular while she poured salt and pepper into their shakers.

"Just look at him falling apart over there," the woman said. "Sure don't look like no hot stuff now."

Buddy glanced over her shoulder at the solitary figure in the corner. The man's body was hunched forward, his head supported in the palm of one hand. The edges of his black, silk bowtie dangled on either side of his crumpled and unbuttoned vest while the hem of the white, pin-tucked shirt ballooned out above his waistband.

The woman was right. The handsome, charismatic man had temporarily lost his appeal, and his fun-loving "posse" seemed to have deserted him.

"You still sweet on him, honey?" the waitress asked as she lowered her ample hips onto the seat of the captain's chair.

A telltale warmth traveled up Buddy's neck. She was grateful her cinnamon complexion hid the evidence of her embarrassment. She opened her lips to respond but quickly closed them. Sweet on him indeed. Who used words like that nowadays? Come to think of it, though, those just might be the right words, for she refused to believe she was in love with David. Love is more than the giddy-up of a heartbeat when the object of one's affection draws near, and that was her only measurable response to him. No, she was definitely not in love with him.

So why was she finding it difficult to even acknowledge the woman's question?

Swallowing deep, Buddy shrugged her response and hoped it was sufficiently nonchalant to stop the woman from probing further. How many other people had guessed her secret?

Not that she was alone in carrying a torch for the handsome architect. Didn't every woman who came within an arm's length of him do the same? The problem was that their lifestyles were completely incompatible. Whereas she was careful that her actions were always above reproach, David didn't seem to care what anyone thought of him. Even as an infrequent lecturer on campus, his reputation for carousing with his boisterous friends was legendary, and turned her off so much that on the rare occasions when she had been assigned to serve his table, she traded stations with another waitress. Add to his cavalier lifestyle the fact that he did not share her faith, and she had two solid reasons why he was firmly off limits to her.

She'd admired him from the day he guest-lectured her freshman class about his passion for preserving and restoring historical buildings. She was drawn to the way he listened intently to her classmates' questions, making sure he thoroughly understood them before expressing his own opinions. He'd seemed so gentle, so caring, offering no criticism at the simplicity of some of their questions and treating each one with respect.

Buddy returned her attention to her task. The sooner she finished setting the tables, the sooner she could end her Saturday night shift and go home. She had to get in a few hours' sleep before waking up for the early service tomorrow. Then, if she could swing it, she would spend some time doing her laundry before meeting her study group for another intense session.

Hers was a hectic schedule, but one she just had to master if she was going to complete her degree on schedule.

"First time I ever seen him without his boys," the older waitress droned on. "He's a fancy architect, you know. Said he was gon' have a fancy office in the city. Sure don't look it, though. Looks lost, if you ask me. Yeah, lost without all his admirers hanging around him … oops, there's the signal." The woman acknowledged David's waving hand with a nod of her head. "He's ready for another drink."

"You're not going to give it to him, are you?" Buddy was incredulous. The last thing David needed was—

"You got a better idea, girl?"

"Yes!" What was she, stupid? "Coffee."

"Uh-uh. He orders beer, he gets beer. And don't give me any more of them holy-roller sermons about the demon drink. I've heard them all." She flashed a warning look at Buddy, while trying to heave her ample form up from her seat. "'Sides," she continued, "coffee doesn't sober anyone up. That's an old wives' tale."

"Tell you what," Buddy offered in a conciliatory tone. "Why don't I get his order while you finish up the salt and peppers? I'll make sure you get the tip if he leaves one," she offered, knowing the show of generosity would sway the older woman.

"Okay, but if he raises a ruckus it's on your head."

"Yeah, yeah." Buddy dismissed the warning. Truth was, if he raised a ruckus and the manager heard about it, she would be out of a job. And she really needed this job! She was still short on next semester's tuition. But another drink would send David over the edge for sure, and she wouldn't stand by and let that happen. Not to him or to any other customer.

Buddy strode with grim determination toward the coffee station, the soles of her leather sneakers squeaking each encounter with the shiny floor tiles. Pausing only long enough to grasp the handle of the full coffee pot, she made her way toward the table at the back of the room.

She was still a few paces away when David lifted his head from between his linked fingers. "Wha'zat?"

"What does it look like?" Buddy answered quickly and then regretted her sharp response.

David must not have noticed. He was probably too far into his inebriated state to take offense at her tone. She turned over a cup, filled it, and placed it before him.

He gazed down at the cup of coffee, his head wobbling unsteadily, and then looked up at her through glazed eyes. "Want 'nother beer," he demanded, dropping his hand on top of the cup.

"Not here, pal," Buddy replied. "You've already had more than your limit. Time to call it a night." Her eyes dueled with his, urging him to back down. When he removed his hand, she continued. "Coffee's on the house. When you're done I'll call a cab for you."

"Don' need a cab. I walked here ... I'll walk home." He picked up the cup with shaky hands, blew twice across the surface of the liquid, and then downed it without pausing for breath.

Buddy winced, certain it had seared his insides on the way down. Ah well.

Now to get him away from the table. "Come on, I'll help you to the door." Setting the coffee pot on the table, she slung an arm through his and urged him up from his seat. He belched once as he struggled to stand, and she turned her face away from the nauseating odor of alcohol mixed with stomach gases.

"Your hair ... pretty," He squinted and leaned in closer to her.

Buddy pulled back. "The door's this way, pal. Come on." She struggled under the weight of his six-feet-two frame and cautiously steered him toward the double exit doors.

He must have experienced a moment of clarity and realized he was in no condition to walk. "A-about ... about that cab ..."

"I'll get you one. No problem."

Some moments later Buddy was slamming the door of the taxi behind him, hoping he was still sufficiently alert to be able to tell the driver where he lived. As the cab pulled away from the curb, she heaved a sigh and turned her eyes toward the heavens. *Lord, I promised you I will not give my heart away to someone who won't treasure it. I won't break my pledge to you. David doesn't share my faith or my lifestyle. So please keep him away from me, and help me get over him because I really, really like him.*

Satisfied that she had placed her dilemma in the hands of the only One who could solve it she retraced her steps, determined to end this very hectic day and rest up for the challenge of the next.

Chapter 3

Several years later.

David Willoughby scrunched the handwritten telephone message into a tight ball and hurled it with all his might into the black metal trashcan beside his desk. What was Frank, his boss, thinking? No sane person would want to head for the Jersey shore on a day like today. What could be the urgency? The firm had already been awarded the job and the contracts had been signed. Why the hurry to go to the Cape?

For a long moment he stood still in the middle of the office considering his choices and struggling to regain his composure. The display of anger wasn't like him. Typically he was the poster child for self-control, so much so that his colleagues often described him as being cold or distant. If they'd known him in his college days they wouldn't have called him cold. Babe magnet, maybe, for all the chicks who used to hang around him. No, he wasn't cold, far from it, but he took great care not to reveal his warm side to too many people. People flocked to warmth, and he was learning to cherish his solitude. "Flocking" he could do without.

Still, he was lonely. Not that he missed the late nights and party-hopping scene that were part of his younger days, but he did miss the camaraderie of close friends. He hadn't had a close friend in a long time. And no girlfriends. After the fiasco five years ago, he'd sworn off them completely, but with the passing of time, he sometimes felt the yearning for a family of his own: kids who loved him, and a wife who cared about the real David, not his social standing or his bank balance.

Maybe he should get a dog.

He took a breath, deep and slow, allowing his chest to fully expand. As he exhaled he slid his tongue across his upper lip unconsciously searching for the latent flavor of nicotine, a taste that hadn't touched his lips in, what was it? four years now. He was four years into what would probably turn out to be a lifetime of reinventing himself.

He swept his tongue across his lips again, lightly flicking the hairs of his neatly trimmed moustache. Even after four years the desire was still there. Probably would remain with him forever. No, a cigarette was not the answer. Besides, runners don't smoke, and now he got his high on the track.

Coffee. He poured himself a cup from the decanter on his desk and took one mouthful and then another. The liquid brought comforting warmth to his chest and a calming of his emotions.

Crossing to the long, double-insulated glass windows of his New York City office, David gazed down at the activity below. A gray misty rain spat on the heads of pedestrians caught unprepared for the sudden change in weather. They jostled each other, their shoulders hunched against the stinging onslaught, newspapers and magazines held aloft in the hope of providing a modicum of shelter.

No one in his right mind would make a trip to the shore on a day like this. So what if the calendar said it was spring? Outside it had to feel like the middle of fall.

"David?" The voice on the intercom interrupted his musings.

He turned toward the phone on his desk but remained by the window. "Yes, Jennifer." His speech was clipped and formal. He flexed and relaxed his bunched shoulders, but his breathing had returned to its natural cadence.

"Frank wants to see you in the conference room. I think he wants to discuss the Donnelly project at the Jersey shore."

"Tell him I'll be right there."

Even though his response was compliant, he shook his head in frustration. Frank wasn't going to give him a chance to devise his own solution for the shore project. The man was determined to have David oversee the project, and once Frank made a decision he didn't back down. He was top dog, after all. It was his tenacity and sharp instincts that had reshaped the firm, making it the emerging leader in the world of architectural design. David secretly admired the man's drive.

He drained the last of his coffee and set the cup aside. He could go head to head with Frank, but what would be the point? Best to meet him now and get on with the assignment.

Some moments later David was seated across from his boss at the highly polished conference table. He leaned back in his chair and eyed the man whose will to prevail matched his own.

"The bottom line is, we must have a man on site for a few weeks until Donnelly returns," Frank said. "The contractor … his work … if you won't do it, I'll have to hire a consultant."

It was clearly bait, and David took it. "And increase costs? That would blow the budget."

"I'm glad you're still thinking like a businessman."

Frank heaved an exaggerated sigh, but David resisted. From what he'd heard, Cape May was a tourist resort that went into hibernation until summer. He'd probably die of boredom before then. And this had to be the worst driving weather.

"What about Riley? He's capable, and he's about ready to wrap up the Brooklyn school project."

"No can do. His wife's due to deliver any day now and he has to stick close to home. Look, why don't you take the weekend to think it

over? Take a drive down there, look around, get a feel for the place."
Frank slid a large manila envelope across the table and David trapped
it under his palm. "As a matter of fact, if you think you can monitor
the progress with just weekly visits, I'll settle for that."

David pulled the envelope closer, slid a finger beneath the flap,
and ripped it open. He could tolerate a rainy weekend at the shore,
and if the rain moved north as was predicted, it could turn out to
be not so bad after all. But only for a weekend. "No strings?" David
asked.

"Hey, you know me."

"Yeah, that's my point." The two men shared a laugh and leaned
back in their chairs.

"So what's in the envelope?" David shook the contents out as
he spoke. A tourist map of Cape May, driving directions from New
York, and the registration confirmation for a bed and breakfast fell
from the envelope. He laughed again and wagged his index finger at
the older man across from him. "Anyone ever tell you you're a sly old
dog, Frank?"

"Every day, son, every day." Frank's eyes mellowed as they gazed
back at the man he had been mentoring, and David recognized the
genuine caring in them. "Will you go?"

"Can I turn you down?"

"You know you can. And I know you would if I was asking you
to do something unethical."

"In a flash." David replaced the contents of the envelope, scooted
his chair backward, and stood. "But you wouldn't do that, would you,
Frank? Or I wouldn't be here."

It felt good to know the man he respected recognized the changes
in him. Only over the last two or three of his thirty-something years
could he have considered himself a man of high ethical standards.
That had been the direct result of moving back home to care for his
widowed mother and being under her influence again. He was grateful

he'd been able to reestablish the routines he once considered boring. Healthy meals, fewer late nights and a regular exercise program had returned his body and mind to peak performance. Frank's simple observation filled him with a sense of pride and self-worth that he hadn't known as a younger man.

"I know that too." Frank stood with his friend. "But like I said, no strings. I mean it. If you say no to the project after scouting around Cape May, I'll accept your decision."

David gathered his maps and notebook and tucked the manila envelope under his arm. In spite of his reluctance to take on this project, he was feeling pretty good about himself. As he left the conference room he squelched the urge to whistle.

Back in his office he spread the drawings out on his drafting table. The firm had been contracted to convert a two-story office building into time-share units. The challenge had been to design a complex that was functional yet appealing and Victorian in design to fit in with the architectural flavor of the Cape May area. Their firm's designs had been accepted without alterations.

He should go. He really had nothing better to do this rainy weekend. He gathered the sheets of paper, some pencils, and a note pad and tossed them into his briefcase. Reaching for the telephone, he punched out a three-digit extension and waited for his secretary to respond.

"Jennifer? Give Frank a message. Tell him I've decided to go to Cape May for a look-see. I'll be back by Saturday. Of course, if the weather improves, I could stay through the weekend.... No, I'm not agreeing to take on the project yet.... I'll let him know when I return. Oh, and, uh, confirm my reservation at the Magnolia Manor B & B in Cape May.... Yes, he can e-mail me. I'll have my laptop."

There was no doubt in David's mind that he was the go-to guy when a job called for an overnight stay. He had no encumbrances:

no family, not even a pet waiting for his return. He'd wasted the last decade avoiding commitment. Was he now destined to be a bachelor for the rest of his life? He hoped it was not too late.

Surely she was still out there, the one person who could fill that gaping void in the center of his heart.

If Buddy Madsen hadn't given her word that the redecoration of the Merritt Mansion would be completed in time for the spring tourist season, she surely would have quit work early and spent the day basking in the magnificent Cape May sunshine. What a gorgeous day it turned out to be. The tropical storm had passed over their shores during the night and left in its wake a clean, cloudless afternoon, and she longed to be outdoors.

Forcing herself to refocus, Buddy turned away from the inviting scene outside the music room window and continued her final inspection of the house. She was happy with what she saw—a completely renovated Victorian mansion restored to its stately elegance. A smile of satisfaction slowly spread across her face.

"All done, Buddy?" Zaccheus Madsen, her father, interrupted her inspection.

"All done," she echoed. "What d'you think?"

Her father surveyed the room as she had done, doing a complete 360-degree turn before facing her. "I think your work will pass muster!"

Buddy beamed at his words. It was high praise indeed when he slipped into navy language.

"So, kiddo." He placed a hand on her shoulder and Buddy raised her eyes to meet his. "How long before you start decorating your own place, eh?"

Although her dad's voice held a hint of teasing, Buddy recognized the somber tone that had been creeping into many of their conversations lately. Still, she couldn't resist the urge to feign surprise. "You want me to move away from home?"

"Now, you know that's not what I meant."

"I know, Daddy. It's just that … well … I'm determined to have a marriage like you and Mom have. A forever marriage." She looked away.

Outside the window, the limbs of a stately Magnolia tree boasted ripe, full buds ready to burst into flower. Two bright red cardinals played tag on the branches. Buddy's eyes followed their antics, but her brain registered little of it.

When she spoke again, her voice held a faraway wispiness. "I want someone who will love me enough to tolerate my ups and downs but strong enough to stop me when my emotions get the better of me. Someone who will laugh and cry with me, someone I can share my work with, someone I can lean on but who isn't so self-assured and independent that he can't lean on me. Most of all, I want someone who shares my faith. Most of the guys I know, Daddy, they just …"

"They fall short, eh?"

"Yeah, Dad, way short. I know God has the right man for me tucked away somewhere, and I'm willing to wait for him to show up. I made that commitment in junior high, and I plan to keep it. I refuse to marry someone who doesn't love the Lord. I won't settle for less. I can't."

She leaned her head on the shoulder of the man whose opinion she valued so highly. "Think I'm setting the bar too high?"

"Not at all, sweetheart. Personally, I don't think there's anyone out there good enough for my Rosebud." She grinned at the childhood nickname. "Still, another grandchild or two …"

"Give me a break, Pops." She tossed her head back and laughed out loud. "Didn't you tell me just last week that you're getting too old to keep up with the four you already have? By the way"—she glanced at her watch—"they should be arriving for the reunion weekend any minute now. You should go."

"You're right, I should go. I promised your mother I'd be home in time to help her with the chores. If I time it right"—he winked—"she'll be done before I get there."

Grinning at his contrived reluctance to assist her mother, Buddy followed her father down the polished wooden stairway to the street. "C'mon boy." She snapped her fingers at Ensign the family's aging yellow Labrador, who was stretched out on the welcome mat. The dog stood lazily, yawned, and stretched before strolling over to his master.

"Don't work too late," her father whispered as Buddy leaned in for his kiss.

Watching her father walk away, twenty-seven-year-old Buddy was reminded of his advancing years and the demands the sea had made on him. His body, once erect, now listed to one side, and his hand-carved, ebony cane, purchased during his ship's last docking in Singapore, had made the subtle transition from comfortable appendage to walking aid.

Buddy shielded her eyes against the bright sunlight as she watched her father's retreating back. At the end of the block he turned and she raised her hand in a final wave.

"I love you, Daddy," she whispered into the air.

Turning, Buddy's noticed a man gesturing at her from across the street. She shoved her hands into the back pockets of her jeans and waited for him to get closer.

She was impressed by his height and his easy gait. The man was tall, taller by a head than her own five feet eight. His shoulders were broad, but his polo shirt and khaki shorts sat loosely on his shoulders and hips as if he had recently lost weight. The plastic strap of a camera case hung around the wrist of his left hand, which also grasped a badly folded map.

Buddy looked up at his face. There was something familiar about him. Mentally she stripped away the neatly trimmed moustache that adorned his mouth and the wire-rimmed, aviator sunglasses that shadowed the laugh lines at the corners of his eyes. In an instant her insides somersaulted in recognition.

David.

"I-I'm sorry, did you say something?" The warmth of his voice revived emotions in her that she thought were quelled forever. She resisted the urge to pat her hair. She was sure she looked a mess.

"Yes," he said, "I asked you to point me toward Perry Street. I parked my car there, but I walked farther than I planned." Removing his sunglasses with one hand, he held out a map to her with the other. "I guess I'm lost," he added sheepishly. "I'm trying to get back to Magnolia Manor."

He didn't recognize her. Good.

"Yep. You're turned around all right." A nervous giggle escaped with the words. "You're in the right area, but you're heading in the wrong direction." She took the map and moved to his side. "You're actually closer to the manor than the car park. I hope you enjoyed your walking tour." She pointed out the correct route and then quickly returned her hands to her hip pockets, wishing for the umpteenth time that her fingers didn't bear the nicks and calluses that were the battle scars of her work.

"Actually, I did. I've been walking around for quite a while." David paused. "Is it always this quiet here?"

"Hardly." Buddy scoffed and immediately wished she hadn't. David was obviously a first-time visitor to the Cape and she certainly had no desire to send him away thinking the residents were unfriendly. She had no desire to send him away, period! Besides, any minute now he might recognize her.

She wanted him to recognize her.

She was afraid he would recognize her.

For years she'd tried so hard to put him out of her thoughts, and here he was again, turning up just when she thought she had finally suppressed her feelings for him. *God, you promised to keep him away. You promised.*

"If you're still here Monday, you'll notice a big difference," she continued, trying to quell her heightened awareness of him and keep her voice from wavering. "The weekend after Easter is usually pretty busy, what with schools being closed. Lots of families come down for a few days. Spring break. Most of these shops will be open by then." She swept the area with her eyes. "You're not from around here, are you? Of course not, or you wouldn't be lost." She was babbling and she really ought to stop. And why was she deliberately prolonging their conversation? Of course he didn't seem to be in much of a hurry either.

"New York. Actually, I work in the city but I live in Bergen."

"Your first visit to Cape May?"

"Yup." He folded the map and stuck it under his arm.

"You should stick around for the weekend. We're not New York but I'm sure we can hold your interest for a few days."

"You have museums? Theater? What?

"Not on the scale you're thinking." Buddy's response was guarded. "For those things, you should have stayed in the city. Here we have the best beaches, clean air, saltwater taffy, Victorian architecture, and the greatest Italian water ice this side of Italy. You can climb to the top of the lighthouse, take a trolley tour of the town, go whale watching, visit the bird sanctuary ..."

"All right, all right. I get it. Simple pleasures, huh?" He rocked back on his heels when he smiled, and Buddy experienced a resurgence of that powerful emotion that had been her constant companion a lifetime ago. "Maybe I'll stay for a few days. "Thanks for your help, uh—"

"Rose. My name is Rose," she said, telling him her given name and reluctantly offering her hand. With an inward grimace, which she hoped was not projected onto her face, Buddy allowed her hand to be engulfed in his and prayed he couldn't feel the hard calluses on her fingers or see the purplish bruise developing on her thumb.

"Nice to meet you, Rose. I'm David Willoughby."

She caught his eyes sweeping her face and she looked away. She relished the warmth of her hand securely ensconced within his grasp but quickly wriggled them free.

"You have nice hands, Rose," he said.

Buddy pulled them back. He knew.

"Like my mother's hands," he continued. "Hard working. Honest."

She raised her eyes to his and a current of energy darted between them.

"I don't suppose you would agree to be my tour guide while I'm here?"

Buddy hesitated. He appeared to be so different from the last time she saw him. Five years ago he'd been so plastered he was barely able to stand. This David seemed kind, perceptive, gentle, and sober. And he was alone! Rose didn't notice a ring on his finger.

Had there been other changes? She wondered about the condition of his heart.

Wishing for a moment that her family reunion was scheduled for some other weekend and she could take the time to find answers to her questions, she lifted her chin resolutely. "I'm sorry, I can't."

"My loss." David shrugged away her rebuff. "Thanks again for your help." He accompanied his words with a smile that didn't quite make it to his eyes and walked away in the direction she'd indicated.

Buddy almost called him back but caught herself in time. What would be the point? She'd sat through his college class, had waited on him in a restaurant, even held him close to her when he was unable to stand on his own. Yet for all that, she hadn't made any lasting impression on him. He hadn't recognized her.

The real question was, Would she be able to get over the impression he had made on her?

Chapter 4

$\mathcal{B}$uddy pedaled hard, swerving her bicycle around two workers who were hanging a poster about the upcoming jazz festival. She whizzed past the water tower and made the turn into Maple Drive. She couldn't be late. One additional rite of spring was in progress. The Madsen family—Zach and Mary: their daughter, Buddy; three sons; two daughters-in-law; four grandchildren; and a yellow Lab named Ensign were gathering for the annual Easter weekend reunion.

She was within a half block of house number forty-four when she spied her brother's RV parked in the driveway. Excitement and anticipation urged her forward. Feeling like a teenager again, she stood on the pedals of her racing bike and pumped her denim-clad legs. The additional energy thrust the bike forward. It leaned right, left, right in response to the movement of her body. She loved this mode of transportation, and it was still the fastest way to navigate the narrow roads when they became traffic-snarled during the tourist season.

Home at last. Buddy made a wide swing into the driveway, squeezed the hand brakes, and dismounted all in one move. Like an errant child, she dropped the bike in the driveway, vowing to return for it later. She climbed the four steps to the front porch while unfastening the straps on her safety helmet and tossed it carelessly on the white Adirondack chair as she walked past.

Bounding unceremoniously into the living room, she squealed her brother's name. Without warning, she propelled herself into his arms. "Sam-eee."

"Hey, brat," Sam teased her, both enveloping each other with a bear hug. "How've you been?"

"Long time no see."

They spoke at the same time and then laughed again.

Buddy turned to Sam's wife, Becky, who sat beaming at them from the armchair in the corner of the room.

"Hi, Beck." She warmly greeted her sister-in-law and leaned over her chair to kiss her on the cheek. "Love the new haircut."

Becky ran her fingers through her short, curly hairdo before responding. "Thanks. I try not to mention it in the presence of a certain gentleman, who shall remain nameless."

"Sam?" Buddy questioned, inclining her head toward her brother.

"He hates it. He says I don't look like *his wo-man* anymore." She winked at her husband. "But this is way easier to care for than long hair, especially with three kids who demand my attention all the time."

Buddy nodded in understanding while her brother shrugged and raised his hands as if to ward off the combined attack of the women.

"Speaking of kids, where are my nephews and niece?" Becky asked. Not waiting for their response, she peered through the kitchen window at the rear of the house. Four-year-old Sammy and three-year-old Tyler were sitting cross-legged on the wooden deck, fascinated by the workings of a new fishing pole that their grandpa was demonstrating. Seven-month-old Julie was nowhere in sight. Buddy turned back to the couple, her eyebrows raised in question.

"Upstairs with her grandma." Becky answered Buddy's unasked question.

"Then I'll run out and say hi to the boys while you two enjoy some time alone." As Buddy made her way through the door and out onto the deck, she whispered a prayer of thanks for being part of this loving, exuberant family.

An image flashed before her: the image of a man who had traveled alone in the wrong direction. She remembered the strength of his hand as his fingers circled around hers and the way her own hand, for a brief moment, nestled comfortably within his.

I wonder if I'll see him again.

She couldn't deny she was still powerfully attracted to him. Time and distance had not put a dent in her feelings toward him. Apparently, neither had her prayers, or her determination to quell any memory of this man. And now he was here in Cape May. They were bound to meet again. What on earth was she going to do?

Doesn't matter, she reprimanded herself sternly. *He's not from my world. He wasn't right for me before, and he's not right for me now. Nothing's changed.*

The sun was beginning its slow descent over the western shore when David slammed the door of his Jeep and sprinted up the red brick walkway of the Madsen family home. He wasn't really late. His dinner invitation was for six o'clock, and a quick glance at his watch confirmed he still had five minutes.

He'd really lucked out this afternoon. What were the chances of meeting his college buddy, Roger Madsen, his wife, Anna Faye, and their daughter, Susan, in the lobby of the same bed and breakfast where he had registered? He and Roger had become good friends during their college years, but after graduation Roger joined the coast guard, leaving David behind without a clear vision of what his next step was going to be. Except that he wanted to build buildings—big buildings and lots of them.

Glancing up at the house, David caught a glimpse of Roger leaning against the doorpost. As he got closer Roger pulled the door open further and extended his hand.

"Hey, man, I was beginning to think you were going to pass up the invitation to dinner."

David grasped the outstretched hand. "Pass up a home-cooked meal? Not on your life. I'm still thanking my lucky stars I ran into you when you were checking in." David grinned.

"Both of us staying at the same inn. Talk about coincidence, eh? Mom has a place all set for you. We're about ready to sit down."

As they spoke, Mary Madsen approached them, wiping her hands on the front of her pretty floral apron.

"Come in, come in, David. Welcome. Roger, take his jacket. Glad you could join us. It's been, what, nine, ten years since we met you?" David leaned toward her to receive a welcoming hug and a pat on his back.

"Hi, Mrs. Madsen. Ten years, I think. You visited my parents' home when Roger and I graduated." Past her shoulder he saw Zach approach, and David turned to greet him.

"Nice to see you again, Mr. Madsen." The men shook hands heartily, and David allowed himself to be pulled forward for another back-slapping hug.

"Everyone, this is Roger's friend, David," Mary announced, waving her hand in a wide, inclusive arc. Although no one interrupted their chores, they all greeted David with a chorus of "hi" and "hey" and "hi, David." Smiling at the casual yet comfortable introduction, he raised his hand to acknowledge the welcome.

Behind him, someone entered the room from the kitchen and Mary greeted the newcomer over his shoulder.

"Buddy, come over and meet Roger's friend."

Buddy set the large stoneware bowl on the dining table and slipped her hands from the quilted oven mitts. "Well, hello again."

David's brow furrowed for a moment and then his face crinkled into a smile of recognition. "You're Roger's sister? I should have seen the resemblance."

"Small world, eh?" Buddy replied.

"No kidding." He couldn't keep his eyes from sweeping down and back the length of her. She had replaced her jeans and casual shirt with a very simple but feminine shirtdress, and the thick, braided ponytail, freed from its restraints, now fell in waves on her shoulders. She was beautiful, but not in the New-York-City-fashionista way. Her dress enhanced her figure without flaunting it, and if she was wearing makeup, it complemented her features and flawless skin without calling attention to them. This woman exuded an air of quiet self-confidence and a sweetness of spirit that his city girlfriends hadn't a chance of emulating.

He caught himself staring.

"You'll learn all our names soon enough," Mary's voice interrupted. "C'mon, kids. Let's say grace before we sit."

Reminding himself there would be opportunities to chat with her later, David grasped Becky's outstretched hand and watched amused as the children jockeyed for favorite positions. When all hands were joined around the table and the clamor diminished, Zach asked the blessing:

"Father in heaven, you have seen fit to bring us together one more time to taste of your bounty, not just of food, Lord, but of the closeness and fellowship of family. As I look around this group, I can see you have, indeed, poured out your blessing on the Madsen family. Each time we meet, we are larger in number than the time before, and yet we all are not gathered here." He paused, cleared his throat, and continued. "I thank you for baby Julie, our newest addition, for Roger and Anna Faye's new baby expected in the fall, and for all our precious grandchildren. I thank you, Father, for allowing David to share this meal with us this evening. Bless this meal and the hands who prepared it. May it nourish our bodies and strengthen us for your service, amen."

David felt the friendly squeeze of his fingers before Becky released his grasp. Surprised at his emotional response to the simple gesture, he swallowed the rising lump in his throat and focused on the lively chatter coming from the kids' table in the corner.

"Chili, David?" Someone handed him a plate.

"Just dig in or you're likely to go home hungry," another voice chimed in while passing a serving dish and reaching for another. "It's every man for himself here."

He'd never known the camaraderie of a large family. This teasing and bantering among siblings and cousins was new to him, the drawback of being an only child born late to aging parents. From Mary's blustery welcome and introduction to the family's immediate acceptance, he'd felt at home. It suddenly occurred to him that he wanted this for himself.

No sooner had the thought formed than he looked up at Buddy and caught her staring at him. She dropped her eyes and turned away.

"I'm surprised you didn't take up that offer with Satsuko," Roger said, claiming his attention. "I know several guys who would've jumped at the chance to work with them."

"I would have grabbed that opportunity myself, except I didn't want to be too far away from the folks," David replied. "Dad was already sixty-three when I graduated, and since they had no other kids but me ... well, I just didn't think I should make a commitment that would take me to all the way to Japan for an uncertain period of time."

"How are your folks, David? Do they still live in Bergen?" Zach asked.

David swallowed the last bite of salad and rubbed a napkin across his lips. "Dad died three years ago last winter." He took a sip of lemonade, swallowed hard, and then continued. "I buried Mom last Tuesday."

Crash! Before the group could express sadness at David's announcement, the sound of a milk glass falling to the tiled floor caught their attention. Becky immediately sprang up to calm Tyler, followed quickly by Anna Faye, who grabbed a sponge from the sink and proceeded to sop the milk from the table.

"Who's ready for dessert?" Mary asked. Several tiny hands immediately popped up, and Mary rose to take care of them.

Buddy began gathering and stacking the dirty dishes. She scrunched her paper napkin into a ball and executed a perfect "free throw" into the trash can. "Two points," she shouted as the rolled-up napkin landed squarely in the goal.

The two little boys immediately squeezed their own paper napkins into a ball preparing to imitate her.

Becky shook her head in dismay. "I spend the better part of each day trying to teach these two some table manners, and then Aunt Buddy comes along and undoes it like that." She snapped her fingers. "All right, you can each have one dunk."

"I know." Buddy laughed. "I'm a troublemaker, huh?"

Sam and Travis ran closer to the trash can, jumped, tossed in their balled-up napkins, and shouted, "Two points."

Buddy fell to her knees and "high-fived" them both, winking at Becky.

"I'll get the dishes, Buddy. You get the pies," Becky offered.

Buddy retrieved the apple pies from a cooling rack on the kitchen counter and placed them in front of Mary with several plates. Then she gave each of the kids a popsicle and ushered them out to the back deck.

David found himself eagerly awaiting Buddy's return to the table. Although he answered the questions the others directed toward him, his attention was in the kitchen with Buddy. His mother would have approved of her—her simplicity, her sincerity. He liked the way she squat down to the kids' level to talk with them, the way she interacted with her parents. Not impatiently but with kindness and respect. He wanted to know more about her.

Buddy returned to her place at the table. She helped herself to pie and took a bite. When there was a lull in the conversation, David turned to her. "So, which is it really, 'Buddy' or 'Rose'? I'm confused."

Buddy set her fork on her plate and licked away a flake of pie crust from her top lip. It was a question she'd been asked often. "Well, legend has it ..." she began dramatically in a falsetto voice. One of her brothers snorted and her audience erupted in giggles. She glared at the offender and waited for the snickers to end. "Legend has it Joe took one look at my chubby cheeks when they first brought me home from the hospital wrapped in a pink blanket, and nicknamed me Rosebud. Everyone called me Rosebud until I was in the fourth grade. One day I came home with a black eye and had to explain how I'd had a major fight with a classmate who said I was a sissy, and Rosebud was a sissy name."

"Tell him the whole story," Joe interrupted. "She decked the kid, a boy—"

"—who I had a crush on—"

"—and knocked out his front tooth—"

"—for which I was severely punished," Buddy finished. "After that I begged my family not to call me Rosebud anymore. Dad and Joe shortened it to 'Bud' or 'Buddy,' which was perfectly okay with me, since I was still a tomboy at heart. I've been Buddy ever since." She took another bite of pie.

David stroked his mustache while looking at her, a mischievous twinkle appearing in his eyes. "Do you deck all your boyfriends, Rose?"

"Depends on what they call me," she said without missing a beat and brandished her fork in his direction in a veiled threat.

"Sometimes we call her 'Rambling Rose,'" Roger teased.

"Or 'My Wild Irish Rose,'" Sam added, digging her with his elbow.

"After the way she threatened you, *you* should call her Briar Rose," Joe joined in.

"Actually, I was thinking of 'American Beauty Rose,'" David said, adding his own flavor to the teasing.

"Whoa-a-a-a," the whole table chorused.

David kept his eyes focused on Buddy. He'd wondered how she would respond to his joining in with her brothers' taunts. It was all in fun, the kind of give-and-take he'd missed from not having siblings of his own.

"Well, it is a pretty name," he added. "A delicate rose in a Victorian setting. Very appropriate, I think."

"I'm just happy they didn't nickname me 'Snapdragon' or 'Wisteria' or some other flowery but unflattering name." Buddy laughed.

"And who keeps the bees away, Rose?"

"Well." She paused as if taking care to select the right words. "Until 'Mister Right' comes along, I'll do the job myself, thank you very much." Her voice was subdued but her tone steely. There was no mistaking the subtle message: no "players" allowed. Only serious contenders for her hand would be tolerated. She would not waste her time on frivolous relationships.

Taking care not to let her disappointment show, Buddy levered herself up from the table, gathered the dessert plates, and walked away.

What had just happened? David racked his brain, rehashing the conversation of the last few minutes. She'd taken offense at his answer, he was sure of it. But why? She hadn't objected when he joined in her brothers' teasing. In fact she'd laughed when he called her a delicate Victorian Rose. Was it the buzzing bees metaphor? Had he crossed the line from simple teasing to flirting?

As he watched her carrying the armful of dishes to the kitchen, David wondered if he'd made an enemy of the one member of the Madsen clan he wanted to know better. *Who keeps the bees away? I guess it won't be me.*

The temperature had fallen steadily with the setting sun, leaving the air cooler but not uncomfortable. Inside the Madsen home, David wondered at the family's wholehearted and unquestioning acceptance of him. He had been allowed to help the other men wash and dry the dishes and was given the freedom to help himself to additional cups of coffee without waiting to be offered. The children, who had struggled to pronounce his last name, were told to address him instead as "Uncle David." He felt a special contentment when Roger's precocious six-year-old daughter, Susan, after trying out the new combination of words several times while skipping around the coffee table, threw her arms around his neck and declared, "I love you, Uncle David."

Without their orchestrating it, David and Buddy had been left to entertain each other. Seated together on the comfortable sofa, they had long ago abandoned their feigned interest in the children's game on the floor in front of them. Yet in spite of the camaraderie between them, David sensed that Buddy wasn't as relaxed as she was trying to portray. There was a lingering tension in her limbs that suggested an inner struggle, and her smiles, the ones she occasionally offered him, could only be described as prosaic compared to those that spontaneously erupted in response to the children's antics.

He wanted her to feel relaxed with him. He wanted to hear her laugh again as she had laughed earlier. She bothered him—no, captivated him—for reasons he didn't quite understand. And why did the feeling persist that he'd known her in a previous life?

"Now that you know I won't bite"—David's eyes met and held Buddy's as he spoke—"will you reconsider showing me around town?"

Buddy let out a long breath. "I'd love to, except—"

"Uh-oh, here comes the bomb."

"—exceptI'm committed to the family this weekend," Buddy continued. "It's the one time of year we all get together as a family. It's almost sacred to us. We never miss it."

"I get it." David stroked his moustache and sighed deeply. "And 'no strangers allowed.'"

"That's it," she agreed. "No strangers allowed." Buddy lowered her chin to her chest and nibbled on a thumbnail. "Of course, no one here thinks of you as a stranger."

"No one?"

"Uh-uh." She hid a bashful smile, her muffled voice coming from behind her hand.

"Well, that's really good to know." David felt a keen satisfaction at her response. It might be just wishful thinking, but he was sure he sensed in her a reflection of the attraction developing within him. It had been a long time since he'd permitted himself to feel anything for any member of the opposite sex. Buddy was not like the kind of women he'd known in his past life. She was … he didn't know what she was. But one thing was for dead certain: he wanted a chance to find out.

Chapter 5

The weekend was passing much too quickly for Buddy. Already it was Easter Sunday morning, the last full day of the family reunion. The muted chords of the organ prelude filtered through the ceiling of her basement classroom. The Easter Sunday service was in progress. She was late.

She ended her Sunday school class and watched the teenagers rush from the room, leaving a smattering of leaflets and books for her to return to their bookshelf. Deciding to return later to clear away the clutter, she gathered her purse and Bible and headed for the stairs leading up to the foyer. She was really late.

At the entrance to the sanctuary, a smattering of worshipers waited for the ushers to seat them. Inside, the choir started singing the first anthem. Additional folding chairs had been placed behind the back row and at the window end of the pews, leaving the center aisle free. Buddy squeezed through the group outside the main door, whispering "excuse me" as she passed them.

Ahead of her another body blocked her path.

"Excuse me," she whispered again, encouraging the man to step aside and let her through.

The man turned. "Rose." David greeted her, his smile of recognition brightening his face. "I'm late. I couldn't find a parking spot."

"Shhh," an usher cautioned them.

"Sorry," Buddy said.

"Can you see your folks?"

"No, but they're probably sitting front and left where they always sit. Follow me." Without looking back to see if he was following, Buddy made her way through the worshipers, grateful that their late arrival was hidden by the standing congregation.

Easing her body around a wheelchair that almost blocked the left aisle, she patted the head of the occupant, a seven-year-old girl with muscular dystrophy. At the second aisle from the front, she stopped. Sure enough, her family was seated there, and Mary had saved enough room next to herself for her daughter.

Buddy leaned close to her mother's ear. "David's here. Can we fit him in?" Without responding, her mother gave the signal for the others in the pew to squeeze together. She passed her open hymnal to Buddy, who immediately shared with David.

The hymns and choruses were some of Buddy's favorites, and she sang heartily. She was delighted to hear David singing the tenor line of some of the older hymns, and she blended her alto with his voice on the ones he knew. When he was unfamiliar with one of the newer choruses, she sang the melody line to help him along.

Pastor Miller spoke clearly and simply on the events leading up to the crucifixion and then went on the resurrection. He compared the sacrificial lamb, promised in Isaiah, to Jesus Christ, the Lamb of God, who became the atonement sacrifice for our sins, and then detailed the evidence that Jesus was indeed the Lamb, the Messiah. At the end of the message he gave an invitation for all who wanted to trust Jesus for the first time to raise their hands and then to come forward. Counselors met them at the front and took them into a back room. The service concluded with announcements, a hymn, and a closing prayer.

Several friends rushed over to the Madsens' pew and offered Easter greetings. They introduced themselves to David, welcomed him to their gathering, and invited him to visit again.

After the well-wishers left, Buddy sat and leaned forward to retrieve her purse, which she had placed on the floor by her feet.

David sat as wel, turning his body in the seat so that he faced her, his arm stretched across the back of the pew. "Do you really believe all of that?"

"All of what?"

"The message. The crucifixion and resurrection."

She replied simply, "Every last word."

David's eyes searched her face. "Tell me why."

Buddy placed her purse on the seat beside her and placed her Bible next to it. She made her movements deliberately slow, using the time to pray for the right words to speak. She sneaked in a wish that he was not using his curiosity about her faith to coerce her into developing a relationship with him.

"I was six years old when I recognized my need for a savior," she began. "I was quite a prankster in those days. I guess that comes from having to contend with three older brothers and a baby sister. Anyway, after one particularly difficult conference with my teacher, my dad sat me down and explained that, no matter how hard I tried, I could not be a good girl without a very special helper. He explained that because of my sinful nature, I was choosing to do wrong even when I wanted to do right. Jesus would help me make the right choices if I acknowledged my need of him.

"To my six-year-old mind it made perfect sense. Dad left me to think about what he'd said, and that night, alone in my bedroom, I asked Jesus to be my Savior and my special helper.

"I wish I could say I was the perfect child after that, but that wouldn't be true. I still got into scrapes and still had to be punished for making foolish choices, but the escapades became fewer as I got older. As an adult, knowing God is always watching what I do helps me make the right choice even when that choice is the most difficult or least pleasant one. Because I want to please him I am willing to do what he wants."

She was not aware of the passage of time. Buddy continued speaking, her eyes burning brightly with the intensity of her effort to make her points understood. "Let me tell you about how God has proved his faithfulness to me. The ultimate test for me came during my mother's illness. Three weeks before the end of my junior year in college, Mom was diagnosed with breast cancer. My immediate thought was to leave school and go home. I knew it had to be a stressful time for Dad and I badly wanted to be with both my parents, probably more for my own comfort than theirs.

"When I telephoned my parents with my decision, they insisted I remain in school and complete the semester. I knew they needed me and that I could be helpful at that time. Roger was at sea and Anna Faye would have had to bring baby Susan with her if she came home. Becky was nearing the end of a very difficult pregnancy and was not allowed to travel. There was no one else.

"We had no idea where my sister, Violet, was. We hadn't heard from her in about six months. My parents admitted that I could be of some help to them, but they wanted me to stay in school. My choices were clear: honor my parents' wishes, which is what God tells us to do, or do what I thought would be best. I decided to stay in school and allow God to deal with the situation in his own way and his own time. That was really hard for me." Buddy's eyes glistened with tears as she relived the emotions of that time, and her voice broke. "I couldn't stop picturing my mother alone in the hospital and in pain."

David leaned forward in his seat, removed a folded white handkerchief from his hip pocket, and offered it to her.

Buddy whispered thank you and dabbed at her eyes, sniffed, and continued. "On the day of the surgery, Dad stayed at the hospital all day. He planned to keep Joe posted on all that was happening, and the rest of the family would call Joe at the firehouse for updates. Joe was on desk duty at the station. Get this: the day before the surgery, he injured his thumb while playing basketball with the youth group. Since he wouldn't be able to get a good grip on the fire hose, the chief assigned him to dispatch duty. So he was in the office when Vi called. I think she was somewhere in New York or Philly, but we don't know for certain.

"That call was the first contact we'd had with her in more than six months. Before that call, no one knew if she was alive or dead or where she was. Joe told her about Mom's surgery, and Vi called back the next day to talk with Mom."

Buddy raised her eyes to meet David's. "You see, we'd all been praying for her return for months. We wanted her home, but we wanted her to come home willingly. We don't want any more of the fights and arguments that she used to have with Mom and Dad before she stormed out. We'd been carrying this burden for six months and were managing fine. But coupled with my mother's illness, it became almost unbearable for all of us, especially for Mom. Vi's telephone call reassured us, and we could put aside our concerns for her for a while and concentrate on Mom's needs. We haven't heard a word from Vi since then. We all believe she'll return home eventually, but in God's timing, not ours. He has all the answers and we have to rely on him to arrange events according to his timetable."

Her tears were falling silently but steadily. Buddy made no attempt to wipe them away. She reached for her Bible and flipped through the pages. "It says here God is able to provide exceedingly, abundantly more than we could *ever ask or imagine*. I'm holding on to that promise. He has all the resources at his fingertips because he is the creator of the resources. If he doesn't answer the way we want, so be it."

Buddy closed the Bible gently and zipped its leather case around it. She looked up at David, who seemed pensive, but said nothing.

She continued softly. "If I had returned home against my parents' wishes, I probably would have been the one working with the youth group instead of Joe. He would not have been injured, and he would probably have been away at a fire. If I had come home from school, I would have been waiting at the hospital with Dad, and we would have missed Vi's call. Who knows? The point is that when you trust God and are obedient to his Word, you don't have to wonder about the 'what ifs.'" Buddy wiped her eyes and blew her nose into the handkerchief. "Yes I believe, and he shows his faithfulness to me in simple ways every day of my life."

David's eyes moved over the features of Buddy's face and then settled again on her own eyes. "Thank you," he whispered. Leaning forward he gently flicked away an eyelash that had settled on Buddy's cheek and then tenderly caressed the spot with his thumb. "Thank you," he repeated.

Slowly, David stood and stretched his cramped back. "I'd better take you home before I'm banished from your house forever." He held out a hand to Buddy. She grasped it and pulled herself up from her seat.

"New boyfriend, Buddy?" The voice came from behind them. Turning, Buddy met the twinkling eyes of her pastor.

"Hi, Pastor Miller. No, a new *friend*," she corrected. Buddy introduced the men, who heartily shook heads.

"David, if you need to talk give me a call," the pastor offered. "My home and office numbers are in the visitors' packet." The pastor pointed to the envelope David carried. David thanked him and all three walked slowly toward the exit.

Buddy looked at her watch. Late again. "*Yikes*. Can I bum a ride?"

"Sure. How'd you get here? On your bike?"

"No, I walked with Mom and Dad. We always walk. Parking's pretty tight around here at this time of year."

"Yeah, I can imagine what it's like during the tourist season."

"No, you can't imagine. It's horrendous."

Within minutes they were pulling up outside the Madsen home. It was too soon to say goodbye. Buddy wanted to spend more time with him. "Stay for dinner?"

David slipped the gear lever into *park* but left the motor running. "You can't imagine how much I want to stay, but …"

"We'll have more than enough ham and fixings to share," Buddy coaxed. "Mom always cooks for an army."

"Rose," David interrupted. He slid the back of his hand along her cheek, setting off a tingle that ran down her neck to her toes. "I won't intrude on your family gathering, but you haven't seen the last of me. Not by a long shot."

"Okay." With more reluctance than she should have been feeling, Buddy gathered her purse and Bible and stepped out of the car.

You haven't seen the last of me. The words reverberated inside her head as she watched him drive away. She folded her forearms across her chest and fervently hoped he would keep his promise to see her again. And soon.

In the beautifully decorated bedroom on the second floor of the Victorian bed and breakfast, David sat on the wicker armchair, rehashing all that had happened since he'd arrived at the church that morning: the family's enthusiastic singing, the glowing faces of the men and women in the choir—even the young girl in the wheelchair seemed happy to be in that place. He remembered the child's parents smiling a welcome at him as he walked past.

The pastor had not shouted his message or pounded on the pulpit as David had anticipated. In fact, he seemed to be a reasonably normal man, proclaiming a reasonable message: man sinned, God demanded a sacrifice for atonement, and Jesus paid the price with his life. Take it or leave it.

He was touched by Buddy's sincerity and the simplicity with which she shared her belief. It was the kind of response to his question his mother would have given. Not the quoting of long passages he didn't understand but the simple evidence of faith played out in her own life.

David placed his hands flat on his thighs and pushed himself up from the chair. He strolled over to the dormer window and looked down on the deserted yard, his mind still mulling over the morning's message. He'd heard it all before and dismissed it. Yet today the same message permeated his consciousness for the first time. For the first time he felt it demanded a response: embrace one side or the other. Accept or reject.

Running both hands through his hair in a gesture of frustration, he turned from the window and surveyed the room. In his absence the bed had been remade and his clothes folded and placed on the desk chair. He reached for the slacks he had worn the day before and then tossed them aside in favor of his favorite attire: shorts, polo shirt, and sneakers. He loosened the tie at his neck, unbuttoned the shirt, shrugged them off, and tossed them on the bed.

His parents would have approved of the worship service. Pastor Miller, although he was a younger man, did not come across as an intellectual know-it-all, nor did he apologize for his message. He was forthright and spoke in simple, everyday language. No showing off his theological education. His wife too had sincerely welcomed David. Nice folks! He remembered that the pastor had invited him to call on him.

He made himself a promise: *I'll call him tomorrow.*

Reaching for the discarded shirt, he retrieved the church bulletin from the breast pocket and found the telephone numbers for the pastor's home and office. He tore the information from the bulletin, stuck it inside his wallet, and placed the wallet in the hip pocket of his shorts.

Stretching his arms over his head, David realized he was hungry. He should have accepted the Madsens' invitation to dinner. Too late now. It would have been nice to spend the evening with the family. He enjoyed the warmth of their company, their camaraderie, and the freedom he felt to just be himself with them.

He thought immediately of Rose and how sweet and unspoiled she was. He was so sure he'd met her before, but it was unlikely she'd been one of the crowd he'd hung around with in the past. Those people had essentially been thrill-seekers who would go to any extreme for a good time, a good time they could barely recall the next morning.

Rose made no apology for her commitment to her family and her dedication to her Lord. She was *sweet*. He stopped short of describing her as plain. She wasn't plain. He almost hadn't recognized her this morning, dressed as she'd been in a suit, high heels, and makeup. Seated next to her in church, he'd smelled the gentle aroma of her perfume. A nice, flowery fragrance for a nice, simple woman, he thought, and then caught himself.

Nice, yes. Simple? Who knows! She's probably as complicated as any of the women he'd dated.

His memory flitted back to the one encounter in his past that had left him swearing off women forever. He had been more angry than hurt by that woman's rejection, but his life was returning to normal. Well, maybe not normal, but at least bearable.

Halfway out the bedroom, he turned back to pick up the John Grisham novel he'd set aside earlier. Instead of going to a restaurant, he would stop at the deli in town for an Italian hoagie and spend the rest of the evening eating and relaxing on the beach. His beach chair was in its usual place in the back of the Jeep.

He was smiling—not at a joke and not because someone had said something to cheer him up. He was smiling just because! The realization caused him to stumble as he was going down the stairs. He grabbed hold of the polished oak banister and steadied himself. *I'm going to be okay,* he assured himself. *Everything's going to be okay.*

The beach was almost deserted. David parked his Jeep in the designated areas on Beach Drive. He reached into his pocket for change to feed the parking meter and then realized parking was free before Memorial Day. Great! He crossed over the promenade, removed his Reeboks, and settled himself just close enough to the water for the waves to gently lap at his feet.

The repetitive motion of the waves lulled him into a hypnotic daze. His body became lethargic. He closed his book, adjusted his hat so it shielded the sun from his face, and dozed off.

Two hours later, David woke to the sound of seagulls fighting over leftover scraps. He shooed them away and shifted his cramped body until he gained some relief. Sleeping in the sun was foolhardy, especially when he had not used any sunscreen, but he must have gotten away with it. He couldn't feel any burning on the exposed areas of his skin.

Behind him on the promenade a group of teenagers was showing off their skill on Rollerblades. Ahead of him a few brave souls bobbed in the chilly ocean. *Must be members of the Polar Bear Club.* He opened his book again and settled down to read.

Unable to concentrate, his mind wandered back to the church service, but he forced it to think of something less intense. Rose. He couldn't think of her as "Buddy." He ought not to think of her at all. He already thought about her too much.

His mother. Now there was a saint. A more caring, compassionate soul never existed. Strange that he never realized how much he loved her until she was gone.

He pictured her singing with the angels, walking heaven's roads with his dad and the baby his parents had lost before he was born.

Will I ever see them again? The thought was fully formed and seeped through to his consciousness before he could stop it. "This is crazy. I've got to get out of here," he shouted with annoyance into the wind.

You can't hide from me!

"I don't want to hide," he shouted. "I just want to understand." David shouted again before he realized he was arguing with the voice inside his head. Or was it outside his head?

Frustrated, he threw his arms over the top of his chair and winced at his deltoid muscles' reluctant contraction. His eyes gazed unseeing at the expanse of the heavens above him. He looked at but didn't see a distant airplane puncture unmoving clouds and leave a jet stream like a needle trailing yarn through puffy balls of cotton. He missed the seagulls diving repeatedly into the water searching for a meal of fresh fish rather than the scraps tossed to them by errant sunbathers. He was deaf to the sounds of laughing children playing tag with the waves.

"Help me to understand," he whispered into the wind. Then louder: "I want to understand!"

Chapter 6

"*It's* David." A child's excited voice roused David from his slumber. "It's Uncle David." From the beach chair he squinted in the direction of the voice and recognized Susan running toward him. Travis and Sammy stumbled along in the sand after her, with Ensign behind them straining at the leash in Zach's hand.

"I knew it was you," she stated proudly as she caught up to him. She perched on the arm of the chair and threw one arm around his neck as if to hold him captive. "See, I told you it was Uncle David," she bragged to Sammy when he caught up.

"We were just leaving when Susan saw you sitting here," Zach explained, breathing hard after chasing the children across the sand. "Can we hitch a ride home with you?"

"Of course," David replied, stretching his cramped body before standing. "Who's gonna give me a hand with these things?" He looked pointedly at the children. They eagerly offered to help him with his towel, book, and hat. David retrieved his sneakers, folded the sand-covered chair, and led the troop toward the parked vehicle.

In the Jeep, Zach suggested they take the scenic route home. David drove along Beach Drive as Zach pointed out the new homes that were being built in the nineteenth-century design to maintain the area's Victorian flavor. As they drove up one street and down the other, David admired the restorations of the older buildings and the detail that was required of the craftsmen in order to maintain the authenticity of the buildings.

The Gothic arches, entrance columns, and cupolas all testified of the city officials' efforts to keep the area "Victorian," even though several different styles had been incorporated into the same building. The moldings and architectural details were painted in bright, contrasting colors that were typical of the Victorian penchant for variety and abundance. David agreed that what he had seen of Cape May so far was a feast for his architectural appetite. What the buildings lacked in stature and magnificence, as in the large glass and steel buildings and office complexes that he usually designed, was made up in technique and artistry.

As they navigated the roads leading away from Beach Drive, Zach told him that Cape May was the country's first seaside resort and had long been the summer resort for privileged visitors. Even in the town's infancy, visitors came by train or steamboat from Delaware and Philadelphia and as far away as London to spend their holidays near the ocean.

After returning to the family home, David accepted Zach's invitation to spend the rest of the evening with the family. They planned to watch the sun go down over Sunset Beach. David needed no further encouragement. He'd had enough of being alone.

One hour before sunset, the Madsen family drove west on Sunset Boulevard to where the road ended on a sandy beach skirting the Delaware Bay. As soon as the cars stopped they piled out, carrying an assortment of chairs, light jackets for the children, and a blanket for the baby.

Standing with Roger, David watched Buddy take charge of the children. She held on to the hands of the two littlest ones and give directions to Susan, who walked ahead of them. After the other women claimed a downed tree trunk as their own, Buddy gathered the children around her.

She crouched and sat on her ankles until she was at their eye level. "Susan, Sammy, Travis—I want you to listen to me very carefully." She waited until three pair of eyes made contact with her own. "You may play along any part of the beach except for three places." She touched her index fingers to each other.

"Number one, you may not go into the water."

"No water," the precocious Susan repeated, shaking her head several times.

Buddy held up the middle finger of her left hand and touched it with her right index finger. "Two, no climbing on those rocks over there." She pointed to the rocky ledge jutting out into the river. The children turned to look at the area she indicated then turned back to Buddy.

"No rocks," Susan echoed.

"No rocks," Sammy repeated.

"No wock," Travis added.

David covered a chuckle. She was good with the kids.

Buddy pointed to a man standing behind a camera mounted to a tripod. "See that man over there?"

All three kids looked toward a photographer, who had his camera delicately perched on a tripod.

When the children looked back at her, she continued. "He's taking pictures of the sunset. Number three, no going close to that man."

"Or his camera." Roger interjected from beside David. Buddy looked their way, nodded in agreement, and turned back to the children.

"Or his camera," she added. She pressed her hands on her knees and levered herself into a standing position. "All right, who wants to hunt for Cape May diamonds?"

As she led the excited children away to search in the sand for tiny quartz nuggets, David quizzed Roger about the possibility of finding diamonds at the New Jersey shore.

Buddy had been helping the children sift through a pile of sand when she became aware of a long shadow stretching across their little collection of "diamonds." Looking up, her heart lurched as her eyes encountered David's. He was standing still, feet slightly apart, his hands stuffed casually in the side pockets of his khaki shorts. As he watched their play, a bemused smile played around the corners of his lips.

"You're enjoying that, aren't you?" he asked.

"I'm having a blast," she confirmed, grinning back. "Wanna join us?"

He shook his head and turned to the man approaching them. "But maybe Joe—"

"Why don't you let me watch the kids, Buddy?" Joe plopped himself on the sand. "David's been itching to have you to himself ever since we got here."

"Joe!" Buddy was aghast. How could he embarrass her so? She felt the telltale warmth creep up the back of her neck. "Joe ..."

"He's right, you know," David intervened, grinning at the mortified look on her face. "I've been silently plotting to get you away from the munchkins without upsetting them."

He took a half-step closer and a puff of wind guided the subtle scent of his aftershave toward her. Lowering her eyelids, she took what she hoped was an unobtrusive breath, savoring the pleasant perfume. If she'd had any lingering doubt that her attraction to him had returned in full measure, her heart's immediate response to his scent put them to rest.

And, she acknowledged to herself, Joe was right. David had been itching to spend time alone with her. His frequent glances in her direction had testified to that. And while she'd made an outward show of resisting him and pretending not to notice his interest in her, inside she'd already capitulated.

David was holding out a hand. "Come on. Tell me about that concrete ship stuck in the river."

Buddy's self-conscious glance over her shoulder confirmed that she and David were already the object of scrutiny by the other adults. She caught her mother's not-so-discreet nudge to Anna Faye. And surely Becky would pop a vein if she had to hold back her giggles for another second. Roger even had the audacity to wink at her. Buddy had to go with David or become the object of even more teasing, and she knew once they started they'd never let up.

Grasping David's outstretched hand, she pulled herself upright, her heart still pounding from Joe's comment. She immediately pulled her hand away from his grasp and made a big deal of slapping away the sand from her denims, using the extended time to steady her breathing and control the erratic beating of her heart.

"Well, as you can see for yourself, the ship sank," she began, and they walked toward the shoreline. She was being impolite. He didn't deserve that. She tried again. "Some ingenious but horribly misguided person thought he could build a ship out of concrete and float it down the Delaware River. This is as far as he got." That wasn't much better.

"Wait a minute," David suddenly exclaimed with excitement, his history lesson forgotten. "I remember you now. You sat in on one of my lectures. I asked for a show of hands from the architecture students. Only about three people raised their hands, and when I asked why the others bothered to be there, some cheeky kid shouted, 'Because you're a hunk.' Then I looked your way and you were … I don't know … sneering. I tried to talk to you after the class but you'd left. I never saw you again. That was you, wasn't it?"

"The one and only," Buddy admitted through clenched teeth. "But my sneering wasn't directed at you. I mean, was I sneering? I didn't … I just didn't want to be lumped with the gawkers, you know? I was there for a serious lecture."

"I understand, and you're forgiven."

They had arrived as close to the river's edge as they dared go. Grasping her elbow, David guided her to a seat on a large boulder, the surface of which been naturally smoothed by years of pounding by the wind, rain, and sand.

"So why'd you take my class?" He squeezed in next to her.

"I needed the extra credit … and I heard you were good," she answered simply. "I believe my friend described you as being, um …" Her eyes swept across the heavens. "'Passionate about the restoration of historical edifices.' No, really," she insisted, bursting into laughter at his wide-eyed incredulity. "Those were his exact words. He was a nice guy but kinda nerdy."

After a moment, a curious shadow replaced the laughter in his eyes. "I never saw you again."

"I saw you … around." She wondered again if she should mention their last meeting. He was sure to be embarrassed when she described his helplessness and the part she'd played in getting him out of the restaurant and into a taxi. The chances were good he'd been so far under the influence that he would have no recollection of the incident. She decided to keep her secret.

"You're missing the sunset."

They sat in companionable silence as the ball of fire slowly descended from the sky and slipped into the water, spreading its bright, orange-colored rays for miles across the horizon. Throughout the show, Buddy was keenly aware of the muscled shoulder leaning into hers. Not only that, she was well aware that quite often his eyes contemplated her profile rather than nature's display unfolding before them. She felt vulnerable under his gaze. Could he tell that her heart was beating unusually fast in his presence? Did her closeness have a similar effect on him? He seemed quite at ease as he watched her, and she hated that she was unable to mask her own feelings.

A spontaneous burst of applause erupted from the people on the beach at the conclusion of the spectacular display. Buddy joined in. It had been a marvelous sunset—what her brain had registered of it.

"I want to get to know you better." David's softly spoken words called Buddy's attention back to him. She turned from the panorama and found that his face was so close to hers she could not look at him directly without giving in to the urge to lean closer. So she lowered her eyes.

"I want to know what motivates you, what kind of music you enjoy, why you and your family find the answer to every question in God, the Bible, or the church. I want to know how you can be so sure of heaven, of being together after death as you are together in life. I want to know why everyone loves you—yes, everyone," he added quickly when she opened her lips to protest, "and why none of the men I met this morning and none of your brothers' friends have staked a claim on you. I want to know—"

"I hate to interrupt." Zach Madsen's voice intruded, and Buddy wished Zack hadn't chosen that moment to come over to where they were seated. She had a feeling that she was seeing the heart of David Willoughby for the first time, and she wanted to see more. Although maybe the interruption was for the better, for she surely had been losing herself in the voice at her shoulder and the man who owned it.

Buddy was unaware that she had been holding her breath. She slowly exhaled as to not give away her feelings. It wouldn't do for David to know just how completely his confession was penetrating the barriers she had erected. Torn between a sense of relief for the interruption and a curious disappointment, she smiled up at her father.

"The kids are getting fussy, so we're leaving," Zach said. "No need for you two to come with us. David, if you'll bring Buddy home...?" Clearly, Zach was waiting for a response from David, not his daughter, but David turned to Buddy.

"I think that decision is up to Rose ..." His shoulder gently brushed hers as he turned back to her, raising his eyebrows in question.

Buddy hated it when her heart pounded out of control as it was doing now. It made her voice sound breathless and excited, and she was trying hard to keep it at a normal pitch. Her thoughts raced. Should she go now with her family and prevent what could turn out to be a deep inspection of her very soul? Or would running away just delay the inevitable? And could she trust him to be gentle with her very vulnerable heart?

Like a distant observer who has no control over the unfolding events before her, she heard her answer erupt from between her lips before she had a chance to properly examine the words.   "I'll stay."

"Before you say anything else," Buddy cautioned David when they had waved their last wave to the family, "there's something I have to tell you."

Although the temperature and darkness had fallen with the setting sun, the night was still comfortable, and Buddy and David remained in their seats on the boulder near the river's edge. Sufficient light radiated into the night from the rising moon that the two were swathed in its soft glow.

Can David hear the pounding of my heart? she wondered. She felt vulnerable, seated so close to him that their shoulders brushed with her every movement. She had not been prepared for his announcement that he wanted to get to know her better, but it had been so spontaneous, so sincere, she felt she owed it to him to come clean about their last meeting. She had to take the chance that he would walk away in embarrassment and end any budding relationship. She had to take that chance, for there could be no friendship between them with that dismal cloud hovering overhead.

"We met a few times after that lecture," she said, "but I think our last meeting is the one you're struggling to remember."

David's brow furrowed, but he remained silent.

"Think back to about five years ago. The Whistle Stop Diner … a little after midnight …"

Like a slide projector clicking away myriad scenes, David's expression flashed through rapidly shifting emotions: fear, anger, pain, pride, loneliness as he relived, one by one, the events leading up to their encounter. His fingers stroked his mustache, stopping occasionally as he clarified some thought while his eyes darted back and forth, trying to recall the hours that had passed him while he'd been in a blind fog of his own making.

Buddy remained silent. There was nothing more to say, no way to help him recall those foggy hours, no way to wipe away the painful events that had brought him to that point. What if he hated her for taking him back to that time?

Slowly, David's agitation ceased and he drew closer to her. She felt his breath, warm and moist, brushed her cheek even as the rest of her body was chilled by the evening air. "It was you." He reached for the hands that were twisting nervously on Buddy's lap. "It was you," he said again. "Do you know what you did for me that night?" His eyes bored his question into hers.

Buddy didn't think he needed a response, and it was just as well, for she seemed to have lost her voice.

"You saved my life. I'd been planning to drink myself into a stupor that night, but when I ordered another drink, you gave me coffee."

Buddy cleared her throat and tried to speak. Relief washed through her. He didn't seem angry. He seemed amazed that she was the one who had helped him. But not angry.

"Yes, you got coffee, and I got fired."

"You were fired? Because you gave me coffee?"

"Uh-uh. Not because I gave you coffee. Because I didn't give the customer what he ordered. Because the other waitress didn't believe me when I said you didn't leave a tip. You had a reputation of being a big tipper and she didn't believe me when I told her you left without tossing some bills on the table. See, you'd been seated at her station. Slouched over it, really. I offered to cover for her because I knew that if I didn't, she would ply you with drinks until you were incapable of walking out of there. When you didn't leave a tip, she reported me to the manager."

"And you were out on your—"

"Yup. Got canned."

"Now it's my turn to apologize."

"No, don't be silly." Buddy dismissed his efforts. "I have no regrets. I'd do it again in a heartbeat."

David slowly shook his head. "You're an amazing woman, do you know that?"

Buddy was pleased but dismissed the compliment. "No, I'm not. I think most people would have done the same thing. But why were you so determined to—"

"—drink myself into oblivion? Well, I, uh, I'd had a really bad day. The worst."

He paused and Buddy waited, sensing there was more. A spasm of something that looked like pain crossed his face, but it was gone before she had time to analyze it.

"I'd just come from a wedding." His voice was so low Buddy wasn't sure he had spoken. "Big wedding. Important people everywhere. The governor, politicians, you name it. We were all standing around

57

outside after the ceremony when a motorcycle screeched into the driveway. The rider started shouting for the bride. Leila. Before anyone could figure out what was happening, she was running across the driveway, and then they were gone. Just took off"—he snapped his fingers in the air—"like that. She ran out on her own wedding."

Buddy's lips mouthed "wow" but no sound escaped her throat.

"Afterward, everybody fell apart. Leila's mother was hysterical, naturally. Her father, well, let's just say he went ballistic. The groom … the groom turned his back on the mayhem and just walked away, out the driveway, down the street, across town. And when he couldn't drag his body another step, he found someone to ply him with drinks. He'd decided to drink himself into forgetfulness or die trying."

Silence stretched between them. David seemed to be wrestling with painful memories, but some sixth sense told Buddy she should not intervene but allow him to break through to the other side without her assistance. She watched the play of emotions across his face, heard his shallow breathing, felt the tension within him.

When he was ready to continue his story, David slowly turned his head in her direction. Through the darkness lit only by the moonlight, their eyes met and held while he ended his story.

"I would have succeeded, had it not been for the angel who brought me coffee."

Chapter 7

Seated on the edge of the boulder, her body held taut, Buddy struggled to maintain her composure. Whoever said you shouldn't let your adversary see you sweat didn't have a clue. This wasn't about sweating. This was about controlling her heaving stomach. Any minute now she was going to be violently ill.

David had a wife. She had carried a torch for this man for years, and all that time he was married. She swallowed several deep breaths and fought to gain control.

Several seconds passed before she felt in sufficient control to speak. "You're married." The annoying heaving had started again.

"No. No, listen," David's fingers crushed hers as he attempted to arrest her runaway thoughts. "Rose, listen to me. We exchanged vows but that's all we exchanged before she ran away with the man she really loved. Honest. We never made it to the honeymoon. Not even to the reception."

With more strength than she thought she could muster, Buddy yanked away the hand that was ensconced in his. "But you're married!" She leapt to her feet and spun around to face him, the loose sand underfoot impeding her movement. Her eyes fired darts at him, and while her voice never rose above a hush, the vehemence with which her words were delivered could leave him in no doubt as to intensity of her anger.

"How dare you make advances toward me while you're committed to another woman? How dare you impose upon my family's good nature without letting on that you have a wife tucked away somewhere? How dare you, David? How dare you!"

She wanted to kick and scream her frustration. Over the years he had stirred such conflicting emotions within her: love, pity, admiration, but now the only emotion she could dredge up was anger. And maybe hate.

In the recesses of her being she knew she was overreacting. More than that, she was being a poor example of a woman of faith. But she was livid, and she wanted to vent her fury on him. Anything to wipe that smug grin from his face.

He was grinning.

"This isn't funny!" She stormed at him.

"You're not sitting over here," he said calmly, the mirth creeping up his face to his very expressive eyes. A moment later, his face sobered. "I never saw Leila again. About six months after the wedding, her parents called me with the news that she'd been killed in a motorcycle accident."

"Oh." Buddy felt her body relax by degrees. What must David think? She knew her ardent response to his story had given away her feelings for him. Sheepishly she returned to her seat on the boulder.

"I'm not married," David uttered the reassuring words for her, although they were now unnecessary, and then repeated them, as if for his own comfort. "I'm not married."

"You're a widower?"

"Yes."

"Why didn't you tell me before?"

"When? How? I guess I could have introduced myself, 'Hi, I'm David Willoughby and you should know I used to be married.' It's not the sort of thing you drop into the middle of a conversation, especially not with someone you're trying to get to know better. That sort of information could be a turn-off, you know? Besides, since I met you, we haven't been alone long enough to have a serious conversation. There wasn't a chance. I'm kinda surprised I'm telling you now."

"But you would have told me?"

"Yeah. Sooner or later. After I had a better sense of where we're heading."

"And do you know where we're heading?"

"No, but like I said earlier, I want to get to know you better. The real you, not just Rose the daughter, or Aunt Buddy. I want to know *you*. In a man-woman kinda way."

From the corner of her eye, Buddy saw his features tightening. She was secretly pleased at his declaration, but he seemed to be having misgivings.

"I'm making a mess of this," he said, his voice subdued. He ran his open palms over his head from forehead to nape in an act of weariness before turning back to her. "Look, it's been years since I dated anyone seriously. The kind of experience I had left me feeling—I don't know—beaten up. Deflated. Like I'd been kicked around and left to bleed. Funny thing is, I think I deserved it. The way she treated me was about the same as I'd treated girlfriends in the past. I used them and then tossed them aside. It left me questioning myself, questioning all women. I just didn't trust them anymore. I didn't like them, and after some honest self-examination, I didn't like myself either."

He inhaled deeply and continued. "Now you, the way you are with the kids, your family ... I never looked for those traits in the women I dated. They had to be gorgeous and witty. In fact, they were shallow. You're not like them. You're, well, different. I admire the way you listen to your mom's opinions and take your dad's advice, things like that."

"You make me sound unreal, but I know what you mean," Buddy agreed. "With me, it's a little different. I look for similar qualities in the men I date, but I won't date someone who doesn't share my faith."

"That's another thing I don't understand. Your faith. I was taught the same principles, but in you it's different. Your faith is not something you pull out on Sunday mornings and put to rest after the church service. You live it. It's part of you. I admire that, but I don't understand it."

He ran his hand over his head again and sighed, the plaintive sound emanating from deep within him. "I have an appointment with Pastor Miller tomorrow morning. I'm not saying I'm ready to make a commitment yet, but I get the feeling I can talk with him man to man and not have him preach at me."

Buddy sensed his sincerity. *He means what he's saying. It's not about getting to me. He really means it.* She prayed, *God, soften his heart. Reach him at his deepest need. Make him understand that you love him and that you want him for your own.*

"You're on the right track," she encouraged. "If you want to talk some more after you meet with Pastor Miller, let me know."

He had linked their fingers again. He unconsciously caressed the back of her hand with his thumb.

"Just make sure this isn't just about getting to know me," she said, and then whispered, "I'll be praying for you."

The soft intonation of her voice made her promise sound very intimate. He must have felt it too, for his anguish receded, and his eyes radiated such intense warmth that it touched Buddy to her very core.

Wanting to reduce any sense of gathering intimacy, she spoke quickly. "We could meet for lunch afterward?"

David pondered her offer for some time. "You don't know how much I want to say yes, but I have to spend some time at the construction site after my appointment with the pastor. I haven't done an ounce of work since I arrived here and the contractor's expecting me tomorrow. By the time we're done working, it'll be time to head up north again."

Buddy hid her disappointment well. "You're right. We did monopolize your time this weekend, but my folks enjoyed getting to know you again. They're not going to take it well when I tell them about your marriage." *They aren't going to like it one bit. Especially Dad.*

"Would you mind letting me tell them? I think I owe them that. They've been very gracious to me. Besides, I'd like to hold off telling them for a while. For selfish reasons, I admit. I don't want them thinking I'm making a play for their daughter after knowing her only one weekend. It's how I got into trouble with Leila in the first place. I'm less impulsive now. That experience taught me to think things through. Act less on emotion and more on hard knowledge and intellect."

"Emotion's not bad."

"No, but if the relationship is only being held together by emotions, it's doomed to fail. It's a little like the buildings I design. The larger the construction, the more solid the foundation has to be. In a relationship, the foundation has to be something more dependable than feelings, and I'm still trying to figure out what that something is."

Buddy was feeling more and more like a wizened old sage as he spoke. She could end his questioning and tell him what that foundation was, but he'd be better off discovering that on his own. No, not really on his own, because such knowledge could only come directly from the source of all knowledge, and by the looks of things, David was well on his way to tapping into that source.

She would honor his request to delay telling her parents about his past, even though she was a little uncomfortable withholding that information. It went against her usual practice of telling them everything. Still, there was nothing to be gained by enlightening them now rather than later. Either way, Leila was history. Dead. Relegated to the past. From the ashes of that marriage would emerge a newer, stronger man. God willing he would be the one who met Buddy's criteria for a life mate.

Every time David made the three-hour trek from his Bergen home to Cape May, it seemed longer than the time before. He just couldn't decide if this was because he hated to drive long distances alone or because he so desperately wanted to be with the woman he had come to love.

The last twenty minutes were always the worst. He found himself counting off the final landmarks: the end of the Parkway, the bridge, the coast guard base, the water tower, and finally, Maple Drive.

He swung into the driveway and leaped from the Jeep, chuckling to himself when he realized his heart was pounding like that of a love-sick schoolboy.

The living room was deserted except for Mary.

"David, you naughty boy," Mary scolded as he hugged her and swung her off her feet in a wide circle, but her smile softened her words and she grinned at him as he put her down. He held both her wrists for a moment until he was sure the wild movement had not upset her equilibrium.

"Happy Fourth of July." He kissed her cheek and sniffed her neck. "Nice perfume, Mary. Smells like barbecue sauce. What's cooking? Ribs? Chicken?"

"Both." She snapped him with her dish towel. "And that's not my perfume." Without pausing for breath, she shouted, "David's here!" to no one in particular.

A moment later, Buddy made her way downstairs. She held out her hand to him. "David, nice to see you."

"I thought we had gotten past the handshake stage, Rose." He grinned at her, using the outstretched hand to pull her close.

Blushing, she offered him her cheek.

He kissed her without releasing her hand and then used it to twirl her around in front of him. "Nice outfit. New?"

"Mmm, sort of."

"For me?"

She hesitated and he sensed her lack of experience in casual banter. "What if I said yes?"

"I'd say, 'You done good.' I like it."

"Thank you." She tried to turn away, but he used the hand he still held to bring her back to him.

"So did you?"

She caught the sparkle of mischief in his eyes and boldly decided to play along. "Did I what?"

"Get dressed up just for me?"

"Are you flirting with me?"

"You didn't answer my question, and yes, I'm flirting with you. Does it bother you?"

"Should it?"

"Don't you know you shouldn't answer a question with another question?"

"Why not?"

"You're still doing it. Okay. Let's start over." He blew out an impatient breath, but the twinkle in his eyes told her he was enjoying this. "Look at me, Rose."

She raised her eyes to meet his.

"Did you get dressed up just for me?" David thought he would drown in the depth of the eyes that bored into his. He watched her take a deep, steadying breath before responding.

"Yes. I bought this outfit because I thought you would like it. I put it on today hoping you would like it."

"Thank you." His eyes still held hers. "And in case you're wondering, I don't just like it, I love it."

In the span of silence that followed their teasing, his face drew close to hers. A sense of longing bubbled within him. Would she let him kiss her? The pulse at the base of her neck throbbed so fiercely, he was sure he could hear it. He drew closer, but at the last second, she turned her head aside.

"Chicken," he whispered, kissing her temple. He casually threw an arm across her shoulders and they walked toward the back of the house, through to the deck. At the door, Buddy attempted to reach for the handle, but David beat her to it.

"Allow me, ma'am." He turned the doorknob and pulled the door toward them, allowing her to go through ahead of him, but he maintained his connection with her shoulder.

On the deck, Pastor Miller and his wife, Anne, immediately engaged David, eager to learn about his spiritual growth since their last meeting.

David's arm slipped from Buddy's shoulders. Instantly, he missed the cozy warmth and sense of oneness.

"May I say the blessing?" David later asked Zach when they were seated around the long picnic table. With a nod, Zach gave his permission. David clasped Buddy's hand in his larger, left hand and Mary's in his right.

"God, my Father in heaven," he began in a bold, steady voice. He paused, distracted by Buddy's thumb, which had unconsciously started a sweeping caress across the back of his hand. He felt a welling inside his heart such as he could not recall feeling before. The woman whose hand fit so snugly within his own had given so much of herself to him and asked for nothing in return. He wanted to respond to her openness by giving something back to her.

Give what? His heart? His love? Did he dare?

"Father in heaven," David began again in a barely audible voice which wavered slightly. "When I first sat at this table a few months ago I was miserable, lonely, and lost. But in your infinite mercy you saw me and touched my worthless life. You picked me up from a path leading to destruction and you set me down in a quiet place. You've given me friends who nurture me and support me and guide me on my journey. God, how can I thank you? Words just don't seem sufficient."

He drew a steadying breath and continued. "I ask for your blessing on this country of ours whose birthday we celebrate today. I ask your blessing on this meal before us. Use it to nurture and strengthen us. And bless this family gathered here ..." He opened his eyes and focused on the bowed heads, naming each of them as they were seated around the table. "Mary, Anne, Pastor Ed, Zach, and Rose." David's voice softened as he said Buddy's given name.

Buddy lifted her head. Their eyes met and held.

"I love them all and I thank you again for bringing them into my life. Amen."

Several moments lapsed before he and Buddy released hands. He recognized her struggle to portray a relaxed composure she didn't feel. He immediately offered her a glass of iced tea. She accepted it with an unsteady hand.

She nodded her thanks.

He winked his response.

"Who's up for the fireworks?" David asked later.

With none of the others interested, Buddy and David decided to drive to Wildwood to see the display there.

Before he started the engine, David turned in his seat to face Buddy. Gone was the giddiness from earlier. He looked serious. "I told your father I'm very attracted to you, and that I think you feel the same toward me." He didn't wait for her to confirm or deny her feelings. "I want to tell you right now before we become more involved that I am committed to keeping our relationship pure. My men's group at church taught me that praying with my date at the start and end of an evening is the best way to make sure that we don't, uh, cross the line. Will you pray with me now?"

Buddy nodded her agreement. She couldn't speak. Her heart was just too full for words.

After the fireworks, David pulled into the driveway and immediately turned off the ignition key, stilling the engine. Without lingering, he exited the Jeep and quickly walked around the front to the passenger door. He opened it wide but placed his body in the opening, blocking Buddy's exit. Raising his arms to the top of the vehicle he planted both his hands firmly on either side of the door frame.

With a satisfied grin he told her, "I can't remember when I've enjoyed a day as much as I enjoyed this one." His eyes roamed over her face, which was visible in the amber glow of light that spilled from the porch.

Buddy tilted her head, a mischievous twinkle in her eye. "Didn't you tell me you were accosted by one of New Jersey's finest this morning?"

David flashed her a saucy smile. "Even with a hefty fine for speeding, it was a wonderful day. The best!"

He was going to kiss her. She could feel the energy sparking between them. His eyes caressed her face. Her hair was a mess and the salty sea air had ruined her makeup. Still, she sat unflinching under his gaze, allowing his eyes their fill. Her heart pounded blood through her veins, the swish-swish echoing deep inside her ears. Surely he could hear it? She needed air. Her nostrils flared, her lips parted. He bent his head and gently brushed her lips with his own.

He withdrew his head only far enough so that she could see him clearly without crossing her eyes and feel his warm breath on her heated face. Then he lowered his head a second time. She met him halfway.

Afterward, she couldn't distinguish the words, but she knew he was praying. When he was finished, he stepped back and lowered his arms from the door frame, wincing as his shoulder muscles retracted.

Buddy reached down for her sandals she had kicked off during the drive. Slipping them on, she stepped out of the vehicle onto the driveway. David slammed the door shut and they climbed to the porch, their steps in time with each other. She handed him her key; he unlocked the front door and returned the key to her. They faced each other, reluctant to call it a night.

Finally, David inhaled deeply and blew out a breath. "I'll see you tomorrow. Sleep tight." He flicked her nose with his finger, winked, and retraced his steps.

Curiously disappointed that he hadn't attempted to kiss her again, Buddy turned the lock and slowly climbed the stairs to bed.

Later, lying between the cool sheets, she relived the last moments of their evening together. The fireworks had been spectacular, but they had missed most of the display, preferring to revel in the warmth of each other's company.

There was no doubt in her mind that she was completely and irrevocably in love with David. She was ready to make a commitment to him, but she knew that his experience of the past had made him cautious. She couldn't fault him. Given similar circumstances, she knew she would feel the same way. So she would wait patiently, until he was as sure of her commitment to him as he needed to be.

And her final prayer before her eyes closed, continued to be, *Let it be soon.*

Chapter 8

On the Sunday of the July Fourth holiday weekend, David rose early, showered, shaved, dressed, and left Magnolia Manor in plenty of time to arrive at the Madsen family home for breakfast. He didn't want to be late for Mary's famous light and fluffy blueberry pancakes with maple syrup and tiny link sausages. He knew how much it thrilled her when he asked for additional helpings.

After breakfast, the family set out on the short walk to the church for the Bible-study hour followed by the morning worship service. Buddy invited David to sit in on her youth class.

The kids' wealth of biblical knowledge and the passion with which they spoke truly amazed him. Then his own experiences in a youth group flashed before his eyes. He had been like most of these teenagers, eager to give his opinion, to quote and expound on favorite verses. Yet until a few months ago, he had not truly made the commitment to turn his life over to Christ.

Within his heart David felt the need to share his own experience with the class. From his seat at the end of a sofa that had seen better days, he raised his hand to get Buddy's attention. "David?" she acknowledged him.

"I wonder if I might share some of my own experiences with the group?"

Several pairs of curious eyes turned in his direction.

"Fine with me, David. How about it, class?"

The group nodded and murmured their consent.

David moved to the front of the large room and began to talk about his teenage and young adult years. Withholding nothing but the most intimate details of his life, he spoke about his need to belong to the "in" crowd and how his activities and friends in high school often resulted in conflicts with his parents. Yet, he acknowledged, he had been in church every Sunday, and his conservative attire, his speech, and his mannerisms had led everyone to believe he believed as they did.

He cautioned the class against playing the game and not being serious. "Play the game long enough," he warned them, "and even you will start to believe the lie."

He could see from the intense gazes and the squirms from some of his audience that his words were having the desired effect. Nothing made an impression like speaking from real-life experience!

Finally he stepped away from the center of the room. He thanked Buddy for allowing him to speak and thanked the young people for their attention.

Two beeps of the electric bell announced the end of the session, and Buddy dismissed the class. A couple of the kids hung back to thank David for his candor and to disclose some of the challenges they faced in school. He encouraged their renewed commitment to stand firm in their beliefs.

"Hang on to that one, Miss Rose," one cheeky young woman shouted across the room on her way out the door. "He's a keeper."

Buddy blushed delightfully and turned her attention to gathering her papers and erasing the white board while David restored the chairs to order.

"You're an amazing teacher, Miss Rose," David remarked as he turned off the light and closed the door behind them.

"You're not so bad yourself, Mister David," she responded. "Sally Jacobs's eyes never left you for a moment."

"Sally Jacobs didn't hear a word I said," David countered. "I know the posture. Make eye contact. Make the teacher think you're taking it in. I was there, remember?"

Buddy nodded in agreement. "We've all been there. But for the grace of God …" She left her words unfinished.

The couple climbed the stairs to the main level of the building and turned right, crossing the foyer and moving toward the doors of the sanctuary. Several members remembered David from his previous visits and stopped to shake his hand.

Inside the main sanctuary, they made their way up the left aisle toward Mary, who was already seated in the third row. As before, they passed the young girl in her wheelchair who grinned back at David when he winked at her. Buddy slid into the pew beside her mother, leaving room for David at the end.

As the song service progressed, David's strong baritone swelled in chorus with the other congregants. Four months earlier, his voice had been all technique. Today it was all heart. Buddy's heart swelled in thanksgiving.

During the prayer, he snaked his hand across the seat to cover the back of hers. She turned over her palm and allowed their fingers to intertwine. While the pastor prayed for the turning back of the hearts of the nation, for those members of the congregation who were ill, for countries at war, and for the homeless and hungry, his own prayers were for his relationship with the woman seated beside him.

The pastor spoke on the sanctity of marriage and the obligation that a husband and wife have toward each other. He ended the message by challenging the married couples in the congregation to assure their spouses of their love and commitment to their marriage. Then, he said, make the same commitment to your children. A rather subdued congregation stood for the closing hymn and prayer.

Back home, the four sat down to a dinner of cold roast beef and an assortment of salads. When they were done, David pushed away his plate, patting his too-full stomach. "As usual, you outdid yourself," he told Mary.

"Thanks, dear. So did you." Mary gleamed. "Do you have room for dessert?"

"Don't I usually?" He laughed back at her.

"Wait a minute," Zach interrupted, tapping the tines of his fork on the rim of his glass. "Sometimes Ed Miller asks us to do some cockeyed stuff, and this morning I thought he was really going off the deep end. Then I remembered our good friends Rich and Lynn Waters. Divorced after, what? Thirty years?"

"Thirty-two," Mary confirmed.

"Thirty-two. So I said to myself, 'It happened to them, it could happen to us.' Maybe this recommitment thing isn't so farfetched. So here goes." He cleared his throat. "Mary—"

Buddy interrupted him. "Daddy, you're supposed to take her hand."

Zach smiled indulgently, pushed back his chair, walked over to Mary's end of the table, and took her hand in his. He smoothed the calluses on the palm of her hand, turned it over, and kissed the age spots near her knuckles. He gazed down into her sweet face, at the wrinkles on either side of her eyes, at the slightly sagging jaw that once had been taut.

"Mary Madsen, I've loved you from the moment I set eyes on you, and after thirty-odd years of marriage and five children, I still bless the day we met. I love you as much today as I did then. More. I'm in this for the long haul. This is a lifetime commitment for me." He raised her hand to his lips, kissed the area near her wedding band, and gently returned her hand to her lap.

Zach moved over to Buddy's chair and held out his open hand to her. "Rosebud …"

"Whaaa-aat? Oh, Daddy, don't be silly."

"Give me your hand, Buddy," he commanded in a stern voice.

She reluctantly placed her right hand in his.

Zach's voice resumed its tenderness. "Rosebud, you were such a little thing when we brought you home. You were all wrinkled with a tiny screwed-up face and just the most perfect little rosebud mouth. Your brothers fell in love with you immediately. My heart just about fell out of my chest the first time you smiled at me. Sweetheart, be assured that I love you too much to even considering leaving your mother."

"Oh, Daddy," Buddy said again, tears welling in her eyes. She blinked rapidly to keep them from spilling over. Zach kissed the top of her head and returned to his seat.

For a while the others sat silently, too emotional to speak.

"Okay, my turn," David announced. Three pairs of questioning eyes turned toward him.

"Zach …" David started.

"Wait a minute," Zach interrupted, grinning. "Did you and I ever exchange vows?"

"No, sir," David chuckled. "But I think the time is right for me to express my commitment too." He started again. "Zach, Mary." He looked at each as he spoke their name and then paused. His heart was full but he wanted to make his intentions clear, not just ride the wave of emotion that enfolded them. He picked up his fork, made a few circles on his plate, replaced the fork, and looked up at his hosts.

"This is not the way I intended to declare my hand," David continued, "but it just seems like the right time to say what is in my heart." He directed his words to Zach and Mary, but his eyes met and held Buddy's. "Some day soon, really soon, I intend to ask your daughter to marry me. If she accepts my proposal as I hope she will, I promise to cherish her all the days of our lives. I promise to do everything in my power to make sure she will never want to leave me or any children who might be born to us …"

He had barely formed the words when Buddy burst into tears, pushed back her chair from the table, and sped up the stairs two at a time.

"What did I say?" David looked from one to the other, consternation sweeping his face. Had he spoken out of turn? He could hardly hide his confusion.

"Let me tell you something, son." Zach casually motioned him to regain his seat. "Some women cry when they're sad, some cry when they're hurt, but they all cry when they're happy. The happier they are, the harder they cry. Don't try to understand it and don't worry about it. She'll be down before you know it.

"And by the way," Zach continued, "Mary and I are way ahead of you. We've seen this coming for some time and we've discussed it. You have our permission to court our daughter."

"I have to ask her first."

"That's just a formality, son. Just a formality. She feels the same about you."

True to her father's prediction, Buddy returned to the table after a few moments. Although her eyes bore the traces of weeping, her smile had returned and within moments she was again joining in the dinnertime banter.

A wild mix of emotions surged within her. She hoped they had moved on to discussing some other topic. She hoped they continued in the same vein. She very much wanted to hear more of David's declaration but felt apprehensive at the same time.

Having swallowed his last bite of peach cobbler and ice cream, Zach leaned back in his chair, patted his bulging stomach, and turned to David with a serious face but a comical twinkle in his eye. "Son, there's one more key ingredient for a happy marriage. Find yourself a woman who can put together a really good peach cobbler."

MAXINE THOMAS

Without missing a beat, David turned to Buddy. "How are you in the kitchen, woman?"

"I make a *mean* peach cobbler," she teased.

"All riiiiiight!" He held his hand high for a high-five, and Buddy, not wanting to disappoint him, slapped her own hand against his.

David lifted the last bite of peach cobbler to his lips and lowered his eyelids as his lips curled around the tines of the fork. His tongue savored the complementary flavors of syrupy-sweet peach juice laced with brown sugar, cinnamon, and nutmeg. This was really good stuff! He resisted the temptation to lick the last crumb from the fork and instead lowered it to his plate.

As he slowly and methodically chewed, he mentally recounted his words of commitment: someday soon, someday soon …

Chapter 9

$\mathcal{R}$eplete from the delicious dinner, David relaxed out on the deck with the family in the warm afternoon sunshine. Buddy poured four glasses of ice-cold lemonade and passed them around with a napkin and coaster and then returned to the webbed deck chair close to David's. Across from them, Zach lounged in a matching chair, one hand lazily scratching a spot behind Ensign's ear, while Mary lay half asleep in a green canvas hammock.

David felt at home. This family had welcomed him into their fold without question, embracing him as one of their own. He'd been aware for some time that their complete and unquestioning acceptance of him left him with the responsibility of divulging the tidbit of information about his past he'd shared with Rose, and only Rose. He owed it to them to be completely candid about his marriage. If he had any intention of holding on to their love and respect, he must tell them about Leila. Now. Today.

David's fingers tightened around the hand that lay casually in his own. Sensing the tension growing within him, Buddy sent him a questioning look. He raised her hand to his lips and placed a gentle kiss on her wrist. Buddy's frown deepened.

"Zach, Mary," he began, "I told you a few minutes ago that I would like to court your daughter, but there's something I should have told you before I declared myself." His eyes swept from Zach to Mary and back again. Their expressions hadn't changed. It almost seemed as if they hadn't heard him. "Five years ago, I married a woman I barely knew." He heard Mary's quick intake of breath. Buddy's fingers tightened around his. He continued quickly. "It happened at a time in my life when I was feeling lonely and vulnerable. My parents were ailing. I knew they wouldn't be around much longer. I was bored, between jobs, searching for a good time.

"I met her at a nightclub. She was dancing on top of a pool table. Her long, jet-black hair was flying, her skirts twirling. I remember thinking that she spelled trouble. But she looked like fun, and I was looking for fun." He inhaled deeply, anticipating comments from his audience. When no one said anything, he continued.

"Later that night she begged me to drive her home. Said she'd had a fight with her boyfriend and he drove away without her. I took her home. She lived with her parents in a really upscale neighborhood in Bergen. The next day she telephoned me—I don't know how she got my number. She invited me to dinner at her parents' house. She said they wanted to thank me for seeing her home. It turns out they were hosting some big social event. A charity fund-raiser or something.

"I found out afterward that her parents encouraged her to invite a friend to their party because they wanted to show Leila—that was her name—show her that her friends didn't fit into their social circle. They'd expected her to invite one of her biker buddies. Instead, she brought me. I was dressed appropriately, was educated, articulate. I was the kind of husband they wanted for their daughter. I fit the mold. They loved me. We were married fewer than two months later.

"After the wedding ceremony, while we were standing outside in the receiving line, her boyfriend rode up on a motorcycle shouting for her for all he was worth. It took her all of thirty seconds to decide to go off with him. I never saw her again."

"You must have been very hurt." Mary's tone was commiserating and David felt heartened.

"No, I don't think I was hurt," David responded. "At least, I don't think so now, but I was angry. Angry at her because of the embarrassment she caused her family, my own family, and me, but angry at myself most of all." He leaned forward in his chair. "See, I knew I wasn't in love with her. I was lonely and I was using her. What I didn't know at the time was that she was using me too. She was only nineteen, and I guess from her perspective, marriage seemed like the best way to get out from under her parents' control. I just wish she'd run away before the marriage instead of afterward.

"About six months after the wedding, I got a telephone call from her parents. It seems Leila and her boyfriend were killed when their motorcycle was in a head-on collision with an oil tanker. She was pretty badly burned, they said. She was still wearing the rings I'd given her when we married."

"Why did you wait until now to tell us about this?" Zach spoke for the first time, his voice stern.

"I wanted you to get to know me first. I didn't want you to think my overtures toward your daughter were ..."—he searched for the right word—"cavalier."

Zach leaned forward in his chair and his eyes targeted David. "No, I wouldn't say cavalier. I don't think that. But inconsiderate?" Although he did not raise his voice, David knew he was upset, and disappointed. He couldn't answer the older man. Zach was right. He should have been up front about his marriage from the very beginning. He realized that now.

"And did you think you owed it to Buddy to tell her about your marriage?" Zach continued.

David felt the pressure on his fingers from the hand tightly ensconced in his own.

"I did know, Daddy," Buddy blurted out before David could speak. "I chose not to tell you."

"You chose not to tell us." Zach swung to face his daughter. "You chose not to tell us."

David sensed the angry tide building within the man. He watched him clench and unclench the muscles in his jaws. A blood vessel on his forehead grew larger with each muscle clench. Any minute now, steam would surely come shooting from his ears. *Say something,* he prodded himself. *Anything.*

"Sir, I asked Rose not to tell you because I wanted to tell you myself. I—we—I wasn't trying to deceive you, sir. It's just that, I don't think of myself as a widower, probably because I didn't ever feel married. As a matter of fact, I was about to petition the courts for an annulment when I'd heard she'd been killed."

"An ... annul ..." Zach was not being calmed by David's words.

"Yes, sir, an annulment. Just to be sure that she ..."

"What do you mean, 'Just to be sure'? She's dead. How much surer do you need to be?"

"Well." David paused, searching out Rose's face. Why hadn't he told her everything? Was this going to be too much for her? Would her love for him take a nosedive because he hadn't been completely honest with her? He couldn't blame her if she walked away. He should have been completely candid. What had he been thinking? He should have told her everything. Stupid, stupid, he mentally berated himself. "There's more."

"There's more?" Zach looked at him in astonishment. His forehead knit together even as his lips hung open after his question.

"More?" Buddy echoed her father.

"The authorities couldn't be absolutely sure the body was hers. She was burned very badly. It was a huge fire ... gasoline from the wreck ..."

"Did they issue a death certificate?"

"Yes, sir, but in the name of Jane Doe."

"Why not in her own name?"

"Er, her parents disowned her after she'd eloped. They refused to fly out to Florida to identify her body or to submit her dental history."

"But *you* are willing to accept that the body was hers?" Zach persisted.

"Well, no, sir, which is why I went through with the annulment. That way, if the body wasn't really hers, I'd have taken the steps to end the marriage."

David could not believe his simple announcement had taken such a turn. What on earth had he been thinking? And why was Zach quizzing him about the circumstances surrounding Leila's death? If the state was satisfied with the accident report and the follow-up conclusions, shouldn't the family be satisfied as well?

"Well, now, son, you know very well how this family feels about ending a marriage. What if she isn't dead, son? Have you thought about that?" Zach demanded. "What if your wife is walking around somewhere with amnesia? What if you marry my daughter while you have a wife in, I don't know, Timbuktu or somewhere?"

David watched the man rise from his chair and pace back and forth across the width of the deck, a look of both anger and pain painted his face.

"But I have a decree of annulment, which—"

"—which means *nothing*," Zach insisted, his voice escalating.

David strode across the deck after him. "Okay. If I conduct a search and come up empty, will it mean something then?" The volume and intensity of David's tone rivaled Zach's. "This all happened more than five years ago. When do I get to say, 'It's over and done with'? When do I get a chance to move on with my life? *She* did this, not me! *She* walked away. I was perfectly willing to—"

"Stop, stop! Both of you." Mary jumped up from the hammock, waving her hands frantically toward them. "Zach, calm down before you do yourself an injury! Sit, David. You too Buddy," she said as Buddy started to rise from her own seat. "Sit, I said!"

Zach perched on the edge of the chair he had just vacated. Realizing Mary would not continue until he obeyed her command, David meekly returned to his seat and placed his elbows on his thighs, his head in his palms.

"Now then! This is a big problem. A doozy! Why don't we all spend a few days praying about it and wait for God's lead? Zach, we'll discuss this with Ed. See if he has some advice on where we go from here. David, you talk with your pastor. Ask your men's group to start praying about what we should do. Let's not jump off the deep end yet. David, will you be able to make another trip down here in a week or two, or should we plan to come north?"

"I'll come back. I don't know when. I'll rearrange my schedule." David responded in a barely audible voice. His shoulders slumped forward in defeat. He hadn't anticipated this response. This had gone south really fast. "I'll give you a call."

"All right. Then it's settled. We'll wait to hear from you." Mary dismissed him, but David did not move from his chair. How could he? To walk away would be to accept defeat. He'd only wanted to declare his love for their daughter. What had happened here?

"David?"

Although he heard Mary speak his name, David was too distraught to respond. His body felt leaden, welded to his seat. He'd expected this to be so simple. Some questions, yes. Some expressions of disappointment at his casual treatment of his marriage vows, certainly. But not this dismissal, this banishment from their home.

"I can't leave like this." His empty hands reached out to them, begging for understanding. "How can I leave here like this?" His bleak eyes searched the group, seeking some sign of empathy.

"You can't." Buddy addressed him for the first time. He recognized the tension in her, although her voice remained amazingly calm. He had withheld much of the details of his marriage from her and she ought to be hopping mad.

"Why don't we take a walk around the block?" she added.

Circling around to the back of David's chair, she placed her hands on his shoulders and gently massaged them until they relaxed beneath her fingers. Then she reached for his hand. "Let's drive down to the beach. We can talk there."

Grasping the slender fingers that were held out to him, David stood. His eyes darted back and forth between the two older folks. He searched unsuccessfully for the words that would bridge the chasm that suddenly separated them. How quickly had they been split apart, he from this family he had adopted and who had embraced him as their own. He wanted to cry out, to protest his innocence, to ask their forgiveness for his folly. He wanted to plead with them for their understanding and for absolution. He had been young and headstrong. Was there no mercy for him?

But no sounds emanated from his parched throat, no words of comfort landed on his deafened ears, and the gentle tug on his fingers insisted he turn away.

A million platitudes whizzed through Buddy's head, but she dismissed them for what they were—platitudes. Clichés that sounded intelligent but did little to comfort the hearer. For the life of her, she couldn't think of a single thing to say that would lessen the tension inside the car. What could she say that hadn't been said while they were seated on the deck? Nothing could assuage the intensity of their emotions and the turmoil of their thoughts.

Buddy laid her head against the back of the seat. She closed her eyes, feigning relaxation. The act did not reach up to her fiercely knit brow or down to her lips, one corner of which she nibbled unconsciously. Inside she was a bag of twisted nerves.

She touched the fingers of one hand to her temple and gently massaged it. A vein throbbed along the side of her neck. She tried to stop the restless finger picking at the cuticle of her thumb. She feigned a semi-relaxed pose but knew it didn't fool David for a minute. She, who was typically in control of her emotions, was a mass of nerves, and it was *his* fault.

This pit, this mess was of his own making, but she'd fallen in love with him and therefore fallen into the pit with him. Now they were both suffering.

David's thoughts must have been similar to hers because he slammed the heel of his hand hard on the top of the steering wheel, startling Buddy. The car swung to the right and she grabbed the dashboard for support but remained silent.

At Sunset Beach, David swung the vehicle into a vacant parking spot. He switched off the engine and turned in his seat toward Buddy. "Rose …"

"Shhh." Buddy touched a finger to her lips. "Let's walk." She led the way past the gift shop, across the warm, pebbly beach, and onto the cooler, wet sand. Buddy slipped off her sandals, holding one in each hand, and continued along the water line so the waves gently lapped at her ankles. David followed a half step behind her, his hands buried in the side pockets of his slacks.

A young couple lay on a large blanket sunning themselves. She side-stepped them, turning her gaze toward the river instead, where two passenger ferries inched their way across the Delaware Bay toward Lewes, the port city on the other side. Would she and David ever share that trip together?

The gentle walk, coupled with the hypnotic rhythm of the water, slowly eased her tension. Buddy switched her sandals to one hand

and shortened her steps. As David drew alongside her, she slipped her hand into the crook of his arm.

"David, earlier today you told my parents you had certain intentions toward me?"

"Yes, and I meant every word. There's so much more that I want to say to you."

Buddy wrestled with her words. She didn't want to add to David's pain, but she knew she had to release him from his declarations. "You didn't ask me about my feelings toward you."

"Rose, be serious." His tone was dismissive.

"I've never been more serious about anything in my life." She stopped walking and turned to him.

His eyes wildly searched her face for some sign of jesting. He turned away, staring.

Buddy would have given anything to help him turn his back on the turmoil and uncertainty he was feeling. She could think of nothing more satisfying than to spend the rest of her life in the company of this strong, warm man who'd turned back to her, his heart in his hands.

"I love you, Rose, never doubt that. But your father is right. We can't … we can't plan a life together when these questions about my past remain. Five years ago I made a commitment before God to love and honor someone else through good and bad times. The law nullified the agreement. But at the very least, I need to try to find out if she really is dead before I can even think about a future with you. I know God has forgiven me for entering into a marriage without consulting him, but …"

"David, all this happened before you came to Christ …"

"No, no it didn't. That's another part of my life I've kept hidden from you. I knew Christ as a child, but I turned by back on him in my teens. I questioned everything I had been taught as a child. I wanted proof; he asked for faith. I didn't understand then, but now…. Well, he's forgiven me. Thanks to Pastor Miller, I know that for sure, but I still have to face the consequences of my bad behavior. I'm just so sorry that what I've done will cause you to hurt right along with me."

He wriggled his shoulders for relief. She waited for him to continue. "If I can't find proof that Leila died in that accident, or if I find that she is remarried … well, either way, I'll let you know. In the meantime, we both need to trust God for direction in this."

"I know, I know. You're right," she answered. "And I need to honor my dad too. Sometimes I think he is way too legalistic in his beliefs, but I know he loves me. And if he's coming across as dogmatic, it's only because he wants to protect me."

In spite of her determination to follow David's lead, she could not let the subject end. She needed to hear the words. "So, what if you find proof that she died in that accident?"

"Honey, you and I will be married so fast, your head won't stop spinning for a week."

Recognizing the need to lighten the atmosphere, Buddy held out her open right hand to him. "Then it's a deal. Shall we shake on it?"

His sudden, full-throated laugh healed her heart more than any medicine could have. So much time and so many tears had passed since they had shared laughter together. She joined him, their heads thrown back, faces lifted to the skies.

Tears of hope and gratitude trickled down Buddy's face. Her body sagged in relief. The strain of the last hours fizzled away. The sound of their happiness echoed across the waters and was carried on the wings of the wind, lifting in spirals up to heaven.

"Shake hands? Not a chance, Rose." He opened his arms to her and she closed the gap between them. "Not a chance."

Buddy felt herself being gently folded into the strong arms she had been dreaming of from the first time he'd called her name. She burrowed her head into David's chest.

He continued to hold her close, his arms wrapped securely around her, his chin resting on the top of her head. He protested when she tried to put space between them. "Not yet." He gently massaged her back.

"David?" His hold relaxed and she tilted her head back to gaze into his face. "David, you know I love you." The question might have been rhetorical, but he nodded. "We can't see each other until this is cleared up. We'd be dishonoring your marriage if we continued to have a relationship while you search for Leila—no, please don't interrupt." She held a finger to his lips when he started to protest. "If she's alive, that makes you her husband and you will be off limits to me. But, David"—her voice broke on his name and a wayward tear started its course down her cheek—"if that should be the case, please know that if you ever need me as a *sister* in Christ, I'll be here for you. Always."

Chapter 10

At the fitness center the next morning, David checked his time as he started his second lap around the outdoor track. A morning run was something he had craved. It was part of his routine now, a routine that changed little from day to day regardless of the state of his emotions. He used to think he could take on anything and anyone after a good run. There were times when he felt the urge to beat his chest and do a Tarzan yell. He glanced at the other runners on the track—well, maybe he'd channel Tarzan another day.

Overtaking a slower jogger, David shouted, "Morning," and swung back into the lane. His thoughts turned to the subject that was never far away. Rose. Leila.

Well, Lord, how do I start a search for someone who has been missing for five years and is presumed dead? And if I search for a while and find nothing, is that proof she's dead? And if I can't find her because she's dead, how do I know when to end the search? And if I marry Rose and Leila shows up later…? What a mess I've made.

Approaching the starting point for his final lap, David picked up his speed and ran hard around the track. This was not going to be one of his better times. His preoccupation overshadowed his desire to exercise. His heart was no longer in it. Too much on his mind.

He slowed down before ending the lap, reached for his towel and jogged down the path leading to the gym and the showers. A quick glance at his watch confirmed there was still enough time for a quick breakfast before heading to the office. He planned to get an early start on some designs he had been working on the night before and allow himself time for a lengthy lunch with Frank and his wife, Cyndy. He'd scheduled a meeting with his own pastor, Dr. Jessup, for later in the evening. Surely one of the older, more world-wise men would have a better sense of how to start the search.

By the time David arrived at the office he had made some preliminary plans. He'd start with the simplest method first: the telephone book. Mentally, he enumerated his choices. Try to find her parents, for one. At least they would know where the accident took place. Florida, yes, but in what area? He could hire a private detective, check out police files and whatever other means existed. He would do a thorough search. He had to. With his future happiness at stake, he could not afford to leave any stone unturned.

The phone on his desk was ringing as he opened the door to his office. He was early. Only a few conscientious draftsmen had already arrived. He punched the flashing button.

"Willoughby," he answered, tossing his briefcase aside.

"Wow. Bad morning?" It was Buddy. He picked up the receiver.

"Sorry, honey, I just had my mind somewhere else. Everything okay?

"Everything's fine, or as fine as it can be under the circumstances. Dad's still scowling and Mom's going overboard in the other direction to compensate. She's running around and chirping."

David laughed at her description but could picture the very plump Mary flitting about the house and singing in an attempt to lighten the mood.

"David, I've been thinking about this all night. I want to help in the search—"

"No," he interrupted before she could complete her sentence.

"Now wait a minute, David, let me finish."

"I don't want you to be involved in this, Rose. This is not your problem."

"How can you say that? I have a stake in the outcome too, you know," Buddy countered.

"I know," he admitted, "but I created the problem, I'll work on the solution."

"In other words, 'Back off'? David, I don't want us to fight about this, but at least listen to what I have to say. Please."

"I'm sorry," he apologized. "Go ahead."

Buddy laid out the specifics of her plan to him. If he would give her the details as he knew them, full name, age, date of the wedding and accident, and so on, she would start reviewing the back issues of the larger newspapers at the library for any related information. In addition, she would attempt to do some searching on the Internet.

"I guess there's no harm in that," David acquiesced. "You'll call me if you find anything?" His voice became husky.

"I'll call every evening, if you like." He could hear the warm smile in her voice. How he loved this woman. He could talk with her forever, but the day's duties called.

"No, I don't think you should do that. Remember our pledge to be honorable. I gotta go. I love you, Rosebud."

The upper east side Lexington Avenue apartment, the scene of many swank affairs in the past, came across as cold and ostentatious to David now that it was devoid of "beautiful people." David found himself comparing the opulent rooms to the cozy quarters of the Madsen family home. Whereas in this place there were glass-topped tables, chintzy curtains, and marble statuettes, there the furnishings were overstuffed, comfortable, and kid-friendly.

Cyndy, dressed in a silky, zebra print hostess jumpsuit "kissed air" as she greeted David and led him to the living room. As she shouted for Frank, she poured a glass of white wine from the well-stocked bar and held it out to David.

"Cyndy." David shook his head, declining the drink. They went through this charade every time he visited. For some reason she seemed determined to see him slip back into his old lifestyle. *Well, that's not gonna happen,* he assured himself.

"Just checking." She grinned. "One of these days you'll come back to the dark side."

"Don't hold your breath, Cyndy-girl." He shook a finger at her. "I'm a changed man."

"Yeah, well, that's a challenge if ever I heard one." She set the glass aside. Reaching for a larger glass, she plopped in two ice cubes, filled it with ginger ale and a cherry, and slowly held it out to him. "And I do love a challenge."

David stepped away from her just as Frank entered the room.

"Back off, Cyndy," Frank warned. "I mean that."

The woman picked up her own glass, held it aloft, said, "Cheers," and left the room.

Frank greeted David with a hearty handshake. "So, what's up, bro?"

"I need your advice," David started. "It's personal." He filled him in on events leading up to his marriage and the annulment that concluded it. "So essentially, what I need is advice on how to find someone who might not even exist."

As he finished speaking, Cyndy announced that lunch was ready. She led them through the formal dining room and out to a glass-enclosed morning room where a small table was spread with broiled salmon, warm croissants, various cheeses, and a fresh fruit salad.

"Help yourself, David," Cyndy offered as they were seated.

David served himself a portion of salmon and fruit and waited for the others to help themselves. As his hosts started to eat, he bowed his head and silently offered thanks for the meal.

When he raised his head, Frank continued as if they had not been interrupted. "Work backward." He bit into a croissant. "Assume she's alive. Ask yourself where she might have gone. Who would she have turned to? Family? Friends? Work colleagues?"

David passed a scurrilous remark under his breath. "I didn't know her well enough or long enough to have met extended family or colleagues."

"Could she have returned to her parents?"

"No. They weren't on good terms when she left."

"Go back to the places she hung out. Pass around her picture at the bars or clubs. If those don't pan out, check out hospitals, homeless shelters, the Y." Frank cut a piece of the salmon with his fork.

David gave him a moment to chew before asking, "Any other suggestions?"

Frank nodded thoughtfully, swallowed, and continued. "My army buddy, Nick Calisandro. He's a private eye. Like Rockford. Remember that TV show? After you get through all the other options, I'll call him. He's expensive but thorough. If Cal says she's dead, you can believe she's dead.

"You know, David," he went on, "this is gonna be a humongous task. Expensive too. Could be months before you see results. Lemme know if you need money or time off from the office."

David thought about the offer. He'd be spending time, effort, and money in the search when he would rather be with Rose. How effective would his search be if he continued working at his present pace? Better to hire an expert. Have it over and done with. "I'll let you know if I do, but I think I'll call your guy. Thanks, Frank."

After a few more pleasantries, David thanked his hosts for lunch and the advice and went in search of his car.

Instead of returning to work, David drove home. The magnitude of the task ahead of him threatened to become overwhelming. He decided to spend some time alone in prayer. He felt the need for more guidance than any human could deliver.

Forty minutes after leaving Manhattan, he turned into the driveway of his housing development. Because of his architectural training, David's gaze tended to seek out buildings and large structures first, viewing the trees and shrubs and grasses only as enhancements to the buildings. Today he took the time to admire the landscaping around the building and the great effort of the gardeners to keep the lawns weed-free and the shrubs neatly trimmed.

Parking in the allotted slot outside his townhouse, he picked up his briefcase from the backseat and stepped out of the vehicle. He fiddled with the keys, selecting the brass-colored key, inserted it, and pushed the door open.

The kitchen reminded him how quickly he'd left this morning. Picking up the glass now crusty with dried milk, he placed it in the sink and filled it with warm tap water. Ignoring the rest of the mess, he crossed the hallway to the bedroom, tossed his briefcase on the bed, and threw the keys on top. His body followed, half kneeling, half lying across the crumpled bedspread, his heart crying out in confusion.

God, what am I going to do? It all seems so futile. The choices go 'round and 'round in my head, and I still end up with no answers. Why didn't you stop me? Why did you let me marry her? Why didn't you bring Rose into my life earlier? Are you even hearing me? Oh, God, why don't you answer?

Even as David's mind cried out for understanding, his body succumbed to the pressures within him, and he fell into a fitful sleep.

Some hours later, he woke and stretched his body from its cramped position. He glanced at his wristwatch and catapulted into action, intent on keeping his six o'clock appointment with his pastor, Dr. Jessup, in the church office.

David turned on the hot water faucet and allowed the water to run while he selected clothes for his appointment. Deciding on tan slacks and a dark-green, short-sleeved sweater, he made a mental note to sort through his winter clothes before too much longer. The evenings were already getting cooler and he had not gone through his winter wear since moving them from his parents' home earlier in the year. In fact, they were still in the packing boxes in the spare bedroom that doubled as a home office.

Having showered, shaved, and dressed, David reached for a comb and ran it through his hair without much finesse. He slapped on a few drops of aftershave, smoothed his moustache, and reached for the keys that lay on the briefcase where he had tossed them. Before going out the door he flipped on the switch for the overhead light in the kitchen and turned on one lamp in the living room. Locking the door behind him, he entered the Jeep, set the motor running, and steered the vehicle in the direction of the Bergen Community Church.

The parking lot was deserted. From his car, David saw that a note had been taped to the huge double doors of the building. Upon closer inspection he saw that the note invited him to come up to the Jessups' home for their meeting.

Minutes later, David pulled into the driveway just as Mrs. Jessup was leaving. He waved to the friendly woman and parked in the spot she had vacated. Dr. Jessup beckoned him from the front door. Dressed in denim jeans, sneakers, and sweatshirt, he looked nothing like the scholarly gentleman who stood behind the pulpit on Sunday mornings.

"David, come on it. Have you had dinner?"

"No, sir, but ..."

"Please ... call me Matt or Dr. Matt. Or Pastor Matt. But not 'sir.'"

"Peggy—that's Mrs. Dr. Matt—left us a pot of stew, which she expects us to finish off."

He led them to the kitchen, washed his hands at the kitchen sink, and indicated that David should do the same. After they dried their hands on paper towels, the older man handed him a large serving spoon and plate with instructions to "have at it."

They set about eating what David later told Buddy was "the best beef stew I have ever had, bar none."

Their appetites appeased, the men rinsed their plates, stacked them in the dishwasher, and poured themselves coffee. Dr. Jessup led them into his study where they each lowered themselves into a large armchair.

Comfortable in the older man's presence, David repeated his account of how he had met and married Leila, her abandonment of him, his parents' deaths, his reunion with the Madsens, falling in love with Buddy, his growing faith, Zach's questions, his own fears.

The pastor listened attentively without interruption. When David was through, the pastor spoke. "David, put your hands together to form a cup."

He did as he was told.

"All right. Let's bring your cupful of problems before the Throne."

Both men bowed their heads. "Lord, here is your son, David, holding out his burden to you. He just enumerated his problems, Lord, not for you—you were aware of them all along—but for himself because they are becoming so overwhelming. He is here because he wants to let them go. You told him to cast his burdens onto you because you care for him, but he hasn't done that yet, Lord. He's going to do that now, and we trust you to take it from there. Thank you, Lord."

In the ensuing silence, David half opened one eye, his hands still cupped, to see the man staring at him questioningly.

"Well, you planning to tote that bundle forever?"

David looked down at his hands and then returned his puzzled gaze to the pastor.

"Let it go, son, let it go," the older man coaxed.

David rotated his wrists.

"Now see that you don't pick them up again. They're in God's hands now." The man sat back in his chair.

Incredulous, David asked, "Is that it?"

"Do you have a better plan?" Dr. Jessup asked. "Son, I can't think of one question to ask you that you haven't already asked yourself a hundred times, and I can't think of a better person to handle the situation than God himself. So let us just leave him to deal with it, okay?"

Reaching for the Bible that stood open in the middle of his desk, the pastor flipped a few pages until he found the passage he wanted. He spoke as he leafed through the book. "You came here with your hands full and now you've emptied them. Let's see if we can't fill them up with something else, eh?

"Over here in Genesis, chapter 3 starting with verse 14, we read about how God dealt with Adam and Eve because of their sin. He was really disappointed in them. They disobeyed him and then tried to cover it up by lying. But did he forsake them? No. Did he stop loving them? No. In the midst of all of this, he shut them out of the Garden of Eden. Why? To punish them? Perhaps. But I think he did that for their own protection.

"You see, if they had been allowed to eat from the other tree in the Garden, the Tree of Life, they would have lived forever in their sinful state. So even while God was punishing them for disobeying him, he was also protecting them. He was shielding them from themselves, from their own lustful desires, from their own weakness."

Dr. Jessup looked over the rim of his glasses at David, who was nodding. He flipped a few more pages of the Bible. "Now here in

Chapter 37, same book, here's the story of Joseph, who was sold into slavery by his jealous brothers. A tragedy, right? To the casual observer, maybe. But let's look deeper. Years after his brothers sold him, Joseph became governor of Egypt, and from that office he was able to save his father and his brothers from starving to death while Canaan was in the middle of a seven-year famine. Coincidence? Surely not! Could God have intervened in Joseph's abduction? Of course! So why did he allow it?"

"Probably because he could see the bigger picture?" David asked.

"Precisely. So here we have another picture of God's mercy and grace in the midst of adversity. More than that. We see him preparing ahead for the greater calamity down the road. " He closed the Bible and looked intently at the younger man. "Can you see the hand of God in what you've been going through?" he asked. "Look deep, son."

David forced himself to look at the events of his life from a different perspective. How could anyone in his right mind see anything positive coming out of his marriage to Leila and her desertion of him? The whole relationship had been a fiasco from the word "go."

"Well," he said, hesitating while his flipped the pages of his memory, "if Leila hadn't eloped after the wedding, we probably would have been divorced by now. Or worse. We might even have killed each other. Or we might have had children who would be suffering through their parents' fights."

Pastor Jessup nodded. "Has there been a change in your lifestyle in the last five years?"

"Definitely," David confirmed. "After the wedding I moved back home. I was able to spend real quality time with my parents before they died. I became so disenchanted with women that I shied away from serious relationships with anyone. I stayed away from nightclubs and bars, gave up the party scene and the casual lifestyle ... I see what you mean." David was beginning to see that after the tragedy of his marriage he became less sociable, more selective of his friends, more introspective, and less flamboyant, and this prevented further disastrous liaisons.

"By the time you met this young woman, Rose, you were ready for a solid, mature relationship."

"And because of her and her family, my life has turned around." He looked down at his fingers, which were loosely linked in his lap. "I guess my cup is filling up again." He grinned.

"Good. Now one more thing. I suspect you've been praying the 'why me?' and 'where are you, God?' prayers."

David nodded and Dr. Matt continued. "Son, here's a lesson many of us don't learn until we are old and gray. When the complexity of your problems gets in the way of your seeing God's hand at work, start to praise him. In good times, it is easy to believe His promises. It's easy to see his blessings. It's during the bad times that the doubts come. And the enemy delights in that!

"Praise God, son. Thank him for the trees and the mountains, and babies, and light, and water, and for being honest and faithful and true to his children. Praise him for your job and your health, for Rose, and for Leila. Be assured that he has a specific plan for you and that nothing and no one can thwart that plan. Trust him! He loves you so much that he sent his one and only Son to die in your place. He promised never to leave you or forsake you, and if there is one thing you can hold on to, it is this: God always keeps his promises.

"I think you're going to recognize the hand of God in your life in ways you can't even imagine at this point. Just keep doing what he called you to do, and leave him to do his job.

"Now about that cup." The older man nodded toward the hands that were still linked in David's lap. "Is it full yet?"

David raised them toward him.

"Yeah, Dr. Matt." He grinned. "It's full."

Chapter 11

The muffled sounds of pots and pans being pulled from cabinets and set down on metal cooking grates seeped through the open window of his neighbor's kitchen and stirred David from his daydream. At six fifteen in the morning there was a buzz of activity as the family next door prepared to begin their school day and workday.

He found himself matching the muffled sounds with pictures from his past. Someone pulled a pan from a cabinet, left a faucet running, started and stopped the garbage disposal.

No faces were visible on the pictures in his mind. But as he identified the sounds caused by the equipment, the hands preparing the meal became those of his mother and of Mary Madsen and of Rose.

He missed them so much! Mary had telephoned twice to offer her encouragement. Buddy also telephoned occasionally, but their stilted conversations had the effect of leaving them both discouraged, and her calls gradually decreased.

His aloneness today was punctuated by the sounds of life next door. He had not noticed the neighbors' noisiness before. Of course he wouldn't usually have been at home at six fifteen in the morning.

He would have started his morning run, but he hadn't slept well during the night and had fallen into a fitful sleep at dawn.

Leveraging his lanky body upward, David used the back of his legs to scoot the chair further away from him. He picked up the empty milk glass from the kitchen table, filled it with tap water, and set it down on the edge of the sink. Returning to the table, he placed one foot on the seat of the chair he had just vacated and tied the laces of his running shoes. He did the same with the other foot and slid the chair back into place under the table.

Outside, a fine, gray mist cast a pall on the day that matched his dismal mood. Resolving not to dwell on his circumstances, however, he climbed into his Jeep and headed out to the track for his morning run.

As the early morning mist swirled around him, David opted not to remove his sweats. Instead, he reached behind him and pulled the hoodie over his head and started a slow jog around the track. As usual, once he found his stride, his body automatically took over the mechanics of running, and his mind was free to wander. Today he was finding it difficult to channel his thoughts away from this loneliness, this isolation from those he loved.

How long, Lord, before I can call them my family? How long must I wait before your reveal your hand? Seven years like Jacob waited for Rachael? Please, God, not seven years; not even seven months.

David was not sure that he was permitted this verbal wrestling with his Maker, but his heart was crying out for an answer, for solace, for some recognition that God had heard his pleas. Yet he remembered that the psalmist, his namesake, had cried out in similar circumstance from the depths of his own misery, and so David continued his lonely discourse.

Maybe Rose and I are not meant to be! The thought triggered a misstep, and he slowed, adjusting his pace. *Could it be? Could that be what you are telling me, Lord? That I must be prepared to let her go?*

His heart pounding, David stopped in his tracks. *Give up Rose? Give up the light of my life? Would he ask that of me?*

David stepped off the running track and onto the lawn and started the slow trek across the damp grass, taking the shortest route back toward the parking lot. *Give up Rose. Give up Rose.* His heart beat out a cadence in time with his words: *Give up Rose. Give up Rose.*

Defiance swelled within his chest and erupted in one violent shout. "Nooooooo!"

The mournful wail startled him. Realizing it had escaped his own lips, he tossed back his head and cried out to the sky once more. "Nooooooo!"

He tripped, falling headlong on the slick, wet grass. Prostrate, sobs wracked his body. "Give her up? She's the best thing that has happened to me in my life!" His fist pounded the moist earth.

No, I am the best that has happened to you!

"Nooooooo."

Without me, you are nothing! Without me, Rose is nothing. Release her to me!

"Nooooooo."

I love you. I love Rose. Trust me!

Emotionally drained, David's crying gentled, and his heart softened. He recalled his past unwillingness as a teenager to yield to his parents' wishes and to the teachings of the elders in his church. He acknowledged that his own willfulness had led him down the path he was now regretting. He knew he was still hankering after full control of his daily walk but God recognized the wisdom of letting go of the reins of his life in favor of the One who holds authority over all life.

"God, I need you," he whispered. "If this is what it takes, Lord, so be it. I release Rose into your hands. I yield my whole self, my will, into your hands. Thy will be done, amen."

His chest still heaving, David rolled over onto his back. He looked toward the sky. Though he was still unable to see beyond the gray cloud cover, he knew on the other side of the clouds the sun shined brightly and the sky was a vibrant blue. He was blissfully aware of God's presence, had felt the gentle touch upon his brow.

His eyes closed.

His tortured body and his breathing relaxed .

How long he lay on the damp turf David didn't know, but he became uncomfortably aware of the moisture starting to penetrate his clothing, and the fine mist, mingled with his silent tears, trickling down the side of his neck. He rolled to his feet, cold, weakened yet energized, and with renewed determination.

"Yet will I fear thee." He quoted the psalmist out loud as he began the walk across the field toward his car. Like David of the scriptures, he resolved to hold fast to God no matter what lay in store. *I turned my back on you as a teenager, Lord, and you turned me around. There'll be no more waywardness on my part. Whatever comes, whatever my future holds, "Yet will I fear thee."*

Back in his bedroom, David ignored the flashing message indicator light on the side of the telephone and opted instead for a long hot shower followed by two cups of steaming coffee and cinnamon toast. Later he retrieved the telephone messages, made some notes on a nearby pad, and planned to respond to them later.

Logging on to his e-mail account, David noted the flashing icon indicating there were messages awaiting his attention. Double-clicking on the first message, he skimmed over the words and then returned to the beginning to read them a second time. Then, still unwilling to believe the message, he read it again, slowly absorbing every word. Finally, he closed his eyes and let his body slump against the back of the swivel chair. His heart thundered in his ears. His hands trembled as the opening words of the message from Cal reverberated inside his pounding head:

I found her. She's alive.

"There's got to be a mistake," he whispered into the empty room. "She can't be alive!"

Denial, that initial, defensive response, provided David a moment of protection against the impending pain, but only a moment. Then the pain pierced and coiled like a sinewy serpent, swirling slowly downward from the center of his brain through to his neck and shoulders, reaching down to his bowels, writhing, squeezing, and then twisting back against itself to coil around his heart.

David's fingers flexed. His biceps bunched. The desires both to fight and take flight wrestled within him. Yet he felt powerless to move on his own.

His mind raced back to the events of the early morning, his yielding of Rose, himself, and their dilemma to his Maker, and as his brain numbered his actions, a sense of peace settled around him, comforting, soothing. Seemingly of their own will, his fingers unclenched. His muscles relaxed. His breathing settled into a steady cadence.

This is no longer within my control, he reminded himself. Remembering Dr. Matt's coaching, he held out his closed fists before him, pictured this problem clutched within their grasp, and then rotated his wrists and splayed his fingers apart.

"This is no longer within my control." Although the words came from his lips the assurance sprang from a stronger core and David acknowledged, "It never was mine. It's all yours, Lord."

Cupping his hand around the computer mouse, he moved the pointer to the X button and pressed his index finger into the groove. *The other messages will keep. First I have to tell Rose.*

In one continuous movement, he kicked the chair out from under him, turned off the computer, and reached for his keys. He dreaded the task ahead. He hated the pain it was sure to cause to the people he loved most in this world, hated it so much he knew it must be done swiftly and without contemplation.

Allowing himself one moment of self-pity, David leaned his head against the open door of the Jeep and wished this lot had not been assigned to him, wished that as a young man he had paid attention to his parents' teachings, wished there was a way to turn back his life's pages and undo his wayward decisions. But that was possible only in dreams and fairy tales.

He took a deep, cleansing breath. His shoulders and chest heaving from his expanded lungs. He entered the car and slammed the door. Driving past the familiar scenes along the Garden State Parkway, David wondered whether this was to be his final trip to Cape May. He couldn't imagine a time when he would not be traveling this route to visit the friends he had come to love as family—in truth, the only family he now possessed on this Earth. Yet he could not see himself visiting Rose as a friend when he wanted her to play a much greater role in his life. So their relationship would have to end.

Shaking his head to dispel the maudlin thought, he reached for a CD from the case on the floor between the seats and inserted it into the player. The melodious voices of the Brooklyn Tabernacle Choir swelled within the vehicle. David made himself harmonize with their praise song, tentatively at first, and then more heartily as the music progressively modulated upward. Before long the sing-along turned to true praise, and that special calming spirit he had come to rely on settled over him again.

Chapter 12

Three hours after leaving home, David crossed the overpass leading into Cape May. His heightened senses took in the gentle ocean breeze that carried the salty scents inland and mingled with the appetizing odor of seafood being cooked on a charcoal grill. On his right, a billboard's invitation to see the dolphins at play reminded him that he had not taken up Rose's offer to take him on a whale-watching excursion. That was not destined to happen now since the outcome of this trip would surely be the end of their relationship.

The Jeep seemed to find the turns without guidance from David. Left on Madison, pass the water tower, right on Maple, and swing left into number forty-four.

Now that I'm here, what do I say, Lord? How do I tell them? What do I tell them?

A delighted Mary greeted him from the porch. "David, Buddy didn't say you were coming to visit. Zach, David's here. You're just in time for lunch. Come on in." David couldn't help smiling at Mary's exuberance. As usual she was including everyone within earshot in her conversation whether or not they were interested.

"Hi, Mary." He leaned down, kissing her cheek. "I didn't tell Rose I was coming …" The rest of his words were lost as she led him by the hand into the great room.

"We're having tuna sandwiches with tomato soup. I'm not expecting Buddy for lunch but she should be back pretty soon. She, um—Zach! Soup's getting cold"—she shouted up the stairs without pausing for a breath—"… had to meet with the architect about renovations to the cottage she's redecorating. Sit over here while I get another bowl … over on the west side. A couple from Philly …"

"You want me to sit on the west side?" David asked, his brow knit at the puzzling request.

"If you like, sit anywhere."

"Mary. *Mary*," Zach interrupted his wife as he approached David. "Slow down. You're confusing the man!" He grasped David's hand in welcome, and David hugged him hard in return. This man had become like a father to him. He would miss the man's frankness even though it was this directness that had triggered the looming disastrous end to his heart's pursuit.

"Buddy is decorating a cottage in west Cape May," Zach explained patiently, "and you're welcome to sit at whichever side of the table you prefer."

The pleasantries continued throughout the meal, and as Zach rose to clear the dishes, Mary announced, "Here comes Buddy now."

David moved toward the entrance, eager to greet his love. Watching her pull her car into the driveway beside his own, David became aware of the rising pressure within his chest. This was not going to be easy.

As Buddy stepped out of the car, David's heart thundered. His eyes met hers and for an instant they were two lovers, alone, with all the time in the world to revel in their feelings for each other.

"God, help me," David whispered, and went forward to greet her. He didn't miss the unspoken questions in her eyes, but his answers would have to wait. Right now he needed to hold her. It might be the last time he could freely experience her warmth. Without speaking, he folded his arms around her and she melted into him. He held onto her, inhaling her unique perfume of spring flowers mixed with fresh paint. He'd never forget that combination.

He finally released her and, taking her hand, led her into the living room. Finally seated, David squirmed under the three sets of questioning eyes that bored into him. He decided to make his announcement without preamble. There was no way to soften what he had to say.

"It seems I'm still a married man." His statement fell like a huge shroud engulfing them.

"David, this isn't funny." Buddy broke the silence.

"No, it isn't," David agreed, and plunged on. "Cal—that's the investigator I hired—Cal left me an e-mail this morning. I don't know where he is, and I don't know where he found Leila. He said he'll be back in New York this weekend, and he'll give me details and proof and whatever else he has ..." David's voice quivered and he coughed to cover it. How was he ever going to say goodbye?

"I'm sorry," he whispered. "I wish, I wish ..." Unable to formulate the words or force them past the lump in his throat, he shook his head and remained silent. He had rehearsed the words several times during the drive, but his memory and his will deserted him.

"What're you going to do now?" Zach ended the prolonged silence.

"Well, I'll meet with Cal ... see what he found ... try to talk to Leila. Cal didn't say if she had married again, just that he had found her."

"And if she hasn't remarried?" Zach asked quietly.

"If she hasn't remarried ..." David gulped, searching for air. *I can't do this. God, give me the strength to do your will* ... "If she hasn't remarried, I'll m-make every effort to fulfill my vows to her."

The deathly silence following his statement was interminable. Without turning his head, David saw the tears coursing down Rose's cheeks. He felt the tremors within her, sensed the raging battle: please God, or please self. The focus of his prayer switched from himself to her.

Lord, give Rose the strength to do your will …

"I imagine you're feeling a little like Jacob at this time." Zach, looking directly at David, interrupted his private thoughts. David had not seen him leave the room to get his Bible from its home on the bookshelf by the door. "Now, I know there is a lot more in this story that doesn't apply to your situation, but I think we can gain some wisdom and some comfort from this." Licking his finger, he flipped through a few pages and paused. David met his eyes and waited.

"Here's a story of a man, a righteous man, who was promised the wife of his choice. But because of some trickery, he finds himself married to another woman. So what does he do? Cast her aside? No, of course not. He remains faithful to her, and after a period of time he is given the wife he had been promised in the first place.

"Son, daughter"—Zach held David and Buddy's attention—"I know your hearts. You think this is the end. Mary and I believe this is a test, a proofing. It may last ten years, maybe longer. It may not play itself out in this lifetime, and you may never know the reasons why these events lined up the way they did. My advice to you is this: be faithful. Be obedient. God will show his hand when you least expect it."

Zach seemed to be waiting for them to comment. David had nothing to say. He wanted to disagree with the older man, but how could he? What argument could he raise? He was wrong. He had made poor life choices and this was the consequence. His mother had warned him he would eventually have to pay the piper. Well, he was paying now. He was paying dearly.

And it hurt.

Zach stood up, held out his hands to David and Buddy, and then helped Mary to her feet. Linking arms in the center of the room, he prayed for God's wisdom, protection, and guidance regarding David, Buddy, and Leila. Then turning to face David, he placed his open palms on either side of David's head and recited from memory the benediction from the Scriptures: "The Lord bless you and keep you ..."

After Zach said "amen," David turned away from the somber group. Clearly he had been dismissed. There was nothing more to be said.

At the door, Mary pulled David toward her for a final hug. "This doesn't change how we feel about you, David. If you ever need us, for anything, anything at all, just give us a call."

David thanked her and, followed by Buddy, made his way across the porch and down the steps. In front of the Jeep, he turned to face her. "I guess this is goodbye."

Buddy nodded without speaking. David could see from the slight tremor of her chin and her pursed lips that she was making a valiant effort to maintain her composure.

Deciding not to prolong his departure and hoping to keep the mood light, he leaned forward, and planted a quick kiss on her cheek. "See ya, kiddo. Take care."

Inside the Jeep he quickly inserted the key and turned the ignition. The engine turned over instantly. He slipped the gear lever into reverse, reached for his seat belt, and checked the rear-view mirror all at the same time. He had to get out of here as quickly as he could. The pain within him was so intense it threatened to overwhelm him, and he knew Rose was close to her own breaking point.

As his gaze returned to the front, he couldn't help but cast one final wistful glance at the woman he loved with all his heart. She stood dejected, hands at her sides, shoulders slumped. Yet to him she had never been more beautiful.

Lord, forgive me this one indiscretion.

Throwing the gear into park, he let go of the seatbelt, which instantly retracted, and threw open the door. "Rose!"

"David."

They met halfway, arms outstretched. He folded her close, swinging her high above the concrete driveway, his head buried in her neck, her head against his shoulder. Tears flowed without restraint. Words of love gushed forth unrestricted. Secret longings found expression never to be aired again. Recriminations. Regrets.

"If only …"

"We should have …"

"I have to do this."

"I know."

Finally, emotions were spent, composure was regained. Stepping back, David retrieved a folded handkerchief from his hip pocket and gently wiped the tears from Buddy's face.

"I must look awful," she grimaced.

"Not to me," he replied softly. "Never to me." His eyes roamed her tear-streaked face, indelibly imprinting its beloved features into his memory. "You will always be my American Beauty Rose."

Fresh tears welled in her eyes again, and again he wiped them away.

Taking her hand in his, David led her up the porch steps toward her parents, who still stood in the doorway. Their steps slowed as they drew closer. As they drew near, Zach pushed open the screen door. The fingers of Buddy's slender hand were entwined with David's. He raised them to his lips, pressed a final kiss into their warmth, and released her hand into the hand of her father.

"This is too much." David's voice cracked. Turning, he sped down the steps and into the waiting vehicle, threw the gear lever into reverse, and screeched out of the driveway and out of their lives.

Following David's departure, Buddy gave way to a fit of tears, which she shed into the shoulders of her two loving parents. Like a baby, she laid her head in the crook of her mother's neck, her ear flattened against the comfortable shoulder, one arm resting loosely on her ample hip. She felt Zach's arms encircle them both. His lips grazed her forehead in a gentle kiss.

Buddy's face contorted with the pain that writhed and twisted within her. The questions and uncertainties of the past weeks had been answered. Her shoulders shook as she vented her emotions. Loud sobs of despair escaped unchecked, propelled by deeply inhaled breaths. Her body sagged from the weight of emotional exhaustion.

She stood secure in the arms of her parents.

When finally her sobs subsided, and Zach and Mary relaxed their hold, Buddy straightened. She swiped at her cheeks with each shoulder. Sniffing, she tossed her head as if to shake away the vestiges of her meltdown. "Well, I guess that's that."

Raising her eyes to her parents, Buddy attempted a watery smile, but her bottom lip quivered, so she pressed her teeth firmly into her lip to curtail its movement. She saw Mary fish a crumpled tissue from her pocket and dab at her own eyes.

"Honey." Mary's voice cut through to Buddy, but she held up her hand, effectively cutting off Mary's plea.

"Mom, I get it. I really do. David has a wife. David is an honorable man. David must fulfill his vows to her. That's that!"

A gloomy silence swelled within the room. Finally Buddy moved toward the stairs. The episode was behind her and it was time to move forward. She was grateful that Zach and Mary immediately became involved in some activity that said they understood her unspoken message and were ready to comply.

Zach picked up his Bible from the coffee table where he had placed it earlier and Mary began rummaging through her pockets for more discarded tissues when Buddy pivoted on the first rung of the stairs.

"What I *don't* understand," she announced loudly, punching the air with her index finger, "what I *don't* understand is why this had to happen to me. What did I do to deserve this? I'm a hard worker. I honor my parents. Haven't I done everything that was ever asked of me? Everything you expected of me? Then why me? Tell me that. Why me?"

A single wayward tear slid from the corner of her eye and down her cheek. Buddy dashed it away impatiently with the palm of her hand and then swiped it across the seat of her pants. "Just lucky, I guess. Just plain dumb luck." Blowing out a resigned breath, she continued her weary trek upstairs, leaving her parents staring mutely behind her.

In the confines of her room, Buddy allowed herself the release of more tears. Gentle, silent tears trickled across the bridge of her nose to be captured by the cool, plump pillow that cushioned her head. David was gone, taking with him the seeds of hope she had planted.

Gone.

Intimate walks on Sunset Beach bathed in the orange light of the setting sun, gone. Long rides on tandem bikes, shared sandwiches in the backyard between assignments, all of it gone.

A gentle evening breeze teased the sheer window curtains, causing them to billow inward, rise on the puff of air, and fall softly back into place. Their easy movement, like the repetitive rhythm of the ocean waves, eased the tension from her body. Buddy's tortured breathing settled to an even rhythm, and finally, sleep engulfed her within its downy folds and eased her into oblivion.

Chapter 13

Several years earlier.

"Go, go!" Leila shouted from the pillion seat into the leather-clad back of the rider. He needed no further encouragement. Gunning the motor, he let in the clutch so that the front wheel of the bike rose from the ground as the vehicle shot forward.

Not stopping to look back at her new husband surrounded by the gaping crowd of family and well-wishers, Leila Amherst Willoughby adjusted her body so that she was shielded by the body of the man in front of her from the onslaught of wind. Her bouquet of flowers wedged between them, she gave her attention to keeping the bridal train bunched in her lap and out of the way of the tires.

I've really done it this time. Dad's gonna be livid.

Not allowing herself to dwell on the image of her father's furious face or her mother's embarrassment, Leila tossed the folds of her bridal veil away from her face and attempted to snuggle closer to the black leather jacket of the man who had rescued her.

The rider slowed the vehicle as they turned into the main highway and eased into the lane of Saturday afternoon traffic. As they sped forward, the wind whipped the bridal veil into Leila's face. Tired of fussing with it, she methodically extracted the bobby pins holding the headdress in place. Freed from its anchor, the mass of tulle was swept up by the rush of wind and took to the skies, spreading its folds above the traffic like a giant crane taking flight.

At the stoplight, Leila tapped her driver on his shoulder to gain his attention. He placed one booted foot on the blacktop and twisted his body toward her. "Where are we going?" Her raised voice successfully penetrated the safety helmet, for he responded with a cheeky grin.

"Where d'ya wanna go?"

"Some place far away from here."

"That's where we're going, darlin'," he shouted back over his shoulder as the light turned green. "Far, far away."

"I'll need some clothes."

"I'm way ahead of you," he replied. The light changed. "Hold on."

In her lap Leila still carried her bouquet of flowers. A sickeningly sweet perfume emanated from the crushed petals. She had to get rid of them. Easing her torso backward, she lifted the bouquet from between them and tossed it without a care to the curb. Free of the bouquet, she embedded her fingers into the waistband of the rider's jeans and laid her head against his broad back.

No turning back now, she told herself with a sardonic grin. *This time I've really done it!*

They had tried to coax her into respectability, tried to convince her she could make a success of marriage with David. David, who came from a solid family and who had a successful career ahead of him. David, who had been schooled in the social graces. David, who could hold an intelligent conversation about politics or the economy or the stock market—all boring subjects in her opinion. The trouble was that no one listened to her opinion. They just wanted her compliance with the plans they made for her. Yes ma'am, whatever you say, sir. Well, no more!

It might have worked. A marriage with David the gentleman might have worked. Except for Sly.

Sylvester Connors was a rebel from the two-inch heel of his hand-tooled, black leather biker boots to the top of his black Stetson, his headgear of choice when he was not astride his beloved motorcycle. Born and raised within the city limits of Newark, he had cultivated the language and hip-hop gait that had gained him the admiration of the neighborhood kids. With seductive eyes and an easy charm, he drew the attention of men and women alike. "Slick Sly," his cronies called him with a mixture of admiration and envy, but to the female members of his entourage he was a hunk to be loved and adored.

Leila squirmed at the memory of how she had flirted shamelessly with him in an unsuccessful attempt to win him away from his groupies. Only when she redirected her charms toward David, the stranger who had started to frequent the Illusions Club, had Sly responded to her wiles. Then she taunted Sly with fictitious tales of wedding plans hoping he would claim her for himself. The ruse backfired when her parents, thrilled at their daughter's choice for a husband, orchestrated the wedding with such alacrity that she and David found themselves agreeing to the plans.

Leila released her fingers from the leather belt and encircled Sly's waist with both arms. In the end he had come for her. That's all that mattered.

The Kawasaki devoured the highway miles, and in a short while they were turning into the wide, semicircular, macadam driveway of her parents' home. Startled out of her musings, Leila pounded delicate fists on the muscled shoulders in front of her.

"What are we doing here? Are you crazy? What if my folks—"

"Shush, darlin'." He slowly maneuvered the bike past the garage and around to the rear of the mansion. He silenced the motor, rolled the bike backward to rest on its stand, and dismounted.

Furious with Sly and frightened of being confronted by her parents, Leila swung her leg over the seat, tangling her dress in the leather cover as she backed away from the machine. "Are you crazy?"

she blared. She yanked the dress free, her eyes open wide in angry disbelief. Gesturing wildly, she lunged toward him. "My parents … the neighbors will … we've got to get out of here. I can't believe you did this."

"Stop!" Sly grabbed her by the shoulders and immediately ducked backward as one flailing arm narrowly missed his face. "Knock it off, do you hear? *Leila!*" He managed to seize her shoulders again from behind and clamped a calloused hand over her mouth. "Listen to me."

Recognizing her struggles were futile, Leila calmed her wild movements. Sly gingerly removed the hand that had silenced her.

"Do you have a way to get into the house?"

"Get into the … I'm not going in there," she exploded again.

"Shut up and listen, girlfriend!"

She breathed hard from her efforts to free herself from his hold.

Sly patiently reasoned with her. "You need clothes. We can't ride around town like this. That dress calls attention to us. We might as well leave a map for your folks." He paused, and Leila nodded. Sly continued. "The house is locked up tight. Can you get in?"

Leila nodded again, remembering the hidden key that opened the rear door of the garage.

"Okay. Get us inside." She felt him let go of her shoulders.

Gathering up the train of her dress, Leila dashed over to the brick patio outside the kitchen. Slowly and carefully she counted off some bricks, leaned over, and firmly grasped one. Giving it a tug she extracted it, turned it over, and removed a key taped to its underside. She held it aloft, grinning at her success.

"Let's try it before you start celebrating."

Together they returned to the rear door of the garage and inserted the key in the lock. It turned easily. Sly withdrew the key and pushed the door inward.

"Close the door. Hurry," Leila warned him. "I have thirty seconds to disarm the security system or the police will be here before you know it." She punched in a four-digit code and watched for the green "disarmed" light to flash on.

On the other side of the door, Sly took charge again. "I'm giving you five minutes to change into some jeans or something," he told her.

She nodded and sped toward the stairs.

"Leila," he called out just as she placed one foot on the first step. She turned toward him. He raised one hand, his calloused palm facing her with his fingers spread wide. "Five."

Leila sped toward her bedroom at the top of the stairs. She twisted her arms behind her to undo the mass of tiny pearl buttons. A sharp pain shot through from wrist to elbow as she stretched hand over shoulder in an attempt to reach the buttons. Realizing that she hadn't a hope of succeeding, she hurried to the bathroom, opened the door of the cabinet above the sink, and took out a pair of cuticle scissors.

Passing through the adjoining door, she entered her bedroom and viewed the unaccustomed neatness of the room. A set of three matching blue suitcases stood on the floor next to the chest of drawers. The suitcases, an engagement gift from her parents, had already been packed in preparation for her departure on her honeymoon. David had told her nothing of their intended destination, only that she should pack for warm weather with as many bathing suits as she cared to include.

Leila turned away from the reminder of the life that had been planned for her and faced the full-length mirror. *What a mess*, she thought, casting a cursory glance over her flushed cheeks and matted hair. Her dress, so perfect this morning, was in total disarray, her satin slippers stained green from newly mown grass. But unlike this morning, there was a sparkle in her eyes and her face glowed. In the end, Sly had come for her.

Sly. The thought of the man waiting downstairs propelled her into action.

Spreading open the tiny scissors, she held the bodice of the dress away from her chest and snipped deliberately through the beaded fabric. *Easy come, easy go,* she thought as she worked away at her task.

"Two minutes," came a shout from below.

Tossing the scissors aside, she forced the garment over her shoulders and down past her hips. She stepped out of the dress, leaving it where it lay. She rolled the sheer white stockings down to her ankles and kicked them aside. Reaching inside the walk-in closet for the denim jeans that had been recently laundered and hung, she quickly pulled them on. Without stopping to do up the zipper, she tugged a T-shirt over her head and inserted her arms.

From the shelf above she retrieved a gym bag that still held a towel and a can of spray deodorant from her last visit to the spa. Emptying the contents on the bed, she refilled the bag with underwear, socks, a pair of sneakers, and two shirts. She bounced across the bed to her dresser, picked up her hairbrush but decided against attempting to repair her damaged hair. Instead she added the hairbrush to the gym bag, grabbed a scrunchie from the assortment on the dresser, and secured her hair away from her face.

"Okay, we've gotta go," Sly called impatiently from the bottom of the stairs.

"I'm on my way," she yelled back, still tossing items into the gym bag.

In the dresser mirror she caught a glimpse of her left hand decked out in its new jewelry. Removing her wedding ring, she gingerly set it down, thought better of it, and returned it to its place on her finger next to the diamond engagement ring.

We'll need money. I can probably hock these later.

Money. She reached into the top, left-hand dresser drawer and grabbed her checkbook and seventy dollars in bills. She stuffed them into the hip pouch that had been hanging from the doorknob and secured the pouch strap around her waist. Momentarily pausing from her frenzied movements, she closed the zipper on her jeans. Snug, she noticed. Too snug, but too late to change.

"Leilaaaa." Sly's impatience was growing.

Hopping on one leg she pulled on a sock while struggling to maintain her balance. She slipped the socked foot into a pair of Oxfords, switched feet, and repeated the action. Not stopping to tie the laces, she reached for the gym bag, added a toothbrush and toothpaste, a razor, makeup, and cleanser, and then zippered it shut. She took one last look around the room.

Will I ever see this place again?

The thought took her by surprise. Deliberately setting aside the budding wistfulness, she turned her back on the nest that had been hers since she'd outgrown the nursery at three years old and sped downstairs.

"I have to reset the alarm." She attempted to detain Sly as they left the way they had come, the habit formed from many years of listening to her father's lectures.

"Hang the alarm," Sly snapped, striding ahead of her. "We've wasted too much time already. We've gotta get outta here."

After a brief hesitation, she pulled the door shut behind her and ran after the man who was already seated on the bike, both legs spread wide and planted firmly on the turf beneath his feet.

"I'm up," she said to let him know when she was seated. Securing the gym bag between their bodies, she lifted her feet to the footrests as the bike leaped forward.

No more than a few moments had passed when Sly leaned the motorcycle into the entrance of a large parking lot.

"Where are we?" Leila asked, surprised they were stopping so soon. She looked around in amazement at the deserted lot and the darkened windows of the store front.

"I have to meet a guy here," Sly mysteriously replied. "This is gonna be our ticket south."

He pulled into a slot close to the building, turned off the motor, and rolled the bike back onto the kickstand. He slowly eased his helmet from his head and dismounted, all in the same movement. Holding the helmet in his left hand, he reached out his right toward Leila. She grasped it firmly and swung her legs around toward him, jumping the short distance to the ground.

Sly's eyes scanned the vacant parking lot and then returned to rest on Leila's questioning face. His eyes darted away from hers. He scanned the lot again, more slowly, searching. Finding nothing to hold his attention, he turned back to her. "I guess we'll have to go inside."

Sly rest his helmet on her gym bag and took another quick look around the parking lot. He wiped his sweaty palms on the seat of his jeans, started forward, but then stopped in this tracks. "Look." He lowered his voice to just above a whisper. His eyes piercing Leila's, he continued. "I don't know who's inside, so just stay close to me. Don't ask no questions, don't talk to nobody, don't look at nobody. You got it?"

"Are you in trouble?" Leila's concern became evident as she drew closer to Sly.

"That's a question. I said no questions." His eyes pierced hers for several heartbeats, and then he said, "Come on." He took her arm and propelled her toward the building.

On the other side of the grungy steel door the odor of stale liquor greeted them. Sly hesitated, allowing his eyes to adjust to the dim interior. Several tables, still bearing empty drink bottles and plastic cups, had been randomly strewn around a small circular vinyl-covered area in the center of the room. A dance floor. The threadbare carpet beneath their feet muffled the sound of their movement toward the door at the end of the large, open lounge where a faint light shined through a tiny porthole.

As they approached the door, Sly's steps slowed then stopped altogether. He turned toward Leila. "Come here." His command was little more than a whisper. Gone was the cocky attitude, the self-assured demeanor. Instead, a fearful reticence had crept into his eyes.

"Let's get out of here," Leila whispered back.

"No." Sly turned his head toward the closed door and quickly looked back at her. "Hey." He inhaled deeply, holding her gaze., "I have to do this. It's too late to back out now." Tossing an arm around her shoulders, he pulled her closer and lowered his head until his eyes were level with hers. "When we get in there"—he nodded at the closed door—"don't say anything. Just play along with me, okay?"

Leila nodded and began picking viciously at the cuticle on her thumb.

"That's my girl." Sly rubbed a thumb over her lips and lowered his head for a quick kiss. "Don't look so scared. Just go along with whatever I say." He slid his arm from her shoulders and folded her clammy fingers inside his own.

Sly's knuckles pounding on the metal door broke the eerie silence that had settled around them. He barely had time to return his hand to his side when the door was pulled open.

"You're late!"

The burly, unshaven man on the other side of the door stepped back, allowing Sly to enter. A puff of smoke escaped with his words while his lips settled themselves around the stump of a well-chewed cigar. He spied Leila and placed his body squarely in front of Sly, preventing their entrance into the smoke-filled room. He peered around the younger man, his hooded eyes surveying Leila, who tried not to meet his gaze.

"Who's this? I told you, no partners or the deal's off."

Leila tightened her grip on Sly's hand. "She's my wife."

The man's eyes darted to Sly. "You didn't say nothin' 'bout no wife." He removed the cigar stump from his lips with a fleshy thumb and forefinger, wiped away a drool of spittle with the back of his hand, and waited for a response from Sly.

"That's because I didn't have a wife when we made the deal. We just got married this morning."

"You just got married this morning?" The burly man echoed Sky's words, disbelief painted all over his face. "You just got married this morning," he said again, starting to slowly circle the couple. "This morning!"

Pausing beside Leila, he leaned closer. "You got a ring?"

Quickly, she raised her hand to display the gold and diamond set that David had placed there earlier. The man lifted her slender, manicured fingers in his pudgy ones. He glanced briefly at the jewelry, scanned her face and hair, and seemed satisfied. He quickly lowered her hand and became businesslike.

"A young married couple. It could work. I like it."

Closing the door that had been left ajar, the man returned to the cluttered desk in the middle of the room and sat in the swivel chair. He rolled the remains of a hoagie sandwich in its brown deli paper and tossed it into a nearby trashcan.

Ignoring the oily residue left on the desk by the sandwich, he pulled forward a note pad, scribbled a telephone number, and tore off the page. From his pocket he retrieved a keychain with two keys attached and handed them over to Sly along with the note paper.

The couple followed the man as he walked out of a back door into the rear parking lot. They made their way toward a beat-up pickup truck.

"Don't let her looks fool you." The man spoke for the first time in several minutes. "She'll get you to Miami without a hitch. Just keep her gassed up and she'll be fine. There's a ramp and some ropes in the back for your bike." He nodded toward the vehicle as he spoke. "Call that number when you get there. My son will pay you for the job. If you want to do a return trip, let him know."

Sly nodded his understanding.

Walking around to the front of the vehicle, Sly released Leila's hand, selected the smaller of the two keys, and inserted it into the door lock. He pulled open the door and helped her into the very clean interior. Slamming the door shut, he nodded at the man, who stood away from the vehicle, watching his movements.

"Hey," the man beckoned.

Sly walked over to him, expecting additional instructions.

The man removed the cigar stump from his lips and swallowed before continuing. "If this is a setup, that birdseed in her hair was a nice touch." He paused. "But if this is a setup, you ain't gonna be married long. You get me?"

"Don't worry, old man." Sly's cocky confidence was returning. "I've got everything under control."

Inside the pickup, Sly reached across the seat and squeezed the hands that lay folded in Leila's lap. "You're all right, girl, you're all right."

He inserted the key into the ignition, turned it, and the engine immediately sprang to life and then settled into a low, steady hum. He slipped the gear lever into drive and eased the vehicle forward.

On the other side of the building they stopped only long enough to roll the bike into the back of the truck and secure it. As they pulled out of the parking lot and onto the road, Leila glanced at the profile of the man who had rescued her from the prospect of a life of convention and propriety in favor of fun, excitement, and heady adventures. A secretive smile hovered around her lips.

"Are we really heading to Miami?"

"No other place, darlin'."

"For how long?"

"Until we get tired of havin' a good time." Sly looked across at her and winked.

"For real?"

"Straight up! We deliver this truck, get paid, and then it's you and me, babe!"

"Fun in the sun. South Beach, I'm there." Leila mimicked Sly's spirit.

"Look out world, here we come."

Leila tossed her head defiantly, as if to dispel some intrusive thought, and turned instead to the man beside her. "Yeah, look out world, here we come."

Chapter 14

Nick "Cal" Calisandro hated this part of his job—not just because it was the end of the chase but because he had to deliver the goods to the client, and in his line of work, "the goods" usually meant bad news for somebody. It had been different when he was in the army. There it was a case of the good guys searching out and eliminating the bad guys. Or that was what he chose to believe. In civilian life, the good guy was the one who could afford to pay, and sometimes when the job was over, it was the bad guy who came out the winner. Sometimes nobody won. Something told him this was going to be one of those times.

Well, he reasoned, he'd been paid to do a job that most people would sneer at, and he'd done it well. Too bad they didn't pay for his advice at the same time. He'd certainly tell this client to forget his good intentions. Walk away. Start over.

Smothering a sigh, Cal gathered the sheaf of note papers, airline ticket stubs, car rental receipts, and photographs that he planned to deliver to David later that morning. *What a waste of a life*, he thought as he peered at one snapshot that had fallen from the pile.

Although the picture had been taken from a distance, the telephoto lens had clearly picked out the woman who had seen better days hunched over on a bench. Her matted, bedraggled hair cried out for a shampoo. Her sunken, jaded eyes were partially squinted against the cigarette smoke curling upward from her lips, past her eyes and into her hair. Not visible in the photograph but forever imprinted on his mind were three equally disheveled toddlers who played nearby in a small, grassy patch that was much too close to the Miami traffic for Cal's comfort.

Shaking his head to dispel the image, Cal stuffed the papers into a large manila envelope and shoved it into the side pocket of his briefcase. He slapped the hip pockets of his Levis searching for his car keys. Spying them on the desk, he picked them up and walked out of his apartment to keep his appointment with his client.

Promptly at nine o'clock David stepped off the elevator onto the fourth floor and headed down the corridor to his office.

"Morning, David." His secretary shielded her coffee and doughnut with her body as he brushed past her. "There's a Mr. Calisandro waiting in your office."

"Thanks, Jenny. Bring us coffee, would you?"

"Already done," she assured him. "And croissants."

"Great." David paused, his hand on the doorknob. "Ah ... hold my calls, eh?"

Inside the office, a burly man sporting a tattoo on each forearm turned from gazing out on the New York bustle as David entered the room.

"Cal, good of you to meet me here," David said. The men shook hands.

"No problem, man. I'd forgotten how crazy the early morning traffic is in the city."

"Where'd you park?" David asked, turning aside to hang his trench coat on the hook behind the door.

"Downstairs in the basement garage."

"I'm surprised they had slots open."

"Lots o' spaces when I came in. I was here at seven." He held his cup aloft. "This is my third cup o' java this morning."

David filled the remaining mug with coffee and sipped the hot liquid. "Early bird, huh."

"Catch a lot of worms that way, man."

"Speaking of birds, did you watch any of the game yesterday?"

"Yeah, the last quarter. Those Eagles don't have a clue," Cal scoffed. "That game wasn't even a good practice for the Giants. Ah well, so much for the Monday morning quarterbacking."

"So what have you got for me?" David led the way to his desk, pausing to return his empty cup to the tray on the credenza. With a wave of his hand, he indicated that Cal should sit in the chair opposite.

"First, fill me in on how much you know." Cal lowered his thick frame into the leather upholstery. David waited for the *whoosh* of displaced air before responding.

"How much do I know?" David repeated. "I know Leila took off with some guy on a motorcycle after our wedding ceremony. I know she didn't care a whit about her parents' feelings—or mine, for that matter. I know she lied about loving me, lied about her intention to 'forsake all others.' Her whole life was one big lie!"

"Sounds like you're still harboring some feelings of anger toward her, man."

David chuckled at Cal's choice of words. "'Harboring some feelings of anger.' What are you, Cal, my therapist? No, I'm not angry at her. You can't be angry at a dead person. Until a few days ago, I thought she was dead, remember? Truth be known, I'm really angry at myself for getting suckered into her little scheme. The quick engagement and marriage, I mean. I wonder what other little plans she had in store for me." David inhaled deeply and blew out an audible breath. "Ah, well. That's history. So, whaddya have?"

"She's in Florida. Miami. Drove there with Sylvester Cannon immediately after the wedding."

"Sylvester. That's the motorcycle guy?"

"Right. Sly. Good name, huh? Near as I can figure it, he left her for another woman about a month after they got to Florida. *She's* the one who was killed with him in the motorcycle accident. Just inside the Texarkana border. Leila has a room in the back of a large tenement house with several other women. Man, you should see this house. Kids running all over the place. Women chasing after them all shouting in different languages. Spanish, French Creole, West Indian accents. I think I even heard German."

David interrupted the commentary. "You saw Leila?

"Yeah, man, I saw her. I talked to her."

"Did you tell her …?"

Cal shook his head. "She thinks I was looking for Sly. Seems a lot of people were looking for him in the early days."

"How'd she look?"

"One word, man: rough. Her hair was all scraggly, and her dress was kinda hanging off her." Cal wiggled his fingers near his head in an attempt to fill in descriptions where words were inadequate. "And the sneakers just … and the stale cigarette odor … she was lookin' bad, man. Like I said, 'rough.'"

As the man described Leila, David's thoughts skipped to Rose, who was always enticing, even with flour on the tip of her nose after making a pie, or with her hair covered with plaster or sawdust from one of her remodeling projects.

"All right." David leaned forward in his chair, willing his thoughts back to the present. "How do I find her?"

Cal removed the manila envelope from the pocket of his briefcase. He pinched the metal clasp together and lifted the flap. Easing the contents onto the desk, he handed each piece to David along with an explanation of what he was seeing.

"Here's the house address. Your GPS will probably get you there but I sketched out directions from the Tamiami area. These are pictures of the house from the back, front and side, and some of the women who live there. I saw a man and couple boys too, but I couldn't tell if they were just visiting. And this—" He handed over the final snapshot. "This is Leila."

David took a few moments to stare at the photograph. It was Leila all right, although at first glance he might not have recognized her. Her hair, that glorious hair that first attracted him, lay lank against her shoulders. Her clothes seemed several sizes too big for her bony body, and her feet seemed to be touting some rubber shower clogs the likes of which the Leila of old would never have stooped to wear. And yet when he peered at her eyes, he had no doubt this was the woman he'd married. She'd left him for this? What catastrophe could have precipitated her into this circumstance? And where was her rescuer, the guy on the motorcycle?

When he'd seen enough, he tossed the last photo onto the pile.

Cal continued. "These notes might come in handy if you plan to do any follow-up on this case. The rest of the stuff is related to travel expenses, telephone calls, motel room, and such. It's all itemized on the bill." He handed the last sheet of paper to David.

Glancing at the figure at the bottom of the page, David whistled. "You don't come cheap."

"You get what you pay for, man, and you got the goods on this one."

Nodding, David reached for his briefcase. "A check okay?"

"Check's fine. Say, David. Why don't you just let it go, man? Why go through this hassle? She left you, man. Ran away with some other dude. No one would fault you for dumping her."

David thought about the man's words. Just dump her. Don't go to Miami. Don't try to see her. It would be so easy. And no one would fault him. "You know, Cal, a year ago ... piece o' cake." He snapped his fingers to emphasize his words. "But now I can't do it. I married her. I gave my word, you know? *I* would fault me." He picked up the pen from his desk, reread the number at the bottom of the invoice, and filled in the blanks in his checkbook. Signing his name with a flourish, he tore out the check and handed it to Cal.

"Finding her wasn't hard, man. She isn't hiding, just existing." Both men stood, and Cal held out his hand. "I just hope you know what you're doing, man. Good luck."

No, I don't know what I'm doing, David thought as he shook the outstretched hand and ushered Cal to the door.

Two nights of fitful sleep did little to improve Buddy's disposition in the light of day. In addition, she pricked her index finger with a needle while attempting to replace a button on the shirt she planned to wear that morning. Angry at herself, she tossed the garment aside and sucked on the injured finger. A moment later she picked it up again, only to discover the needle had slipped free of its thread.

Stupid! Stupid! She chastised herself and dropped to her knees, carefully patting the carpet for several moments. Unsuccessful at finding the needle, and growing more impatient, she rolled back onto the ball of her feet—and stepped on the needle.

Buddy sucked in her breath, the rush of air whistling past her teeth. She hopped back to her seat on the edge of the bed and lifted the injured foot onto her lap. Sure enough, the thin sliver hung where it had imbedded itself in the soft pad of her heel. Slowly but determinedly she extracted it and immediately pressed her thumb against the wound. She refused to give voice to the *ow* that would have provided some release.

At breakfast, she complained under her breath that her scrambled eggs were too runny and the toast too dry. The coffee was cold, and besides, she was really in the mood for tea this morning.

Zach's reprimanding glance said "that's enough" and promptly quelled her complaints but had her walking away from the table muttering under her breath words that sounded like "pity party" and "lack of understanding."

As she was walking from the room, Buddy reached up and slammed the door of one kitchen cabinet shut, but the impact was so strong the magnetic catch failed to hold and the door bounced open again. Doubling back to close it securely, she caught a glance of restrained amusement that passed between her parents.

So they're finding this funny, huh? Well, I'll show them something really funny, she thought. What that "something" would be she wasn't sure, but it would be good. She defiantly dashed the heel of her hand against the edge of her eye where the beginnings of a tear welled. *No more tears,* she admonished herself as she took the stairs two at a time up to her bedroom. *Let it go. Let* him *go.*

Moments later she returned downstairs and announced her departure to her parents. "I'm off." She checked her watch as she spoke. "I'll be at the paint store for about an hour, and then I'll probably stop in to see Joe at the firehouse. See ya."

"Whew." Both parents visibly relaxed when the door closed behind Buddy. Rising from the table, Mary remarked that only once before had she seen Buddy so agitated, and, come to think of it, hadn't it been after she was rejected by a boy? Of course she was only thirteen at that time, but that episode had lasted for almost a month.

"Well, she's *your* daughter," Zach remarked, pushing away from the table to join her at the sink.

"*My* daughter?" Mary countered. "Only one of us has that stubborn streak, and we both know who that is."

"Right! So you admit it?"

"Not me, *you*." She playfully snapped a dish towel across the seat of his pants. "You're the bullheaded one."

Zach caught the free end of the dish towel and yanked on it, pulling his wife closer until their foreheads almost touched. "If I'm bullheaded …"

"You are!"

"Then you must be—"

"—quietly determined," Mary said, completing his sentence, barely able to control a smirk.

"Ha!" her husband bellowed. "Determined, maybe, but quiet? Never!" Zach laughed out loud.

The phone rang, interrupting their banter.

"I'll get it. You see to Ensign," Mary directed.

"C'mon, boy." Zach snapped his fingers at the dog and both went out the back way for the start of their morning walk, Zach still shaking his head in amusement at his wife's response.

Man and dog had barely descended the stairs from the deck when Mary called them back. "That was Roger. There's a problem with the pregnancy. They're admitting Anna Faye into the hospital. He wants me to come down to take care of Susan."

Zach's response was immediate. "Pack for both of us. I'll see if I can catch Buddy. If we hurry, we can leave here by noon."

In the end, it was Buddy who was driving down Interstate 95 at noon on her way to the Virginia Beach Coast Guard station. Having convinced her parents that the trip away from home and the resulting change of scenery was just what she needed, she telephoned the change of plans to Roger, who gratefully accepted her offer to stay with Susan.

Zach did a quick check of oil and water levels and tire pressure on Buddy's aging Toyota and pronounced the car in satisfactory shape for the six-hour drive. After joining in her father's prayer for safe travel, Buddy hugged her parents and backed out of the driveway, thankful for the opportunity to leave behind the familiar scenes that triggered memories of happier times spent with David in her beloved Cape May.

Chapter 15

Through the clouds sunlight glinted across the skin of the silver jetliner as it started its descent into the Miami airspace, but the sunshine was soon replaced by droplets of rain when the big metal bird finally broke through the fluffy clouds.

David returned his tray table to the upright position and tried to ignore the too-sweet smile flashed at him by the flight attendant. She had not hesitated to let him know of her attraction to him, not just by offering pillows and blankets during the three-hour flight but by her lingering touch on his shoulder to gain his attention and by the evocative toss of her hair as she responded to something he said. His gentle rebuff, an explanation that he was on his way to Miami to meet his estranged wife, was met with a pout and a crestfallen face, followed by incredulity, and then a brazen challenge that seemed to say, "What does that have to do with anything?"

My wife! The words left his lips with an ease that belied the churning uncertainty in his heart. *I have a wife.*

The big jet whizzed above cargo terminals, parking lots, and huge steel hangars as it approached the runway. David felt the bump and heard the squeal of tires touching the tarmac, and he swiftly offered up a silent prayer of thanks for his safe arrival. Immediately the engines screamed their protest as the captain forced them into reverse thrust. The big bird slowed by degrees and was steered to its designated gate.

As if in response to the downbeat of a conductor's baton, several seatbelts clicked open in unison while others waited for their cue to join the cacophony. Ignoring the directions of the flight attendants, passengers stood impatiently in the narrow aisle, anxious to retrieve their baggage from the overhead compartments. Unwilling to hurry the moment of reunion, David remained in his seat, eyes closed, until the mob made their exit.

Finally he got up and reached into the open storage compartment above his head for his knapsack and the case containing his laptop. He slipped both arms through the knapsack, settling it securely on his back, and picked up the computer bag. He strode from the airplane, giving a curt nod to the attendants who stood at the exit.

Within an hour, David was seated at the desk in his hotel room, the keys to his Hertz rental car jiggling nervously in his hand. Indecision played across his face. *Shall I go see Leila now or stop first for an early lunch?* He checked his watch. Eleven ten and he wasn't really hungry. He answered his own question: get the initial contact out of the way. No sense in putting off the inevitable. Reaching for the hotel room key card, he stuck it in his breast pocket and strode from the room.

Once again the Miami sunshine had triumphed in its battle with the rain clouds, and David marveled at the sparkling leaves of the dark-green palms and purple bougainvillea as they glistened in the sunshine after the brief squall. Cal's directions were perfect, and several moments later, David eased the rented Taurus alongside the curb across the street from the house where Leila lived.

In the small, fenced-in backyard, a little girl sat silently on the seat of a broken web chair, clutching a small doll close to her chest. A few feet away, a thin mongrel pup barked wildly and pulled at the rope tied to his collar and secured to the fence post. Three small boys fought to gain possession of a soccer ball from their opponent, an older man. David watched as the man, obviously more experienced at the sport, held them off by expertly nudging the ball just out of their reach. As the boys circled the man, he kicked it behind him and faked a forward motion. The boys, having missed the direction of the ball, moved forward with the man, overtaking him. The man dropped back, allowing them to run ahead of him, while he turned around and reclaimed the ball.

Wishing he didn't have to interrupt their play, David stepped from the car, slammed the door shut, and sprinted across the street to the chain-link fence. "Hey," he shouted to the group. "*Hey.*"

"What's up, mister?" The taller of the three boys ran toward him, breathing hard. The others followed at a slower pace.

"I'm looking for Leila. Leila Willoughby. She lives here." Without answering, the boy turned to the man and rapidly said something in Spanish.

The man responded, and the boy turned back to David. "What d'ya want with Leila?"

David wondered how much he should tell them. He decided to say as little as was necessary. "I just want to see her. I knew her when she lived in New Jersey. Is she home?"

The boy turned back to the man, translating David's words. The two conversed together in Spanish before the boy turned back to David. "They took her to the hospital."

"The hospital? Was she sick?" Cal didn't say she looked ill, just rough.

"*Si. En ambulancia. Domingo?*" the boy said to the older man, who nodded affirmation.

"Sunday," the boy translated. "In the ambulance. She was talkin' kinda funny. Really weird. Mi *abuela*, she phoned the ambulance. They took her away."

"Which hospital? Where is it?

"Que hospital? Donde esta?"

"Creo que ..." The man and boy argued about the best way to get to the hospital. Finally the boy turned back to David. "I tell you, Mister. Turn your car around, stay on this road till you get to Publics. Turn right after Publics and you see the sign for the hospital." Behind him the man was shaking his head no, but the boy continued. "You don' believe me, you ask anybody. My school bus drives behind the hospital every day. You ask anybody. I know."

Thanking them, David sprinted back to the car. He sure didn't know what a "Publics" was, but the boy seemed certain he couldn't miss it. *What on earth could be wrong with Leila? Talking funny? Talking weird?* She was too young for a stroke, wasn't she? Could she have been using drugs? David dismissed the notion. No, not drugs. As he recalled, Leila had vehemently sworn off anything that would diminish her faculties and render her out of control. Dancing had been her vice, and while the others of her group imbibed, she lost herself in the headiness of undulating rhythms and unrestrained movement.

Fifteen minutes after leaving the tenement house—and discovering "Publix" supermarkets—David pulled into the rear entrance of City Hospital. He parked the car in the area designated for visitors and walked through the double glass doors to the receptionist.

"Good morning." The gray-haired volunteer smiled at him. "You'll need a visitor's pass to go upstairs. Which patient will you be visiting?" With her fingers hovering over the computer keyboard, she peered at David through wire-rimmed glasses.

"My wife, Leila Willoughby," he answered.

The woman punched in the name and raised her eyes to him again. "We don't have a Leila Willoughby registered. Could she have used another name?"

"Try Leila Amherst. That's her maiden name." The fingers punched the keys again.

"No, no Amherst either. When was she admitted?"

"Sunday, I think. She was brought in by ambulance."

"Hmmm." Her eyes scrolled down the names on the screen. "Nope. Nothing. Unless … I just thought of something." She punched the key pad. "It's Margie at reception. I might have a lead on that Jane Doe from Sunday." She replaced the telephone on its cradle and addressed David. "She could be here after all. Someone will be right down."

At the reception desk, David shook hands with the social worker, Allyson Redpath, and followed her into a small room.

"Coffee?" she offered. David declined as he pulled out a chair at the small round table and sat down. "Tell me about the person you're looking for," the woman began.

"I can't describe her to you because I don't know how much she's changed," David told her. "We were married a little more than five years ago. I haven't seen her since our wedding day. Until a week ago I thought she was dead. I had plans to marry again. I hired an investigator to verify that she was dead. He found her living here in Miami."

David eased his body forward and removed his wallet from his hip pocket. Pulling out three of the photographs Cal had given him, he slid them across the table toward the woman. "These were taken a week ago."

She stared intently at each photograph. Apparently satisfied with what she'd seen, she handed them back to David.

"Well?"

"Well, it seems our Jane Doe is your Leila Willoughby. I take it she doesn't know you're looking for her?" David shook his head. "I'll take you upstairs to her room. Someone from the treatment team will fill you in on her status. You'll need to sign releases and that sort of thing."

David watched her make some notes on her clipboard.

"So now that you've found her, what are your plans?"

"I'll try to build a life with her … if she'll have me."

"She'd be a fool not to take you up on your offer. I read the ambulance reports. I know the area she lives in. Tough neighborhood. Sometimes it seems the only way out of places like those is by ambulance or squad car." She clicked the top of her ballpoint pen, retracting the point before placing it in her pocket. "I hope you're successful. C'mon, I'll walk you upstairs."

Not knowing what to expect but anticipating the worst, David followed the woman toward the elevators.

"Well, well, well. Look who's awake!"

Leila Willoughby heard the annoyingly cheerful nurse and felt her stroke her arm. She did not respond. The nurse's gloves irritated her thin, dry skin. She could ask her to stop, but why bother. It was just one more irritant. Even the cotton hospital gown felt harsh against her dry, flaky skin.

"Rest well?" Nurse Paula asked, but she did not wait for a response.

Leila had refused to speak since entering the hospital, not even telling the registration people who she was. She was nobody, loved by no one, cared for by no one.

The staff had unsuccessfully attempted to coax some response from her. They'd quizzed her about the red and blue ankle tattoo, the letters V and C intertwined and surrounded by a heart. They'd assumed they were her initials. She let them think so.

"I'm so glad you're rested." The nurse continued her monologue. "Here's some lunch for you. Let's see, what've we got?" The woman called out the food items on the tray. "Mmm … protein shake, some nice broth, rice pudding, orange gelatin. Two desserts. They gave you two desserts! You must have a friend in the kitchen."

Leila wasn't tempted. She wished the woman would leave, but she seemed determined to stay and continue a rambling, one-sided conversation.

The nurse placed the tray on the open-ended laminated table that stretched across the width of the bed. She lifted Leila into a sitting position, punched and shook the pillows, and then eased her backward. Leila allowed her body to be lifted, rolled, and propped into position, not making any effort to help. Moving took too much effort and left her exhausted. Why didn't the woman let her be? She just wanted to sleep.

Instead of leaving the room as Leila hoped, the nurse pulled a chair close to the bed. Leila knew what was coming next: the guess-the-patient's-name game.

Leila barely opened her mouth and the nurse placed a spoonful of food on the tip of her tongue. "Very good, dear. Now what d'you say we try the *V* names while you eat, okay?" From the conversations Leila overheard while she faked sleep, the staff had started a contest to see who could guess her name based on the letters tattooed on her leg. "Are you Vanna? No. Velda? No. Verona? No. How about some more broth? You want the drink instead? Right."

Leila was too weak to drink from a straw so the nurse held the glass against her cracked lips, all the time still calling out names. "Catherine? Carmen? Cynthia?"

Leila made a vain attempt to roll her eyes at the ridiculous game, but her eyelids drooped and closed instead. She wanted more sleep, needed more sleep, but her body wouldn't give in. Her mind wrestled with possible solutions to the horrible mess she'd made of her life. How would she start over, or at least move on from here? If she understood the doctor's discussions with the nurses, she was even sicker than she'd thought. Maybe it was too late to start over.

A few more hours on the saline drip and she'd be ready for discharge, or that's what her nurse said. But discharged to where?

Back to the deplorable living conditions that had contributed to her illness in the first place? Back to the drug dealers who waited like vultures on every corner of her neighborhood? It would be better if they'd let her die. But if they did …

She'd overheard the nurses discussing her case while they thought she was asleep. She'd been picked up while roaming the streets. None of the stragglers in the neighborhood admitted to knowing her. No one had reported her missing. But she was beginning to remember: the slum house. The men who came and went. The kids …

"Feel up to a shower?" That voice again. Leila closed her eyes and turned her head away.

"I take it that's a *no*. Maybe a sponge bath? Then you can sit in the solarium for a little while. It's a nice, sunny day."

Another voice interrupted, and Leila listened with her eyes closed. It was how she learned about her status. She was considered indigent, and she'd learned in the last few hours that not too many people took the time for conversation with the indigent.

"Still mute?" the male voice asked.

"Noncommunicative," the nurse corrected. "I know she can speak. She'll say something before she is discharged, you mark my words."

"Hmm." The doctor did not voice his skepticism. "Stick around while I check her out, will you?" He handed the chart to the nurse.

Nurse Paula pulled the curtain on its metal hangers until it surrounded Leila's bed, enclosing them all. The doctor began his detailed examination, poking and prodding while watching for her reaction. As he turned her ankles to examine the tattoo of the intertwining initials, he met Leila's vacant eyes.

"Carlotta? Venus?" Shaking his head at her lack of response, he continued his examination while addressing her directly for the first time since he entered the room. "D'you know that there is a contest on this floor to guess your name. *I* think it's something really odd, like 'Valtrompia' or 'Clarabelle.'"

Leila did not respond.

Reaching for the chart, the doctor flipped open the pages, pulled a pen from the breast pocket of his lab coat, and clicked it several times before beginning to write. He made several notations as he spoke under his breath to the nurse. "I'm ordering more lab tests. I don't like the feel of her abdomen, so I want a pelvic ultrasound as well. Have the blood work done first." He checked the levels of the intravenous bottle hanging by the bed and made more notations. Returning the chart to the nurse, he prepared to leave the room, sliding open the curtain just enough so he could slip through. Nurse Paula opened them all the way and followed the doctor to the door.

"Find out what's holding up those chest X-rays, will you? I can still hear a wheeze."

For a while he clicked the pen open, shut, open, shut, open without speaking. "And about the lab tests"—the doctor continued as if there had been no interruption in his orders—"I want the results stat. I'm discharging her tomorrow."

So they're discharging me tomorrow, Leila thought. *Giving up on me.*

So be it.

Chapter 16

$\mathcal{D}$avid approached the woman in the hospital bed. Except for her head and shoulders and the one hand that had an IV needle, her body was covered by a thin sheet. Her face was drawn and colorless, quite unlike the healthy complexions of the Miami citizens who basked in the never-ending sunshine. Instead, her pallor rivaled the hue of the bleached pillowcase under her head.

And her hair! It was tangled and matted and bore no resemblance to the crowning glory that had been her trademark years ago. David hardly recognized it as the magnet that had first attracted him as it had swirled around her face during one of her wild exhibitions on top of a table in a certain nightclub. This tangled mess left him cold.

Drawing closer to the inert body, David whispered her name. "Leila?"

There was a barely perceptible stiffening of the thin body in the bed. Her eyelids fluttered and then opened barely wide enough for her to see the man leaning toward her. Then the paper-thin eyelids closed again.

He was sure she recognized him. And if it were possible for her body to become more rigid, he was sure she had. She didn't want conversation—that was obvious—but they'd have to talk. He hadn't come all this way to walk away because she refused to talk. "Leila?"

After several heartbeats, Leila rolled over. In an attempt at modesty, she snaked one arm across her body until her fingers touched the hem of the cover sheet and pulled it up to her neck.

"David?" Her untested voice crackled. The tip of her tongue swiped her lips from one corner to the other in an attempt to moisten them. She took several shallow breaths. "How did you find me? What are you doing here?"

"May I sit?"

Leila barely nodded. She raised one hand toward her head in what was probably an attempt to pat some order into her wildly disarrayed hair, but then her arm fell limp and useless beside her head.

David pulled the wooden chair closer to the bed and lowered himself into it, at the same time signaling the nurse that she was free to leave. "Well." David hesitated, searching for the right words. The moment he had dreaded was here. He considered the woman who had captured his attention, if not his heart, several years before, but who now paled in comparison with the heart of his heart, Rose. Rose, whose smile welcomed, energized, warmed, and consoled him. Rose, whose voice soothed and comforted him. Rose, whose family embraced him. Rose, who loved him.

Rose, who was now relegated to his past!

He forced himself to focus on the woman before him. *This woman is my future,* he reminded himself. *This woman is my here and now.*

"I don't think it really matters how I found you." The words sounded harsh even to him. He searched his mind to find a way to soften them but came up with nothing. Better to speak openly. Why disguise his feelings when he'd only have to reveal them later? "Never mind how I found you. The point is that I did. As to why I am here ..." He gulped the lump that had suddenly formed in his throat. "I'm here to take you home."

Leila's muffled response sounded like "puh" to David, but he struggled on without allowing it to divert him. It had been difficult enough convincing himself to follow through with this plan. Now he had to convince *her!* He had to make her believe he was doing this because it was what he really and truly wanted to do, not just because it was the honorable thing. Lord knows he would really rather be with Rose. Wasn't his heart still with Rose?

But that union was not to be. In an impetuous moment he had pledged his life to this woman. Now he must fulfill that vow. It was, after all, the right thing to do.

Of course, by the looks of Leila she wouldn't take too much convincing. The promise of three square meals a day and a comfortable bed ought to do it. Add to that some decent clothes to replace that hospital gown and it would surely be a done deal.

With a twinge of guilt, he hoped he wasn't being callous. He certainly didn't intend to hurt Leila. In time they might even be able to develop some smidgen of affection for each other, and memories of Rose would be locked away in the recesses of his heart to be retrieved only in moments of solitude, and examined, cherished, and locked away again.

David interrupted his morbid introspection. Now that he was facing Leila, he realized he had no further plan. He'd found her. Now what? "I should have come after you earlier," he said. "After the wedding, I mean. I saw your indecision when Sly called out to you. I should have stopped you.

"When you rode off with him I should have jumped into one of those cars and gone after you. I thought about it. Instead, I joined your parents and our guests in denouncing you. It was easier, you see? Easier to condemn you. Easier to feel sorry for myself. Anyway, I want you to come back with me. Patch up this marriage if we can. Start over."

"No."

Had he not seen her lips move, David would have thought he'd imagined her response.

"No." The single word was louder this time, and more vehement than he expected her to produce in her weakened state.

Her effort triggered a coughing spell the likes of which David had never seen before. He leaped from his chair, slipped a muscled arm under her frail shoulders, and raised her into a sitting position. He sat on the narrow bed facing her and tilted her body forward until it was fully supported by his own body, her chin resting on his chest.

The dry, hacking cough continued for several minutes while he held her, gently rocking her like a mother lulls a newborn. She needed him. He knew it. In the past she'd been fiercely independent, proud, a renegade. Now she was an outcast. She needed him.

The coughing spell tapered off. Tears, forced from her eyes by the unrestrained hacking, slid unchecked down Leila's sunken cheeks and seeped into David's shirt as she struggled to regain control of her breathing. Her body relaxed against him. Exhausted, she turned her face and rested her weight full on him. And he held her.

When she took a deep cleansing breath, David eased her away. "Water?"

He felt her nod. David eased her back against the pillows, carefully moving the plastic IV tubing aside. He poured a splash of water into a plastic cup from the bedside pitcher and held it to her lips. She took a couple of sips and pushed his hand away.

"I won't go back!" she insisted." I won't be pampered and coddled and put on show and then reprimanded and scolded for being assertive. All my life I've tried to fit into my parents' mold, but I can't. I just can't. *I won't.*" Her body trembled. Her lips opened and closed as she struggled to speak, but no more words came.

"Shhh." David stroked the meager fingers in an attempt to calm her. "Should I call the nurse? I'll call the nurse."

"No. No nurses. Please." Her strained protests ended with a gentle hiccup. Taking several deep breaths, she plunged on. "I just didn't expect … I mean … I should be apologizing for running away, not you. You didn't do anything. I messed up. I'm the guilty one. I'm so sorry, David. I didn't want to hurt you. There I go again. Seems like I'm always apologizing.

"Sometimes I think everything I do is wrong," Leila continued. "I've hurt so many people. I didn't mean to hurt you, David. You can't imagine the mess I've made with my life." She withdrew her fingers from his hand and turned her head away.

Leila's contrite words touched David's heart. She was right. She had hurt many people, but he found that in her present condition he didn't have it within him to condemn her.

"Look. I didn't mean to spring this on you, but, well, I do want you to come home with me." She started to protest but he continued quickly. "Don't say anything now. Concentrate on getting well first, and then think about it. We could write to each other, maybe telephone, you know, start over slowly. By the way, are we still married?"

Leila nodded.

So there had been no divorce. He felt deflated. No divorce. He suddenly realized he'd been hoping all along that, in their years of separation, she had divorced him. That would have let him off the hook. It would have been her doing, not his.

"Okay. Let's take this slowly, okay? We have all the time in the world."

A young attendant dressed in blue cotton tunic and pants entered the room pushing a wheelchair ahead of him. He removed the intravenous drip from the stand by the bed and helped Leila to the wheelchair. "We'll be in X-ray for about an hour," he told David, offering to show him to the cafeteria or the solarium.

David checked his watch. "I'll go get a bite to eat and come back later. Will that be all right?" He addressed his question to Leila. Her nod was barely perceptible.

At the nurses' station the floor nurse told David of the doctor's intention to discharge Leila the following day and suggested that he collect a change of clothes from her apartment.

Agreeing, David resolved to return to the house he had visited earlier. If they would let him enter her room, he would pack as much as he could so he wouldn't have to return. Something told him that the neighborhood would be very intimidating at night. And unsafe.

At the reception desk, he thanked the receptionist for her help in locating Leila.

"Visiting hours end at nine o'clock," she called out to him as he walked away.

Outside, he adjusted his sunglasses against the bright Miami sunshine and strode toward the car. He had many tasks ahead of him before he returned to the hospital.

There was no time to lose.

Chapter 17

$\mathcal{D}$avid climbed into the rental car, started the engine, and immediately adjusted the air conditioning to full blast. He punched in the address on the GPS and waited for the directions to load. He remembered seeing the familiar golden arches near the Publix shopping center. First he would collect some of Leila's clothes and then stop for a burger before returning to the hospital. The growling in his stomach was becoming more audible and he had no desire to sample the hospital menu. He eased the car forward. It was time to begin the next leg of his mission.

For the second time that day, David maneuvered the Taurus into the vacant space opposite the tenement house Leila called home. Heaving a sigh, he settled back in his seat and surveyed the area.

Viewed from the cool, fresh-smelling interior of the new car, the dilapidated state of the surrounding buildings appeared woeful and abandoned in spite of the bustle of activity nearby. Rusted rain gutters hung disconnected from their counterparts and swung freely at the whim of the wind underneath unpainted eaves. Upended garbage cans, their contents scattered, invited scavenger birds and mangy animals to feast on decaying morsels.

Ahead of him on the opposite side of the street, David watched a scrawny dog challenge a seagull for a half-eaten sandwich. When the bird hopped away with the food, the dog sniffed the rubble for overlooked tidbits, found nothing, and sauntered away toward another pile of garbage.

Why would Leila be willing to return to this squalor? Nothing, as far as he could see, could entice him to spend one moment longer than necessary in this depressing place. Yet she seemed determined to reject his offer of a home, protection and respectability to return to … this? Of course her reluctance to accompany him would mean he was off the hook, wouldn't it? He had done his part. More than his part! He couldn't help it if in her obstinacy she rejected what was probably her only chance to regain the respectability she had snubbed when she rode off with Sly.

His mind drifted back to their earlier conversation. What was it she'd said about being made to fit into her parents' mold? Pampered and coddled. Put on display and then scolded. Could that be it? Could her reluctance to return with him be another attempt at assertiveness?

Recalling that he had not set upon this enormous task of his own accord, David let his head fall to his chest, closed his eyes, and whispered, "Help me, God."

The interior of the car was quickly becoming oppressive. Rather than starting the engine and the air conditioning to gain some relief, he decided to get on with his task.

David stepped out of the car and locked it. A discarded soda can lay by his feet and a small swarm of bees attacked the spilled liquid. He carefully stepped around the can, being careful not to disturb the insects.

Two teenagers circled the vehicle, checking out its lines. Better to befriend than antagonize, David cautioned himself.

"Nice wheels, huh?" he said to the boys. One responded with two upheld thumbs. As David walked across the street toward his destination, he hoped the vehicle was thoroughly insured. He wouldn't be surprised if the car was stripped of the hubcaps and any other removable parts by the time he returned.

He assumed schools must have been dismissed early, for several women and children milled around outside the old building. On the porch an old woman rocked slowly, joining in the activity of the younger people by watching them. A small boy leaned against the moving chair, his arm across the old lady's shoulders.

It struck David that there was a closeness, a bond, in the company of the varied circles before him that was not often seen in many well-to-do communities. Neighbor greeting neighbor, being neighborly. Maybe this was Leila's reason for wanting to live here. In strangers, had she found the connection and the sense of kinship that had eluded her in her own family?

For the first time David thought he might have caught a glimpse of Leila's view of her Miami life. From her parents' perspective she had been doted upon, pampered, indulged, cherished, and loved, but to Leila she had been misunderstood and smothered. He found himself sympathizing with the young woman who'd married him to escape the glass fences of her parents' lifestyle, and then left him for the fun and freedom that Sly offered.

Inside the fenced-in backyard, the young soccer player recognized him and jogged closer.

"You find the hospital okay?"

"Excellent directions, man," David replied. "Thanks."

"Hey, I know my way 'round this town." The kid started to swagger off.

David called him back. "Who's in charge of this place? I gotta talk to somebody about Leila."

"Hey, Belle," the boy shouted at the group of women.

A very rotund woman left the group and waddled over to them. "Whaddya want, boy?"

"This guy, he wanna talk to you 'bout Leila. He knew her from Jersey."

"They took Leila to the hospital," Belle announced without preamble, her sing-song lilt and Creole accent identifying her Haitian roots. "'Bout time, if you ask me. I told her, 'You gotta get outta that bed. Get a job, you know? Fix yourself up. No sense you cryin' and moanin' over your situation. Worser things happen to people, you know? The kid's dependin' on you, I tell her. But I just talk till I'm blue in the face. She don' listen. Pretty soon she run outta food. Then she sells off all her nice stuff, you know? Pretty soon she got nothin', and her mind's gone funny. And what about the kid? Who's gonna take care of the kid? Sittin' there all quiet. Not sayin' nothin.' Who are you, anyway? Why you come aroun' askin' all these questions?"

David didn't point out that he hadn't asked her any questions. "I'm Leila's husband. We've been separated for a while. I'm hoping to take her back north with me."

"Her husband? She didn't say nothin' 'bout no husband comin' from up north. Sly—"

"Sly was not her husband," David interrupted. "When she left me she ran away with him. Look, I just came to get some of her clothes to take to the hospital. If you would let me into her room …"

"Well, now, I can't do that. Private property, you know. Can't do that. Course, if she was to give you a note, you know, giving you permission, like. I could let you in if you had a note. What did you say your name was?"

"Willoughby. David Willoughby. I can show you my driver's license." He reached into his hip pocket, removing his wallet. He handed over his license and his sports club ID card, both with pictures.

The woman scrutinized them for a while and then returned them. "Guess you's who you say you is. But I can't let you in the room without a note." The woman's tone held an air of finality.

As David turned away, his eyes rested on the little girl who sat cross-legged in the white plastic chair as she had done earlier in the day. Even at this distance he could see the worn-out patches in the knees of her scruffy pants. Her braided hair must have been neat at one time but now was a tangled mess. The doll, held so close earlier, lay abandoned in her lap. *Poor little beggar*, he thought. *What does life have in store for a child like that?*

Belle's words suddenly pierced his consciousness. *What about the kid? Who's gonna take care of the kid?* Did Leila have a child? Is that why she was so distraught? The letters on her ankle—a child's initials?

"Belle."

"Mister Willo—" The words collided in mid-air as the woman waddled back to the fence. "Well, now, we have a little problem. Name of Tori." The woman splayed her fingers across her ample hips and looked David dead in the eye. "Much as I feel for Leila, I cannot take on her child. I got enough kiddies runnin' 'round here. Children take a lot of lookin' after, you know? Food and clothes and such. I was gonna call the Welfare tomorrow, but seein' as how her father is right here—I figure you's the father since you have the same last name—seein' as you's here, might as well take her with you, you know? If the Welfare takes her, no tellin' when Leila will get her back, you know? Least I could do is let you take her, seein' as you's here right now."

Deep within himself, the woman's words created a tension that David could not ignore. His stomach heaved. He forced himself to take a deep breath. He swallowed and became calmer by degrees. This was not his child. He and Leila had not been intimate. Leila had had this child with some other guy.

But the woman said we have the same last name.

His stomach heaved again. The increasing pounding within his head and his chest threatened to overwhelm him. Though his outward appearance remained unchanged, rebellion swirled within him, ascended into his chest, and threatened to gush from his lips.

A child? Lord, you tell me to give up the woman I love, take on a woman I don't care a whit about, and now her illegitimate child? You ask too much. You ask too much!

The words remained unspoken. His vehement thoughts never took root, and the protest died a slow death within him.

He blew out a breath and let his shoulders sag. He flexed the fingers of both hands and heard the knuckles pop in quick succession. Feeling the clamminess of his palms, he swiped them across his hips before slipping both hands into his pockets.

I don't want to do this. He was going through the motions of reclaiming Leila as his wife, but his heart wasn't in it. He was being obedient. Did he have to be enthusiastic as well? He confessed he'd been secretly hoping Leila would refuse him, that she would stubbornly disavow him a second time and free him to court his heart's desire, Rose.

But a child, Lord. How can I take on a child?

He felt a response in his heart and mind: *How can you reject a child?*

Deep inside his spirit struggled. He wanted to do what was right. He wanted Rose. He couldn't have Rose; that was clear. What else was there for him to do but to carry on?

David tossed his head back, squinting at the sky.

I'm going all the way, Lord. All the way.

Taking a deep breath to help him regain his composure, David reached out an unsteady hand, lifted the latch of the chain-link gate, and stepped into the yard. He fastened the gate behind him and strode across the yard toward the little girl, brushing past Belle, who struggled to match her stride to his longer legs. When he was within a few feet of the child, he slowed, not wanting to alarm her with his aggressive approach.

"Hello, Tori." The tall man hunkered down and sat on his heels, placing himself at the child's level. He paused, allowing her time to complete her meticulous examination of him. When she raised her eyes to meet his, David felt satisfied she was not frightened of him. "That's a pretty doll. May I hold her?"

The child's soulful eyes roamed his face and then handed over the doll.

David examined the toy and gingerly placed it on his shoulder, hugging it close. "I think she's sad. What do you think?"

The child stared back. David wondered if anyone had ever bothered to ask her opinion or attempted to have a conversation with her. Interaction with the adults in her transient household probably consisted of telling her where to go and what to do.

"She wants her mommy."

"Did her mommy go to the hospital?"

"Uh-huh. She was sick, but they're gonna make her better. Then she'll come back."

David returned the doll to her and watched the child hold it close as he had done.

"Honey, my name is David Willoughby. Can you tell me your name?"

"Tori Wee-oh-bee."

"Tori Willoughby," David repeated. "We have the same last name."

"My mommy has the same last name too," she volunteered.

David nodded in agreement. "Your last name is Willoughby, and your mommy's last name is Willoughby, and my last name is Willoughby."

The little girl seemed to digest this interesting bit of information without comment. David wondered whether, in her innocence, she would be able to string these facts together and arrive at a palatable conclusion.

Her eyes opened wide as realization dawned. "Are you my daddy?"

Daddy. The word caught David off-guard. He found himself blinking rapidly to clear away the moisture that threatened his vision.

I'm going all the way, Lord.

He answered her without flinching and without embellishment. "Yes, child, I'm your daddy."

Tossing the doll aside, Tori Willoughby launched herself into the arms of the big man. He immediately folded them securely around her. He felt her tuck her head into his neck, grasping hold of what must have been the first promise of security offered her in many days. Her tiny hands tenderly stroked the hairs at the back of David's neck, giving and receiving comfort measure for measure.

"Will you take me to my mommy?"

Without answering, David looked up at Belle, who stood silently watching the emotional scene unfold. She'd refused to allow him access to Leila's room and he'd capitulated. But somehow he knew he would not give in so quickly if she argued against his removing this little one from the compound. He was amazed at Tori's immediate acceptance of him as her father. He would honor her faith in him. He would not let her down.

Unfolding himself from his stooped position, David stood, lifting the little girl with him. He turned to the woman who stood silently by, planted his feet firmly, and stared her dead in the eye. "I'm taking her with me, Belle." His voice was firm, daring her to protest.

Belle hesitated only slightly and then nodded her assent.

He nodded in return. Done.

David shifted the child to his hip. He reached into his breast pocket for a pen and into the hip pocket of his slacks for his wallet. Taking out a business card, he scribbled the name and room number of his hotel on the back of the card and held it out to the woman.

Amazing how she fought to stop him taking clothes from his wife's room but willingly handed over her child!

Belle took the business card. David told her he could be contacted there until Leila was discharged from the hospital.

"After that you can reach me at the New York number."

Grasping Tori around her waist with his free hand, he checked the time on his watch before settling her back on his arm. Three forty. Time enough to get a bite to eat before returning to the hospital.

It struck David that he now had in his possession the real reason for Leila's reluctance to go home with him. To return to her own parents with an illegitimate child was to acknowledge her errant lifestyle. She'd be laying herself open for more scolding and admonishment. That must certainly have been her reason for giving the child his own name rather than the name of her real father, whoever he was.

And yet concern for the child's welfare should have been sufficient reason to accept his offer.

Still, if this is what it would take to convince her to return with him, so be it.

Slipping his wallet into his chest pocket, David met the child's gaze. It amazed him that she had so quickly adopted him as her father.

"Hungry?" he asked.

"Uh huh."

"Me too. Let's go get something to eat."

He picked up the discarded doll. His business here was done. He thanked Belle for her assistance and strode out of the yard without a backward glance.

Sometime later, with Tori's hand snuggled in his own, David led the child into the hotel's elevator for the short ride to the second floor. The doors slid slowly together, sealing them off from the noisy bustle of the hotel lobby. Five tiny fingers clung anxiously to David's thumb while a little head tilted backward, allowing trusting but uncertain eyes to search his face. David smiled his reassurance to the child. She didn't respond, but her eyes remained glued to his, her gaze unwavering.

David tried to imagine the feelings of uncertainty that must be circling within the tiny child. First her mother disappears, and then Belle, her substitute caregiver, willingly surrenders her to a stranger. Shouldn't Belle have been more reticent with him? Unless, of course, this scenario had been played out before. Were there other "daddies" in her life? Had Leila ... no! David immediately intercepted the wayward thought and found himself praying that his suppositions were farfetched.

The elevator bell *dinged*. They'd arrived at their floor. The doors parted and the two walked across the slightly worn carpet toward the room at the end of the corridor, the tall man adjusting his stride to match the shorter steps of the little one.

Inside, he turned deaf ears to the child's protests as he deftly scrubbed away ketchup stains from her hands and face. What was it about kids and ketchup? In the restaurant Tori had set aside the nuggets of chicken in favor of the bag of french fries. Rather than biting into the fry, Tori used it as a dipper to scoop up a glob of ketchup. Then with her pinky finger sticking out for balance, she raised it to her mouth, closed her lips around the fry, and licked the ketchup away. She'd kept doing that until the fry was too soggy to support the ketchup. Then she set aside the soggy fry. When she tired of the routine, or when her stomach protested at not being filled, David wasn't sure which, she selected a few pieces that were untainted by ketchup, chewed them thoroughly, swallowed, and sipped from the small carton of milk. Her hunger allayed, she began again to savor the ketchup using the previous technique.

Tori swished and rinsed several times and David made a mental note to pick up a toothbrush for her on their next trip outside of the hotel. He swung her high into the air as they approached the bed and felt curiously let down when he failed to elicit a chuckle. Instead she opened her mouth wide to let out a loud yawn followed by an impish grin at David's look of horror.

He pulled back the quilted spread on the second bed and tucked her rag doll next to her. After punching the TV "on" button, he inserted a rented DVD into the player. The opening credits of *The Little Mermaid* flashed onto the screen and immediately captured the child's attention. Leaving her to watch the DVD, David flipped open his laptop and went online to retrieve his messages.

Tori soon became engrossed in the antics of the engaging Sebastian and his partner, Flounder. Her subdued giggles pierced David's awareness and he found himself paying more attention to her unrestrained responses than to his own work. Finally, unable to concentrate on his messages, he logged off and gave her his full attention.

The little girl's antics were a delight to watch. When Ariel complained to Sebastian about her father's strict rules, Tori's head tilted to one side and her shoulders sagged dejectedly. But when Ariel sang her happy song, Tori's body swayed in time with the heroine's dance. Her tiny feet, free of the plastic "jelly" sandals that had left a checkerboard pattern across her toes, tapped out their own rhythm on the quilted bedspread. *She's a delightful child*, David thought.

Lord, if Leila refuses to return with me, what then? What happens to her, and what happens to this innocent girl?

No sooner had the thought left his mind than David's lips curled into a self-mocking grin. *I know, I know. This morning I wanted no part of this, and now I know I can't leave them here.*

His gaze returned to the child, who had changed position again and now lay across the width of the bed. Her body no longer wriggled but her chest moved up and down in a steady rhythm. Lethargy, triggered by long, lonely hours seated in the Miami sunshine, crept over her. Her hand loosely clutched the doll, four fingers curled around it while her thumb buried itself between her lips. Her eyelids drooped and opened, drooped and opened, each subsequent sequence repeating more slowly than the one before, until finally they remained closed. Before Ariel agreed to the sea witch's bargain, Tori was sound asleep.

Chapter 18

On his evening visit to the hospital, David was greeted by the volunteer receptionist. "Mr. Willoughby. Two South, I believe?"

An arched eyebrow accompanied her question while she wrote Leila's room number on a bright yellow cardboard tag. Reaching for the ticket, David thanked her and accompanied his words with a fat wink. The gray-haired woman blushed and turned to Tori.

"And who is this little lady?"

"This is Tori."

The little girl cast a blank stare at both adults. "Tori, say hello to Mrs. Garcia," David encouraged.

"Hello," she responded, lowering her head. As she spoke she sidled up to David's leg and hid behind it.

"We'd better go." He nodded to the woman and moved down the tiled corridor toward the elevators.

"Where's my mommy?" Tori asked as they stepped from the elevator. Unfamiliar, pungent hospital odors, rubbing alcohol—or was it iodine?—caused them both to wriggle their noses. They walked past the nurses' station and turned in to the doorway of the second room on the left.

David walked past the first bed and slowed his approach toward the other. No sounds came from behind the partially drawn curtain.

"Leila?" David called out.

Peering around the curtain he saw that Leila had resumed her earlier position—lying on her side, facing the window, her back to the doorway. He felt Tori's body huddle closer and grasp a handful of his khaki slacks. He sensed tension building within the child. He reached down and rubbed a gentle finger across her quivering cheek.

"Leila, I brought someone to see you."

Still there was no response from the woman on the bed. He leaned close to the child and whispered, "Say hello to Mommy."

His first indication that Tori was not going to comply was a single restrained sob followed by a vehement shaking of her head and a step backward. When the child realized she had released her hold on David's slacks, she quickly stretched her arms toward him again and grabbed a handful of khaki.

The muted scuffle behind her persuaded Leila to roll onto her back. Jaded, sunken eyes held Tori's fearful ones.

"Tori." As the single word escaped Leila's parched throat, the child, already intimidated by the unfamiliarity of her surroundings, spun away and ran toward the door.

"No, no, no, no, no," she repeated at the top of her voice. "I want to go home. I want to go home." At the entrance to the room she came to a sudden stop on the point of her shoes, arms flailing in an effort to maintain her balance. Tears streamed down her face. "Take me home. I want to go home."

As Tori spun around, David followed her so that when she halted at the door, he was right behind her. Acting purely on instinct he scooped her up into his arms and held her close to his chest.

"Shh, shh, shh," he murmured soft words of comfort. Over her head he spied two nurses rush past him into the room, concern for their patient etched on their faces. Satisfied that Leila was in no danger, they turned to the child, who still cried softly.

"I think she's just been overwhelmed by the events of the day." David said. "She'll be fine in a minute." He turned away from them, continuing to hold Tori close to his chest. Gently and rhythmically he pat her back, still murmuring soothing words, and listened for the return to steady breathing that would indicate the end of the episode. When a slight hiccup interrupted the breaths, he instinctively knew she was ready to listen to him.

Where this awareness came from he had no idea, but it had become important to him that this child felt loved and cared for. She had accepted him as her daddy before he had even imagined himself in that role. Now he would act the part, and, Lord willing, she would never know that it was an act.

He realized their experiences were similar. As he had partied in crowded bars and nightclubs lonely and alone in spite of his so-called friends, so, in the backyard of her home, she had been isolated from the playing children and the grownups who socialized nearby. Both yearned to be included; both had lived on the outskirts. Now they'd found each other, man and child, father and daughter.

"Tori," David coaxed. Tori said nothing but burrowed her head further into the crook of David's neck. He moved to the vacant bed and sat on the edge. "Tori, listen to me, sweetheart." He held the child away from him and reached into his hip pocket for a handkerchief. Gently he wiped away the traces of tears. "Tori, we have to go back to Mommy."

"No, Daddy, no." She attempted to scramble up David's chest and hide herself in the corner of his body where she had found comfort, but he held her firmly on his knee.

"Tori, listen." David stopped speaking until the child raised her eyes to meet his. "We have a lot of things to do before we go back to the hotel, don't we? We have to buy you a new toothbrush, remember?"

Tori nodded.

"And we should get you some new jammies to sleep in tonight?"

She nodded again. David saw that he had finally gained her attention. Maybe she was ready to bargain.

"And we didn't have dinner yet. What would you like for dinner?"

She thought about this for a while. She'd obviously had enough experience with grownups to know that there would be a downside to this new line of questioning.

"Chicken."

"Chicken. Mmmm. Fried chicken? With mashed potatoes?"

The little head bobbed up and down. "No peas."

"No peas?"

"No peas." She was emphatic. "I don't like peas."

"Okay. No peas. How about milk?"

"Uh huh, I like milk."

"Me too."

David allowed her a few moments to savor the prospect of a delicious dinner while he tried to recall something, anything, from his college psychology classes that might be of use here.

"Know what, Tori? You don't have to see Mommy if you don't want to, but I need to talk to her for a few minutes. Would you like to wait here while I talk to Mommy or will you go with me and sit on my lap while I talk to her?"

David waited. Her face was as expressive as her mother's.

"Will you carry me?" She tilted her head even further backward and her trusting eyes pierced his heart. He found himself fully bonded to this child.

"Yes, I'll carry you."

"Okay."

"Okay, you'll go with me?"

"Uh huh, and sit on your lap."

David gave her a swift hug. "Thank you, Tori."

"You're welcome, Daddy," she whispered back.

He held her for another moment, gently rocking her on his lap. Finally he stood, hoisting her into his arms, and entered the cloistered section of the room. He sat on the wooden chair at the foot of the bed and settled Tori on his knee, holding her close.

Viewing the room and its occupant through the eyes of the child, David saw how bleak the room was and how frightening Leila's appearance would be to a child. Leila's hair hung shoulder-length, stringy, and matted. Dark, sunken circles surrounded her eyes and her lips were cracked in several places.

Peeking out from below her collarbone two dark circles marked the site of the leads from an earlier EKG exam. One arm still boasted an IV, the needle securely taped in place and the long tube carrying the life-sustaining liquid connected to the poly bag suspended above the bed. The rays of the evening sun seeping through the tilted slats of the Venetian blinds bounced off the TV screen and cast an eerie orange light around the room.

The poor child must have been petrified, David thought, and vowed to leave the hospital as quickly as he could.

"I heard you through the curtain." Leila's raspy voice interrupted his thoughts. "You're good with her."

David continued to stroke his hand across Tori's forehead and into her hair. They had been through a lot, he and Tori, in the short time they had known each other.

"No, you have it backward." He spoke to Leila though his eyes never left the child. "She's good with me."

How long they sat in silence, David couldn't tell, but every few minutes a bell in the hallway went *ding* followed by someone paging someone else or an urgent voice announcing a special code for something.

"Have you thought about what I asked earlier? About coming home with me?" David broke the silence.

"Some. Not much."

"Did they complete all your tests today?"

"I guess so. They haven't said they need to do more. They might discharge me tomorrow."

"Good. Shall I'll try to make plane reservations for Sunday?"

"I haven't said I'll come back with you," she squeaked out.

David shifted his gaze to the woman he had vowed to make his wife in more than name only. He had spent a small fortune locating his fugitive wife, had walked away from Rose, his true love, had flown south from his home in New Jersey, had assumed responsibility for a waif, and had offered the child and her mother his home, his care, and his protection—all in the name of obedience to his Lord.

David's internal struggle persisted. *Can I walk away from her now? Leave her here in this hospital, satisfied that I did my part and more, and not feel guilty? And Tori? What about Tori? It would be doubly hard to walk away from this child.*

"You haven't said you'll come back with me," he finally responded, "but you haven't said you won't."

By the time David returned to the hospital the following morning, Leila had breakfasted, showered, and brushed her hair, so that when her two guests arrived, they were astonished by the transformation of the woman sitting up in bed before them. Still bearing little resemblance to the spunky spitfire David had married, she nevertheless had cleaned up nicely. A little makeup to conceal the shadows beneath her eyes and a few weeks on a diet that included fresh fruits and vegetables and she would be restored to good health in no time. David was sure he could guarantee that *if* she returned home with him.

During the night, David had spent several hours wrestling with himself, finally conceding that his motives for seeking her out in the first place remained pure. Then he let go of the problem, applying the technique Dr. Matt had shown him. With his hands held out in front of him he prayed for Leila, Tori, and himself, their situation, for guidance in making the right decisions, for strength to accept the outcome of the decisions, and then, right at the end of his prayer, a quick plea for blessings on Rose and her family. Then he splayed his fingers, letting go of this burden. Only then was he able to drift into a peaceful sleep, accompanied by the sound of the child's gentle snore from the bed next to his.

"Is it nice out?" Leila's question brought David's attention back to the present. He recognized her question as small talk, neither of them wanting to broach the subject that was never far from their minds.

"Is it ever not a nice day in Florida?"

"You'd be surprised. Hurricanes, floods, lightning strikes …"

"Blue skies, clean air, warm temperatures …"

"Unbearable heat …"

"No snow!"

"That's true. I don't miss the snow. Sounds like you should move here."

"Sounds like you should leave with me."

They smiled at each other and then retreated into silence.

"I got new shoes." Tori, seated in David's lap held up one foot showing off her brand new pink and white sneakers.

"We left the house without a change of clothes," David explained. "We had to get her some clean clothes at Walmart. The shoes were too cute to pass up.

"By the way." He leaned to one side and grabbed the cord handles of a shopping bag. "These are for you. Tori, do you want to show Mommy what we got her?"

Probably because her mother's cleaned-up appearance made her appear less intimidating and her newfound security in her daddy, Tori showed no qualms about hopping down from David's lap and taking the bag from his hands. Coming to a halt just inches from the bed, she set the bag on the floor and gingerly removed the garments piece by piece, placing them next to her mother.

"It's a dress," she announced, "and some other stuff."

While Leila examined the articles, Tori pressed one elbow into the mattress, balancing her head on her folded wrist. Pleased that the child now felt comfortable enough in her mother's presence to leave the security of his lap, David leaned back in the chair, his body relaxed for the first time since he'd entered the room.

"I wasn't sure about your size now, but …"

"I can't go back with you!" Leila's protest hung in the air between them.

David's immediate thought was for the child. He expected Leila's sudden outburst would send Tori scrambling back to the security of his arms. He could see Tori's eyes darting swiftly between him and Leila. Steeling himself, he denied his body the freedom to react and was gratified when Tori took her cue from him and resumed her previous stance.

Finally he felt able to respond to Leila's declaration. But how?

Challenge her! Say, "You aren't capable of earning a decent wage while you're ill."

Be demanding! Say, "I'm in charge now. You and Tori are coming with me."

Threaten! Say, "I'll sue for custody of Tori. Social Services will take my side."

He said, "Suit yourself."

Denied the opportunity to air the arguments she had obviously prepared during the night, Leila crumpled. "You have no idea what you're asking."

"Then clue me in, Leila." David leaned forward in the chair. "Tell me why you're so opposed to coming back with me when your circumstances say you have no other choice. What am I missing here?"

Leila inhaled several times, the last breath escaping from deep within her chest and exploding in a sob. "This is so awful. I'm so sorry for everything."

"And I've forgiven you. So what's holding you here?"

With her free arm, Leila removed a paper tissue from the box on the tray table and dabbed at a tear at the corner of one eye. "There's nothing for me here. It's just Tori and me."

"So come back to Jersey with me and let's work at being a family." David uncurled his length and slowly approached the hospital bed. Seating himself next to her, he snaked his long arm across the sheet and held his palm open.

Leila stared down at his hand, each rough spot bearing testimony to the effort he would make to provide a decent life for herself and her child. Some day he would tell her what propelled him to come after her, to pursue her in spite of her debilitated condition. Certainly he did not love her. But maybe he would get to know her, truly know her. And he would make sure, as far as it was within his power, that she would not regret placing her trust in him as completely as she had trusted Sly.

His large hand remained open before her. After a brief hesitation she topped it with her own.

"We are still husband and wife," David said.

"Yes."

"You will come home with me?"

"Yes."

Bridging the space between them, two hands and two lives touched, renewed their commitment to each other, and held firm.

Chapter 19

The temperature was dropping on the early October evening when David swung his Jeep into its assigned parking spot outside the housing development and turned the key to silence the engine. Behind the vehicle, a pile of dried orange and brown leaves were swept into the air by a miniature whirlwind and deposited on the car in the next spot. Except for one young man at the end of the lot who was practicing maneuvers on his skateboard, the courtyard was remarkably devoid of activity for a Sunday evening.

For the space of many breaths, no one inside the vehicle spoke. David turned to face the brooding woman in the passenger seat, who stared silently out her window. Turning away, he looked into the rear-view mirror and studied the questioning eyes of the child seated behind him. She raised a tentative hand and wiggled her index finger at the image in the mirror. He did the same, and both smiled.

"Are we there yet?" she asked.

"Yup. This is it. We're home.

David pushed the button to release his seatbelt and at the same time opened the driver's door with his other hand. Before getting out the car, he swung his arm across the seat into the back and unlatched the rear passenger door. Stepping out of the car, he opened the rear door, unhooked Tori's seatbelt, and helped her from the car. He held her hand securely within his own as they walked behind the vehicle around to the front and assisted Leila from her own seat.

After the warmth of the Miami sunshine, they all shivered in the chilly October air.

"Let's go inside where it's warmer," David urged. "I'll come back for our bags when you're settled."

Needing no further encouragement, three Willoughbys entered David's home as a family for the first time.

On the other side of the door, David gathered several pieces of mail from the floor where they had fallen through the mail slot on the door. He glanced over them quickly, and finding nothing that needed his immediate attention, he walked through the arched entry on the right leading to the kitchen and tossed the envelopes on the table.

This is awkward, he thought. *Where do I start?*

"I need to go to the bathroom." Tori's wail provided the gateway to normalcy.

"Right. Bathroom's this way."

On their return, David turned to Leila. "I suppose I should show you around before we do anything else, eh?" A nonchalant shrug was her only response.

This is going to be an uphill battle, Lord, but you said "do it," and I'm doing it the best way I know how.

"All right. Here we are in the kitchen." David started the detailed tour of their new home. They would make changes later to accommodate the new residents. Leila and Tori would occupy the master bedroom until he could convert his office into a second bedroom for Tori. They would have their meals at the round table in the kitchen and David would move his drafting equipment into the dining room, making that his new office.

"I'll sleep on the living room couch until we're all settled. How's that?"

Again Leila responded with an apathetic shrug.

Heaving a sigh, David said, "I guess this is as good a time as any to get the bags from the car." He struggled to maintain his composure as he went out into the chilly evening. After all his efforts to restore some order and improve the quality of their lives, Leila seemed not the least bit grateful and showed little interest in having an active part in their rehabilitation. Didn't she understand that this was as difficult for him as it was for her? He had given up so much. What had *she* given up? Living in the slums? Insecurity?

He removed the two bags and his laptop from the back of the car and then crawled over the seat to retrieve the discarded rag doll.

Walking back toward the house, David spied Tori standing forlornly in the doorway, her eyes wide and searching, her cheeks pumping away at the thumb stuffed in her mouth. He'd noticed that she resorted to thumb sucking when she felt abandoned. He offered up another prayer that she would soon become secure enough in her new environment to quit the habit.

"Help me carry these, baby. They're really heavy." The child reached for the doll. "Thanks a bunch, kid." He kicked the car door shut behind them.

"Mommy's sleeping," Tori announced as David entered the bedroom to deposit their bags. Leila lay stretched out across the width of the bed on top of the comforter. The flight and long drive must have been overwhelming so soon after her hospital stay.

"No, I think she's just resting. Shhhh." Removing a light blanket from the foot of the bed, he unfolded it and covered her. On the way out of the bedroom, David unplugged the telephone, noticing the flashing message light. He bundled up the cord and walked out the room in an exaggerated, Pink Panther-like tiptoe. The little girl giggled at his antics and followed close behind him.

"So what's for supper?" he asked her when they were back in the kitchen.

Puzzled, Tori looked up at him. "I don't know." Her shoulders raised in unison in a shrug similar to her mother's.

"I thought *you* would make supper tonight."

"But I can't cook."

"Sure you can. Tell you what. Why don't we make supper together?"

"Okay."

After washing their hands at the kitchen sink and drying them on paper towels, David lifted Tori up and seated her on the countertop. He handed her a bowl and fork, cracked several eggs into the bowl, added milk, salt, and pepper, and showed her how to scramble them for an omelet. While she concentrated on this task, he placed a frying pan on the stove and turned on the burner. Then he grated some cheese, sliced some mushrooms, and made a salad from prepackaged greens that were still green and edible in spite of their time in the refrigerator.

David poured the eggs into the warm skillet and watched Tori carefully sprinkle cheese and mushrooms. While the omelet cooked, they made several slices of toast together, David inserting the bread in the toaster and Tori pushing down the lever.

I could get used to this.

Next he showed her how to place the silverware: fork on the left, knife on the right but rethought his actions and removed the knife from her place setting. He poured two glasses of milk and made a mental note to purchase plastic cups tomorrow. When they were seated at the table, David made a dramatic motion of inhaling the omelet's aroma and declaring it to be the best-smelling omelet he had ever experienced.

"Thank you for helping with supper, Tori."

"You're welcome, Daddy."

"Let's thank God for supper." David held out his open palm to Tori. Having shared all her meals with him since the fateful day when he had taken her away from the tenement house, she had become accustomed to the mealtime routine. She placed her hand in his and allowed his fingers to close around hers.

"Dear God, thank you for giving us a safe trip back from Miami, and thank you for letting Tori and her mommy come to live with me here. Thank you for giving us this nice omelet and milk and salad. Use it to nourish our bodies. And Lord, I pray that you will restore Leila to full health in your own time. Amen."

"You forgot the bread."

"Sweetie, it would be really nice if you would say 'amen' with me at the end of the prayer."

"But you forgot the bread!"

"No, I didn't. See? Here it is."

"Nooo, Daddy." She punched the air above her head several times with her index finger. "You forgot to thank him for the bread."

David tried not to grin at the concern on the child's face as she forced her fingers to penetrate his closed fist and closed her eyes.

"And thank you, Lord, for the delicious toast, amen."

"Amen."

David cut the child's omelet into bite-sized pieces, added a thick layer of strawberry jelly to her toast, and warned her that she must eat a little of everything when she promptly licked most of the jelly from the toast.

While he waited for Tori to complete her meal, David slit open the envelopes he had retrieved earlier, read the contents, and replaced them. Then he plugged in the answering machine and punched the *play* button to retrieve the waiting message.

"Hey, guy, Roger Madsen. I guess you must be out partying or something. We had the babies. Gimme a call."

The machine's date stamp indicated the call had come in the previous evening. David vowed to contact his friend before the evening was over.

After drinking only half her milk, Tori announced she was finished. David walked with her to the bathroom and watched her wash her hands and face and brush her teeth. Remembering snippets of the routine in his friends' homes, he warned Tori that she could expect to be given a bath in a few minutes, after which he would read to her and then it would be bedtime. Set the ground rules early, he told himself, and avoid confrontation later.

So far, this parenting thing was going well!

Later, David washed and dried the dishes and returned them to their place in the cabinets. He bathed Tori, adding a drizzle of shampoo to her bath water. The child was delighted with her first bubble bath, and David was coaxed into extending her bath time, finding he had no defense against the child's pleadings. As he lowered her into bed beside her mother, she wrapped warm, clinging arms around his neck and whispered, "I love you, Daddy."

David took a sheet and blanket from the linen cupboard and made a bed for himself on the living room couch. After stretching out he remembered he hadn't returned Roger Madsen's call and reached for the phone.

The phone rang twice and a familiar voice answered.

David's stomach clenched. His breathing stilled. He was unable to utter a word.

"Hello?" the voice said. "Is anyone there?"

Say something, he told himself. *Speak, man.* A spontaneous cough jump-started his breathing again. "H-hello, Rose."

"David? David, is that you?" Her voice was hushed. Breathless.

Tortuous thoughts whizzed through David's mind. *Does she miss hearing me as much as I miss hearing her? Does she die a little each time she thinks about me? Does she think about me at all?*

He pictured her as she had been at their last meeting. Soft, sweet, gentle Rose. Giving to everyone and asking nothing for herself. He remembered their last kiss. She had poured out all her love in that kiss, and he had selfishly taken. Then he had turned her over to her father.

"Yes, it's me. How are ... I didn't expect ..."

"I've been here since you left. Helping Anna Faye." Her voice faded.

"Yes, I heard. Twins, huh?"

"Uh huh. Roger called. You were away?"

"Yes."

"Florida?"

He didn't need to confirm her words.

"So you're back from Florida?" Her voice was insistent.

"Yes."

"Alone?" Now she was barely audible. He could hear the breathless hesitancy, knew the hoped-for answer and could not give it. "Sorry," she recanted. "I shouldn't have asked."

David inhaled deeply seeking to steady his wavering voice. "The twins ..."

"Two boys. The first is named David, after you. And the other is Jonathan."

"How's Anna Faye?"

"She's fine. Susan's fine. Roger's fine. Everybody's fine. Look, David, I have to go. We shouldn't be talking."

"Rose." David felt like crying. He was desperate. "Rose ... Rose, I'll always love you."

Click. The call was terminated from the other end. Hugging the receiver, David became immediately contrite. *I shouldn't have said that. God forgive me, I shouldn't have said that. I'm only causing her more pain.*

He replaced the receiver on its cradle. Out the corner of his eye he glimpsed a shadow of movement and turned his head. Leila's frail body leaned against the wall, her gaze perplexed, questioning him through the dim lamplight. Their eyes met and held. No words were spoken for several moments. Then, slowly, she turned her back on him and made her way to the kitchen.

Torn between his desire for the woman who held his heart and his obligation to the one who bore his name, David punched his pillow several times with a tight fist, venting his frustration. *This isn't fair. This isn't fair.* Taking a deep breath and breathing out the tension, he burrowed his head in the well of the pillow, closed his eyes, and prayed for oblivion.

After spending a fitful night on his makeshift bed, David set out for his morning run. His methodical approach to running—the arm-stretching exercises, lunges and squats, the slow jog increasing to a steady, mechanical rhythm ending with a full-out sprint—did not result in the satisfaction that usually rewarded his workout. Instead he found he had to remind himself to keep his arms up and his eyes on a distant goal. When he found himself drifting off the track and unable to concentrate, he slowed to a walk and ended the exercise session.

He loved running. He looked forward to the time alone, using it to meditate and to order his day. Today he felt gypped. He returned to the townhouse, intent on taking a hot shower and putting the wasted event behind him. He slammed the door of the Jeep shut, inserted the key into the front door and, remembering just in time he was no longer the home's sole occupant, stopped himself from slamming that too.

MAXINE THOMAS

Halfway down the dim hallway an unfamiliar bundle lay on the floor. As David approached, the bundle uncurled, stretched, rolled over, and grinned up at him.

"Hi, Daddy. I thought you was runned away."

Placing his gym bag on the floor, David squatted beside the child and slicked his hand over her unkempt hair. "Now what made you think I had run away, little one?"

"You took your bag and you didn't say bye-bye." Tori lowered her chin to her chest and poked her thumb between her lips.

David looked to the slightly ajar bedroom door where Leila lay sleeping, unaware that her daughter had left her side. Placing his forefinger across his lips for silence, he lifted the child in his arm, picked up the gym bag, and headed for the kitchen. He sat her on the countertop and placed the bag next to her. In one smooth movement Tori crossed her ankles and pulled them close to her body, rest her elbows on her knees and her chin on the back of her fingers. Looking him dead in the eye she silently challenged him to explain away his actions.

David met the challenge. "Open the bag and tell me what you see inside."

Tori struggled with the zipper and finally opened the canvas bag. When she pulled the sides apart she placed her face close to the opening to examine the contents. She immediately backed up, turning up her nose and fanning her fingers in front of her face. "Phew. Stinky."

David smiled at her reaction and removed the contents of the bag one at a time. "This my stinky running shoe, and here is my other stinky shoe. And a stinky T-shirt. And a stinky towel." As he withdrew each item he held it aloft between finger and thumb, exaggerating his scorn for the item to the little girl's delight. "Now I'll just throw these stinky clothes into the washer."

"The sneakers too?"

"Yup, the stinky sneakers too." He lifted the lid of the washing machine and tossed the items inside.

"Don't forget the stinky bag."

"Right." He saluted her and reached for the bright, kelly-green gym bag with the Celtics leprechaun embossed on the side. Hoping against hope the color wouldn't run, he tossed the bag in with the other items. "In you go, stinky bag."

Tori's giggles warmed his heart. He was discovering that she was a delightful child, easily pacified, and easy to love. He knew too that whatever it cost him he would devote himself to making a decent life for her. He wanted her to feel secure with him, as sure of his protection of her as he had been with his own father. So secure, in fact, that she would never question his devotion and commitment to her.

David looked down at her and felt his heart swell with love. He placed his hands on her waist and took several shuffling steps backward until his forehead was level with hers. Eye to eye, he carefully explained his early morning jaunts and promised to always return. Then he reached behind her and lifted the electric clock from the hook on the wall. He rotated the knob in back of the clock until the hands read five thirty. He patiently explained that he would leave for his run every morning when the long hand was pointing straight down and the short hand was on five and would return when the long hand was pointing straight up and the short hand was on seven. When he was sure she understood, he reset the clock and returned it to its place on the wall.

Moving his forehead closer to hers until they touched, David stared cross-eyed at Tori. "How about some breakfast?"

Tori nodded and giggled when David's head nodded in time with her own.

"What would you like?"

"Crackers and milk."

"Just crackers and milk? No cheese with that?"

"Uh-uh."

"Cereal? An egg?" Tori shook her head at each offer. "Okay. Crackers and milk it is."

From the cabinet above her head David retrieved a box of wheat crackers, poured a glass of milk from the gallon container in the refrigerator, and set them on the table. Lifting her from the counter, he placed her on a chair and sat opposite. Immediately she folded her hands together. David asked a blessing on the meager meal and waited for her next move.

"That's not the way Mommy does it," she complained, refusing to eat.

"All right. Show me how Mommy does it."

"First you have to get a bowl and then a paper towel."

David complied.

Tori removed four crackers from the waxed sleeve, folded them inside the paper towel, and pounded on the bundle until the crackers were smashed. Then she emptied the contents into the bowl and poured milk from the glass over the crushed crackers.

"May I have a spoon, please?" she requested solemnly.

Again David complied. Telling himself that he dare not gag, he watched Tori devour the thickening glob as if it were a gourmet meal.

What other indignities had this child known? And her mother— to what ends had they gone in their efforts to keep body and soul together?

God, grant me the means and the fortitude to keep them from returning to the life of poverty and humiliation they've endured.

Reaching for the remaining crackers, he did as Tori had done. He smashed a handful between a paper towel, dumped the contents into a bowl, added cold milk from the carton, and forced himself to join his "daughter" in the vilest meal he had eaten since downing a handful of earthworms during a wilderness survival camp.

Chapter 20

Three days after he brought his new family to live with him, David stood with Leila at the door of Tori's new bedroom and watched the child pirouette in the center of the room. Behind them, David's friend Spencer Gooden settled his long, paint-splattered fingers on his hips and watched the little girl's antics. The men had completely transformed David's home office into a little girl's pink and white dream.

"Oooh, it's beautiful," Tori cooed while David smiled in satisfaction.

With the help of his friend, and with occasional input from Leila, David had moved his drafting equipment to the dining room, repainted the office, laid new carpeting, and assembled the child-sized bed, table, and dresser, which he and a designer associate purchased the day before.

Now the three adults watched Tori perch gingerly on the quilted comforter, her fingers moving slowly back and forth, relishing its soft puffiness. She stretched out on the bed, her head bouncing up and down on the pillow. Her eyes, navigating the room from this new vantage point, spied the table under the window. She jumped up from the bed and sped toward it. With one hand she quickly pulled out the matching chair and lifted one knee to rest on the seat while her free hand caressed the smooth, painted wood. In the adjoining book rack she discovered a Winnie the Pooh coloring book and a box of crayons. David had purchased a copy of *Goodnight Moon*, remembering it had been the favorite of that other little girl in Cape May who had once thrown her arms around his neck and declared, 'I love you, Uncle David.'

When David turned to Leila, his eyes were still smiling at Tori's antics. "I think she likes it," he said.

"I should think so. It's beautiful. Only ..."

"Yes? Did we miss something?"

"No, it's just that ... she's never had a room to herself before. I was wondering how she'll adjust to being alone. She's always had me with her."

The doorbell chimed in the distance.

"I'll get it," Spencer told David. "It's probably my ride."

As his friend walked away, David turned back to Leila. "And you've always had her with you." He wasn't sure how he'd come by such insight, but he was at once aware that her concern was for herself, not for her daughter. "She'll do fine," he assured her. "And you'll do fine. We all have to make adjustments, but we'll take it slowly. You'll have your room to yourself for a while. I won't join you until you're ready."

And not until I'm ready. But I'm trying, Lord, I'm really trying.

"Anybody home?" Rhonda Gooden shouted from the doorway, and followed it with "Hey, babe" to her husband. She brushed past him and headed for the kitchen where she deposited a crock pot and a large loaf of Italian bread. "I got supper!" she tossed nonchalantly over her shoulder.

"Who's the voice?" David, entering the kitchen, matched her tone.

"Ta-daa. The one and only." She turned around to greet him, arms outstretched.

"Rhonda."

"I brought your favorite. Chicken and dumplings."

David lifted the lid of the crock pot, leaned closer, and inhaled deeply. "I'm in hog heaven."

"Wait 'til you taste it, babe. Mmmm mm!"

"I guess it's all right to share it with my family?" He held out his arm to include Leila and Tori. "Rhonda Gooden, my wife, Leila." David introduced the two women.

"Would you like to see my new room?" A small voice interrupted.

"Well, well, you must be Tori. And yes, puddin', I would love to see your room." Rhonda held out her hand to Tori, who promptly led the woman out of the kitchen.

Later, after the guests had left and Tori was tucked in for the night, David and Leila sat on opposite sides of the kitchen table reliving the day's events.

"Did you see her face when she first saw the room?" David asked. "She was just beside herself."

Leila nodded.

"She could hardly stand still."

Both were silent while they mentally relived Tori's delight in her new room.

"I can't thank you enough for what you're doing for her. For us."

"It's enough that you share her with me," David responded. Sensing Leila was open to more than their usually stilted conversation, he continued cautiously. "I'm just grateful that you're willing to give our marriage another try. I mean, it's not as if we tried and blew it, you know? We never tried. We never had a chance to try."

"I know. I'm sorry, David."

"No, I'm not criticizing you. Fact is, if we'd stayed together, we might have ended up enemies. I knew very little about you, except that you were beautiful, and fun, and full of life. You knew even less about me."

"I knew you were at loose ends. I knew you didn't belong in that nightclub. You were what my Dad called 'solid.' That's the real reason I invited you home that night, you know. Dad and I always argued about my boyfriends. He said they were losers. I brought you home to show him that I could attract someone solid. Dad had invited some guy to be my partner at his business dinner the next night. When I saw how he took to you, I decided to invite you to the dinner."

"Two weeks later *you* proposed to *me*."

"I don't recall proposing." She smiled self-consciously. "I think I just announced that we were getting married."

"Something like that."

"And you went along with my announcement. Why?"

"I guess I was at loose ends, like you said. And I was drawn to you, not to mention very impressed by your father."

"Yes, people are either in awe of him or scared of him. Usually he scares them off, especially if he thinks they're after his money or his daughter. But not you."

No, not me. I went into this with my eyes wide open. Now I'm paying …

"I have something for you. Wait here." David left the room and returned a few moments later carrying a small shopping bag. "I bought these the day after I brought you back. I wanted to wait for the right opportunity to give them to you. Actually, I was afraid you would give them back, and … well, here."

From the paper bag he removed a small jewelry box. Lifting the lid he revealed a matching set of plain gold wedding bands. "I know you don't have the others anymore. The woman in the fire … well … will you wear this?" David removed the smaller of the wedding bands from the box, laid it in his open palm, and held it out toward his wife.

Leila took the ring into her own hand. She circled it in her palm for several moments and then looked up at her husband. "Tell me about Rose."

In an instant, David's calves kicked the chair away from the table. He strode over to the sink and stood with his back to Leila. *Tell her about Rose?* His hands trembled uncontrollably. He clenched the edge of the sink in an attempt to control their shaking. Blood pounded through his veins. Behind his eyes a red hot throbbing made it difficult to see.

Tell her about Rose? Merge his past with his future? Here in this room? No!

Would the challenges never end? Every time he successfully overcame one hurdle, another loomed ahead. He had pursued Leila, only to find that she came with a child. He overcame his anxiety in the jewelry store and purchased the rings for her when he really wanted to buy them for Rose. And now, now he had to tell her about Rose?

What more do you want of me? His silent cry reached the heavens. *Haven't I been obedient? Haven't I gone the extra mile—miles—without asking for recompense? Must I allow her to delve into every inch of my heart, my very soul?*

Inhaling deeply David struggled to regain control. *To withhold part of me is to withhold all of me.* That insight again.

Turning around he saw that Leila hadn't moved from where he'd left her. Her eyes downcast, she was fondling the golden circlet in the palm of her hand. *She deserves this,* David acknowledged. *I went after her and brought her back here. She has an equal stake in this marriage. There will be no secrets between us.*

David returned to the table, every step more difficult than the previous one. He plopped his body down and stretched his legs under the table. "Rose is the sister of my college roommate," he began. There was a frog in his throat that hadn't been there before. He cleared it loudly and continued. "I met her earlier this year when I spent a few days at the shore. Roger, that's my old roommate, was there for their annual family reunion. He invited me to his parents' home. Rose and I spent a lot of time together, and … we fell in love." David looked up at Leila, but her eyes remained downcast.

"Why didn't you marry her?"

"I wanted to. Turns out I was already married. I'm learning that marriage is forever. I'm married to you. I plan to stay married to you. If you'll have me."

"You want a real marriage?"

"Yes. I thought I made that clear when you were in the hospital. I want a marriage with family, kids, and laughter, and a house with a large yard, and a dog, and trips to the beach. I want it all. With you."

"You telephoned Rose the night we came from Miami."

He spied the glimmer of pain, of rejection, that flashed across her face. "No, I returned Roger's call. I didn't know Rose was there. I think she was as surprised to hear me as I was to hear her."

"You told her you loved her."

"Yes I did. I was wrong."

"You were wrong—you don't love her?"

Complete honesty. No holding back. "I do love her. I give you my word that it won't happen again. I will honor our marriage."

Leila nodded her acceptance of his apology. "There's a lot about me you don't know." She raised sad eyes to him.

"We'll take it slowly. I know we can make our marriage work. I'm committed to this." David closed his hand over hers, stilling their nervous movement. "I'm committed to this," he repeated. "Will you wear my ring?"

Leila extracted her hand from his. Spreading the fingers of her left hand, she held it out to him.

He slipped the small circlet of gold on the third finger of her left hand. "Now, you."

Leila took the larger ring from the box and placed it on the third finger of David's left hand. With their four hands clasped together, David prayed for strength to overcome the challenges that lay ahead and for their renewed commitment to forsake all others, and to love, honor, and cherish each other.

"Let's see how Tori's doing in her new room," David suggested after Leila's hesitant "amen." Together they rose from the table and made their way to Tori's room.

Inside, David picked up the discarded coloring book and crayons from the carpet while Leila pulled the comforter around the shoulders of the sleeping child. At the door they both turned for a final backward glance.

As David followed Leila out of the room, he recalled the verse of scripture his pastor had used as his text the week before: *For I know the plans I have for you …*

David's thoughts returned to the sleeping child. His own plans for her were simple: provide food, clothing, and shelter, things a week ago had been uncertainties in the life of this little one. Create opportunities for laughter and growth and learning. Protect her.

And yet, Lord, it is so little compared with what you have in store for her.

At Leila's door, David slammed his hand against his forehead. "Oh, I almost forgot. The kindergarten principal called back today. She'll see Tori tomorrow morning at nine. We'll need to leave here by eight fifteen."

He placed a peck on Leila's cheek as they separated for their respective sleeping quarters, she in the master bedroom, he for another challenging night on the living room couch.

As he squirmed around to find a comfortable spot, David realized Leila had not seemed pleased about the news that Tori would be starting school next week. This milestone would be somewhat traumatic for the mother as well as the child. Still, the four-year-old program was only three times a week. That would leave plenty of time for them to be together on the other days.

Unable to make himself comfortable, he tossed the pillow and blankets on the floor and rolled off the couch onto them. Soon they would have to reexamine their sleeping arrangements. Sleeping on the couch was going to get mighty old mighty fast.

Chapter 21

avid's eyes swept across the pairs of mothers and children seated in the waiting room outside the principal's office of the Busy Beavers Preschool and Kindergarten. He tugged at the knot in his tie, ran his finger around the inside of his collar, and told himself not to fidget. He felt out of place in this roomful of women and children. This was a mother's chore, wasn't it?

"Victoria, come with me, please."

The slim, young woman with the short, dark hair held the clipboard against her chest and waited for the child to respond.

"Daddy, the lady is calling us." Tori tugged at the sleeve of her father's jacket.

"No, she said, 'Victoria,'" he admonished.

"That's me, Daddy. Victoria is my long name."

As David absorbed this new information, his growing bewilderment became evident by his knitted brow. He reached into his breast pocket, intending to examine the official documents in the manila envelope Leila had shoved at him as he left the house earlier this morning. Documents, she said, that would verify Tori's parentage and readiness for school.

"Victoria Willoughby." The crisp, staccato voice slowly and clearly enunciated each syllable of the name.

There was no response from the other children and parents who sat expectantly in the waiting room. Standing, David replaced the envelope in his pocket and took Tori's hand. How embarrassing it was not to be aware of the child's given name.

As father and daughter approached, the woman held out her hand to David and returned a handshake that was as crisp and clipped as her English accent.

"Victoria?" She offered her hand to Tori who, in a rare show of shyness, tucked her chin into her chest but stuck out her right hand for the handshake.

The proprieties completed, Mrs. Billingsley, the principal, led the way into her office, head erect, back straight, and hips perfectly aligned with her shoulders. After seating her guests, she sat on the edge of the leather upholstered chair behind the desk, her posture perfectly maintained.

"Mr. Willoughby, it's a pleasure to see a father taking an active part in the registration process. We get rather a lot of mothers, and sometimes both Mum and Dad, but rarely do we have dads by themselves. Victoria is very fortunate."

David made a noncommittal response, and Tori tucked her chin into her chest for the second time.

"Now, then." Mrs. Billingsley ruffled the papers on her desk and compared the application form with the notes on her clipboard. "'Victoria Christine Willoughby.' That's quite a mouthful, isn't it? Are you called 'Vicky'?" The principal peered over the rim of her glasses at the child.

"Uh-uh. Tori."

"Then 'Tori' it is. Tell me, Tori, have you been to school before?"

"Uh-uh."

David leaned toward Tori to admonish her, but Mrs. Billingsley stopped him with her upheld hand. "Then you're in for a real treat.

School is fun. You'll make many new friends and learn to read, and count, and there'll be plenty of time for play." She turned to David. "Our curriculum includes several periods of structured playtime. We believe strongly in the value of play for enhancing social skills, such as learning to share, making polite requests, using words such as 'please,' 'may I,' and 'thank you,' building trust, being trustworthy, and so on."

Mrs. Billingsley reviewed the notes on her clipboard. "It seems you gave us all the relevant information during our telephone discussion. I'll just need to make a copy of Tori's birth certificate and immunization record."

Once again David removed the manila envelope from his breast pocket. He pulled out the papers and handed them to the principal, wishing he had taken the time to review them before leaving home.

"Well, well. It seems someone will be celebrating a birthday very soon. How nice." David remained silent while the woman read through the documents, made photocopies, and returned them to him. As she continued to make notations on her clipboard, David read the certificates:

Victoria Christine Willoughby. Victoria Christine. V. C. Well, that explained the tattoo on Leila's ankle. One mystery solved! *Born November fifth to David Willoughby and Leila Amherst Willoughby, Dade County, Miami, Florida.* November fifth. She and Sly eloped on June eighteenth. Had Tori been born prematurely? By more than four months?

His quickly drawn breath drew Tori's attention. Although his mind was distracted, he mechanically smoothed the back of his hand across her cheek, and the child settled back into the chair.

Mentally he counted off the months, sucking in his breath as he faced the conclusions he had earlier overlooked. Leila was pregnant when she married him. Four months pregnant. They hadn't known each other four months. She was pregnant when they met.

Leila had coerced him into marrying her for the sake of the child. For the sake of her own reputation!

"Mr. Willoughby." The clipped accent interrupted his worrisome thoughts. "Unless you have questions for me we will end this interview. And Tori, we'll see you on Monday."

For the duration of the fifteen-minute drive home, David added and subtracted numbers in an effort to reveal a discrepancy in his computation, but each time the results led to the same conclusion: Tori was a year older than he'd been led to believe. Leila had been halfway through her pregnancy when they'd married. One more lie uncovered.

And there had to be more lies, he was sure of it. In her confrontations with her father, she had proven herself to be a master at telling half-truths. It was a flaw that was cultivated by her insecurity. Would she give up this practice as she became more secure in their relationship, or would he have to question every report, every promise, every declaration of hers? Only time would tell. And they had all the time in the world to work on her problem.

In fact, they had all their lives.

That acknowledgement did not sit well with David.

Leila pulled the door open before David had a chance to turn the key. She'd been waiting for him. She tried to gauge his mood from his appearance, but his face was expressionless. What was he thinking?

Although she couldn't recall ever praying for anything in her entire, self-centered life, she'd spent the morning pleading with whatever powers were listening for a chance to come clean with David and for him to forgive her for everything. At least, everything she was willing to confess.

"How'd it go?" she asked David, faking calmness while removing Tori's jacket.

"Fine. We need to talk."

As David strode purposefully into the kitchen, she followed him and sat at the table, watching his movements for a clue as to what he was thinking. David shrugged out of his jacket and tossed it over the back of a chair. He loosened his tie, ran the fingers of both hands through his hair, and took a deep breath. He exhaled audibly but said nothing. He was making her nervous.

On the countertop, the coffee pot still held the remnants of the morning brew. David removed a mug from the cabinet above his head, poured himself a cup, and turned to Leila.

"Coffee?"

She shook her head. Adding anything to her queasy stomach at this point would be asking for trouble. She willed herself to sit still but picked at the flesh on her thumb. He was going to lash out at her, just as her father used to when he caught her in a lie. She knew it.

What is he waiting for? His silence was becoming unbearable.

Pulling out a chair from the table, David turned it around and straddled the seat. He folded his hands across the back of the chair and rested his chin on top of them. His own anger had dissipated. A quiet peace had taken its place. David resolutely tackled his newest challenge.

"When I came to you in the hospital in Miami, I told you I was prepared to bring you home to resume our marriage. I told you I would provide for you and your child. I didn't tell you why. I didn't tell you what motivated me to fly to Miami and seek you out in the first place.

"Earlier this year, I realized the life I was living had no substance. My life was empty. *I* was empty. None of my accomplishments— graduating with honors, a great job in a top-notch architectural firm, a healthy bank account, influential friends—none of those things gave me the satisfaction I was craving. I was empty. Then someone challenged me to return to the faith of my childhood. I surrendered my life to God, and he has slowly and painstakingly turned me around. My values are different. My friends are different. *I* am different.

"When I found out you hadn't died with Sly, I knew I had to make an effort to restore our marriage." He took a large mouthful of coffee and swallowed it in two gulps.

"Last night you told me there was a lot I don't know about you. I learned some of it this morning in the principal's office. I'd prefer to hear it all from you. I won't go back on my word. When this is all over, you'll still be my wife and this will still be your home, but I want the truth, and all of it. Okay?"

Leila nodded.

"So tell me."

Stalling for time, Leila rose from the table, poured herself the cup of coffee she had just refused, and added cream and sugar. She rejoined David at the table, thoughtfully stirring the liquid. She tapped the spoon against the rim of the cup and set it down on the table.

"This is very difficult for me." She raised the cup to her lips but returned it to the table without taking a sip.

"Take your time."

"The night I met you, I had just discovered that I was pregnant."

"Sly's baby?"

"Yes. No. I don't know." She raised fearful eyes to David, looking for condemnation and found none. "I saw your attraction to me that night. After I took you home and saw my parents' reaction to you, I started plotting."

"For a quickie courtship and wedding?"

"Yes. When I told Mom about the baby, she insisted I get married. It didn't matter who I married. She didn't like the guys I'd been dating but she'd rather have a bum for a son-in-law than a grandchild with no name. I had just met you. She knew you couldn't be the father, but she encouraged me to marry you anyway. It was the lesser of two evils, you see. Better to have a baby while I was married, even if my husband was not the baby's father. And if that husband was respectable, so much the better."

"What about your father. Did he know?"

"I think Mom might have told him just before the wedding, but I don't know for sure. He treated me differently. He was colder toward me, but he had already grown to like you. He really looked forward to having you in the family. 'My son-in-law the architect'—you know. He said my other boyfriends were trash but you were solid. That was always the word he used to describe you. Solid."

"So you married me to please them. Yet you left me for Sly."

"Yes."

"And you named me as Tori's father on her birth certificate knowing we had never been intimate."

Linda squirmed under his piercing gaze. "Yes. But I was legally married to you, and I wanted to be sure that if anything happened to me, she'd have you. There was nobody else, you see. I don't think my parents would have taken her. Especially since they don't know her father."

"Okay. That explains Tori. What else should I know?"

"That's it. There's nothing more."

"No more surprises?"

She hesitated briefly before answering. "None."

She hadn't fooled him. She could tell by the way his eyes searched her face. Would he renege on his promise to provide a home for her and her daughter? She waited for the hammer to fall, but it didn't.

He took a deep breath before continuing. "Okay. Since Tori's never been to school, they're placing her with the four-year-olds through the end of this semester and will then promote her to the fives if she does well. I'll drive her to school in the mornings and the school bus will bring her home. You'll meet the bus at the corner?"

Relief swept through her. She couldn't have stood up to more questioning. Not today. Right now she just needed to rest. She would just agree to his plan and deal with the fallout later. "Whatever you say, David. Whatever you say."

Chapter 22

$\mathcal{I}$t wasn't the sound of thunder's reverberations rolling inward from distant regions of the sky and crashing overhead that roused David f0om his deep sleep. Neither was it the accompanying lightning, which barely pierced the heavy, damask draperies hanging in front of the living room's French doors. Yet something unfamiliar had disturbed his rest. Not just disturbed it but sounded a warning.

Holding his breath and his body perfectly still in the hope that the *something* would repeat itself, David tuned his ears to the night sounds, listening, identifying, dismissing, and moving on. In the kitchen, the refrigerator motor hummed through its cycle and clicked off, leaving silence. Outside, large drops of rain, propelled by a rising wind, drove steadily into the door's acrylic panels, but its steadiness soon became soothing—a white noise—that disappeared into the background of his consciousness.

So what had disturbed his sleep?

And then he heard it: three deep, hacking coughs, muffled, yet torturous to the ear, followed by a long, raspy, open-mouthed sigh.

Leila.

Easing his body up from the enveloping depths of the sofa cushions, David took two stumbling steps backward and quickly righted himself. He stood for a moment in the darkened room, willing his body to shed its sleep-induced languor. With thumb and forefinger, he rubbed the bleariness from the corners of his eyes and slid his hand over his forehead, massaging the area between his eyebrows while his other hand lay flat against his chest, tracing circles through the matted hairs.

Now sufficiently awake and with a renewed sense of urgency, David reached for the velour robe he had carelessly tossed across the back of an armchair when he'd prepared for bed the night before, and slipped his arms into its folds.

Picking up his watch from the table, he pressed the little button that lit the dial, read the time, and set it down again. Three o'clock. He had slept for all of two hours. Not bothering to slip into his moccasins, David padded barefoot across the hallway to Leila's room.

All was quiet on the other side of the door. Wondering whether to intrude on the silence or let her be, he paused, fiddling with the belt of his robe. Without warning, the muffled coughing resumed. David pushed the door open and entered.

"Leila? Are you all right?" Stupid question. Of course she wasn't all right. That cough, unless he was mistaken, was much worse than it had been when she was a patient in the Miami hospital. Concern for her propelled him forward.

She was sitting on the side of the large bed, her back to the door, her body crouched over two pillows in her lap. With her elbows propped on the pillows, her head rested heavily in the palms of her hands. By the disarray of the sheets and blankets, David could tell she had been having a restless night. One blanket lay in a crumpled heap where it had fallen to the floor. David picked it up, folded it over his arm, and tossed it to the foot of the bed.

"What is it? Can I get you something? A drink of water?"

Leila turned to look at him, but remained silent.

In that moment, a flash of lightning pierced the darkness of the room and left the image of her gaunt face, angular cheekbones where they had once been ruddy, sunken eyes where they had once sparkled with fun and daring. The thin, blue, cotton nightgown hung from cadaverous shoulders, and her skin—that marvelously smooth, firm skin that had once glowed with health—was dappled, gray, and dry.

A look that held both anger and pain crossed David's face. *She's been lying about her illness. This is more than the flu. That incessant cough. Dehydration. Cancer?* Was her body succumbing to the effects of inhaling swirling clouds of secondhand smoke in crowded nightclubs? He couldn't recall ever having seen her with a cigarette, but neither had Mary Madsen smoked, and she had incurred the dreaded disease. Of course, hers had been a lump somewhere. Her breast, wasn't it?

David's mind flitted back and forth, past to present, searching for something that would confirm or deny his uneducated diagnosis.

She hasn't lost her hair. Don't cancer patients lose their hair? No, that was the chemotherapy. Pills. He recalled that the Miami doctors discharged Leila with medication. But what were they for? What were they treating?

She hasn't been taking them. She hasn't sat through an entire meal with Tori and me since our return from Miami. She nibbles at a slice of bread now and then. Sometimes tea or a glass of milk.

Is she anorexic? Could she be starving herself to death in a misguided effort to make herself more beautiful? From what he could remember from his college psychology classes, low self-esteem and control issues went part and parcel with anorexia, and Leila had confessed that before their marriage she *did* have ongoing battles for control with her parents.

Clearing his thoughts with a violent shake of his head, David brought himself back to the present. Leila's coughing had quieted. She sat, unmoving, on the side of the bed.

"Let me help you back into bed," David offered. His anger had fled and he was feeling only sympathy and concern for the woman who sat dejectedly before him.

She shook her head, refusing his assistance. "The coughing will start again if I lie down." Her protest was mild, her voice barely above a whisper. "It always comes back when I lie down."

"Maybe if we stack these ..." Removing the pillows from her lap, David fluffed them and placed them one on top of the other. Then, slipping an arm around Leila's bony shoulders and under her knees, he lifted her effortlessly and placed her in an almost upright position against the pillows. As he removed his arm, he was amazed at the heat generated by her limp body. She was burning up!

Lifting the hem of the sheet that had been kicked to the edge of the bed, he pulled it up to her chin and then folded it back against itself so that it left her shoulders free. It was probably better to leave her body uncovered.

David felt Leila's eyes following his movements. Without acknowledging her, he walked over to the room's double windows, pulling the cord that closed the heavy drapes over the sheer voile panels and shielded the interior from further bursts of lightning.

David held one index finger aloft, indicating he would return in a short while. Quickly leaving the room, he crossed the hallway and entered the kitchen, flipping on the light switch as he passed through the doorway. He strode over to the refrigerator and removed a pitcher of water. He reached for a glass, changed his mind, and instead took his sport bottle from the dish drainer by the sink, filled it, and screwed the cap in place. Then he went to the bathroom where he selected a small bottle of eucalyptus oil from the bathroom cabinet and headed back to Leila.

Back in the bedroom, David sat on the edge of the bed and tenderly lifted Leila upright. Although she balked, he insisted she take several sips of water. Shaking a few drops of the fragrant oil in his hand, he coated his fingers and gently rubbed the oil into the area under her nose and on her chest. The simple remedy had worked well for him on the rare occasions when he experienced head congestion and a nagging cough. Hopefully it would work for her too. Satisfied he had done all he could to make her feel better, he lowered her back to the pillows and smoothed the sheet into place. With a stern admonition that she should call him if needed, David said goodnight and left the room.

In the hallway he paused at the temperature control gauge and lowered the thermostat by two degrees. It would be a little cool for Tori and himself but they were hardy and could handle the discomfort. Right now it was more important that they meet Leila's needs, and she would be more comfortable in the lower temperature.

A quick peek into Tori's room assured David that she was dressed warmly enough in her footed fleece pajamas. Besides, if she woke up cold, he knew she would promptly crawl into his sofa bed with him. The child had displayed no reticence in seeking him out, day or night, and snuggling close in her search for warmth or security.

Satisfied that his family was settled down for the rest of the night, David slipped out of his robe and tossed it over the back of the chair. He glanced at his watch and groaned inwardly. Three forty-five.

He threw himself on the couch, swinging his legs up and onto the deep cushions in one clean movement. There would be no more sleep for him tonight. In only two hours the alarm would wake him to rise for his morning run. Two hours filled with agonizing thoughts, wishing he had never married Leila, but determined to act honorably toward her; loving Rose, but acknowledging that he must try with all his might to transfer that love to his wife; relishing fatherhood, recognizing that he already cared for Tori as he would have cared for his own child, and grateful that she felt the same about him.

God, it's all so convoluted. Help us.

Three forty-five.

Leila slowly breathed in and out, counting her breaths, waiting for the first sign that the medication was taking effect and the pain was easing. Underneath the sheet she raised one hand to her distended abdomen and gently stroked it. She let her hand lightly rest there without moving. Her lips felt parched, but even water sometimes made her nauseous, so she resisted the urge to take another sip from the sport bottle. Of course, even if she decided to chance a drink, she didn't have the energy to reach for the bottle on the bedside table.

I wonder how long it will take. What comes next?

Her thoughts were chaotic. She thought of the prescribed medications that still lay untouched in her suitcase. That stuff for the nausea tasted vile and hurt the lining of her mouth. *I'll have to come clean with David. He'll need to know sooner or later. He's bound to hate me when I tell him, but I suppose I deserve his hate. Take care of my baby, David. Let her know that I love her. I've made such a mess of my life. I'm sorry. God, I'm a mess. Help me.*

Three forty-five.

Buddy reached over to the bedside table and set down her watch, being careful not to shake the bed and disturb Susan, who was fast asleep in the bunk above her. After three weeks of getting up for the twins' two o'clock feeding, Buddy's internal clock had adjusted to the cycle of waking at two o'clock, returning to bed at three, and waking again at eight.

The prearranged schedule also called for Anna Faye to rise for the two o'clock feeding, nursing one baby while Buddy bottle-fed the other. At each subsequent feeding she and Buddy traded babies so each infant would have some special time with his mother.

Then at six o'clock, Roger would roll out of bed, usually before his alarm buzzed the hour, shower, spend half hour in devotions, and then rouse Susan. The routine allowed the two to have breakfast together, after which he would leave for the naval base while Susan dressed herself for school in clothes that had been set out for her the previous night. By the time Susan completed that task, Buddy was up and ready to walk her niece to the corner to meet the school bus.

So far the schedule was flawless. But for some reason, tonight the twins, David and Jonathan, were sleeping through their two o'clock feeding time. Buddy considered rolling over and getting some more sleep but decided against it. If she did hunker down again, the familiar wails would be sure to wake her the minute she dropped off. Better to wait up for them. How much longer could it be?

Buddy wasn't sure whether to be elated or disheartened. If at three weeks old the twins were already sufficiently mature to sleep through a feeding, how much longer would it be before they were sleeping through the night? How much longer before they didn't need their aunt Buddy?

The errant thought took her by surprise and triggered a longing within her that, lately, was never far from the forefront of her mind. *Will I ever have my own family, my own David and Jonathan? Am I destined to go through life as a favorite aunt?* she wondered. *Will I ever know the joy of holding my own baby at my breast? Of having my husband cherish me as Roger cherishes Anna Faye?*

Immediately her mind darted to the other David, and then she purposefully cast his image aside, knowing such thoughts of him, such longings, were now taboo. *David has a wife! He belongs to her, not me. God bless them. God help me.*

For the rest of the night, Leila slept soundly. After suffering through months of intermittent naps, four uninterrupted hours of sleep left her feeling unusually refreshed.

Lying in bed next morning, she realized her headache, which had been a constant presence for much of her waking moments, was gone. The capsules David had insisted she take must have done their job.

Even her cough, persistent though it had been earlier in the night, had abated.

She touched the back of her hand to her brow and then to one side of her neck. Slightly damp, she thought, but not burning with the intensity of last night's fever.

Pleased at the prospect of a relatively pain-free day, Leila allowed a gentle smile to soften the creases of her face. As her lips relaxed, she became aware of the dry surfaces that threatened to crack from the effort. Hesitantly she swiped the tip of her tongue across her lips, from one corner to the other, moistening the surfaces.

What I wouldn't give for a good facial.

Her mind darted back several years to a time when weekly facials and body massages were part of her routine. She softly lowered her eyelids, remembering.

The delicate scents of creams and secret potions wafted around the salon and settled into warm terry towels and soft velour robes that enveloped the wives and daughters of the pampered elite. Flitting among his patrons, Claude Suchet ministered to the whims of his classy clientele, offering them snippets of smoked salmon or brie on crisp, thin wafers followed by sips of Perrier or Chablis while they sat under a hairdryer or steamed beneath a mass of thick towels.

Aurora and Leila Amherst, his most favored clients, were guaranteed Claude's personal attention at their Thursday afternoon appointments, which they scheduled to follow the morning's round of tennis and brunch at their club. If they arrived at the salon early, Claude set aside his tasks to meet them. And if they were late, Claude waited, refusing to see another client until the Amherst ladies had been thoroughly accommodated.

Leila recalled how Claude's supple fingers were especially adept at smoothing and revitalizing the fragile, sun-scorched tissue around her eyes and mouth. While days spent in the sun on the tennis courts or at the Jersey shore and nights spent in smoke-filled night clubs took their toll on her young skin, Claude had always been able to restore her face to its youthful suppleness. One session with him was like being reborn. How wonderful it had been to bask in those luxurious surroundings, to be pampered and petted and coddled.

Remembering the feelings of languor that Claude's ministrations produced, Leila slightly stretched her legs and wiggled her toes, encouraging circulation to spread to her lower extremities.

Focused as she was on the responses of her body, she became aware of a dull ache in her midsection. The sensation made her pause. Then, realizing she was experiencing real hunger pangs, not the usual stomachache or nausea, she resolved to attempt to eat a light breakfast. Something nourishing. Maybe a boiled egg and, of course, a glass of cold milk, her favorite drink. And if the simple meal went down well, and stayed down, it might produce the added energy she needed to start working on her plan—the plan to devise a way to meet Rose.

The seed had been planted on the first night of her return to Jersey. A quiet hush had finally descended on the apartment. Tori and David were settled down for the night, Tori in the bed next to her, David on the couch in the living room. Parched from her bout with dehydration, Leila had rolled out of bed and headed for the kitchen in search a drink. Standing in the hallway, she'd heard David's anguished voice. Although his words were barely distinguishable, his tone was full of pleading.

Is he in trouble? Her first thought had not been for David but for herself. She had barely survived being deserted by another man who had promised to care for her, a man who had come after her while carrying a passel of his own problems. What was David's problem? What would cause that horrible keening sound when only moments before he had been jocular, playing "horsey" with Tori, bouncing her on his back like a bucking bronco? And who was on the other end of the phone call? Concern and a rising sense of insecurity rooted her where she stood.

The conversation ended. She witnessed his final, anguished cry, and as David replaced the phone in its cradle, their eyes met across the darkened room. Caught off-guard, he'd had no time to shed the look of despair that had been so evident in his voice.

Leila had taken in the series of emotions that flashed across his face. With sudden insight she understood that he was experiencing severe emotional pain, severe loss. For the first time she understood the enormity of the sacrifice he was making for her. His offer of a home for Tori and her had cost him a future with his true love.

Casting her mind back to that night, Leila recalled the bleak emptiness in David's eyes when they met hers. He wanted Rose, but he had Leila. He loved one; he was married to the other. Oh, the injustice. Hadn't she experienced the same pain a lifetime ago? But she had chosen self rather than honor when she'd eloped with Sly, leaving David at the altar. She'd always chosen self. And in the end, it had cost her.

Dismissing the memory of that night, Leila resolved to put her plan into action. This time she would make the unselfish choice. And maybe down the road when she was gone, they would look back and think kindly of her.

Her movements slow but deliberate, Leila swung her legs over the side of the bed. Pressing her legs back against the bed frame for leverage, she raised herself into a sitting position. Her bare feet curling into the cushiony, beige carpet underfoot, Leila ambled over to the window and pulled the draperies apart. A shaft of crisp yellow sunlight sliced through the clear glass, brightening the room's interior. *A gorgeous autumn day,* she thought. *A great day to be alive.*

Many of the leaves of the oaks, spruces, and maples had been torn from the trees during the night's storm, but those that remained painted the outdoors with hues of yellow and red and browns. She'd missed the change of seasons while living in the South.

In a celebratory response to the beauty outdoors, she stretched her arms above her head and inhaled deeply, but winced as her chest hurt from the forced expansion of her lungs. Lowering her arms, she hugged herself instead and made her way to the kitchen, determined to ride this wave of good feeling until it crested, as she was sure it would, and leave her foundering in the billows she knew would ultimately surge and swallow her.

Several hours later, seated on the swivel stool at David's drafting table in the dining-room-turned-office, Leila tilted the arm of the lamp until the beam of light was focused squarely on David's Rolodex. Slowly and methodically she flipped through the card file, her fingers tracing each name, studying it carefully before turning to the next card. She focused her search on one name and one name only: *Rose.*

Leila had already rehearsed her speech, her plea. She made a mental note of the reasons why they should meet, and then, playing out Rose's rebuffs in her mind, she detailed ways of circumventing them. It was imperative they meet. Her peace of mind depended upon it. And once they met, Leila had to win her over. Become allies. There was no other way.

The jangle of the telephone interrupted her task. A glance at the clock told her the identity of the caller.

"David." She answered with a smile in her voice. She was tired, but the thought of talking with him pleased her.

"What? No, 'Hello, who's this?'"

"Well, it's two thirty on a school day. You've done this every day since Tori started school. Why should today be any different?" Her tone was playfully defensive.

"Now don't get smart with me, woman." He teased back. "I'm only trying to do the father thing."

"And may I say you're doing it quite well."

"Yes, you may."

"I may what?" she asked, confused. Had she missed something in the conversation?

"You may say it. You know, 'Doing the father thing.'"

"Oh. You're doing the father thing quite well."

"Thank you, ma'am. But how would you know? Have you ever been a father?"

"No." She paused, her voice losing its previous lightheartedness. "But I've been a daughter."

"Well, you're obviously awake and alert, so I'll ring off."

"Okay. By the way, David, don't bring home dinner today. I cooked."

"You're kidding. I mean …"

"It's okay. I know you're not being insulting."

"Are you feeling better then?"

"Some. I've been up all day."

"Good. Well, I'd better let you go so you can meet Tori's bus. I'll be home soon." He hung up before waiting for her final goodbye.

Shaking off her disappointment at the abrupt end to their conversation, Leila made a mental note of the last name she reviewed and returned the card file to its home in the corner of the desk. She stood, rubbing her hands over the seat of her pants, stomping her feet delicately to dispel the pins and needles that shot up each leg.

In one movement she retrieved a sweater from the hall closet, released the automatic locking mechanism on the door so that it would shut but not lock, and pulled the door behind her. She rushed toward the intersection.

Slow down, she told herself when her breath came fast and shallow.

Realizing her hair was caught beneath the sweater, she bunched the strands together with one hand, lifted it from the confines of the sweater and let it fall free it behind her. As she reached up to her neck to fasten the buttons, she was aghast at the sight of several clumps of hair caught in her palm.

Leila felt her heart plummet. Her feet remained rooted to the pavement, oblivious to the movement of life continuing around her. She stared, transfixed, at the evidence in her hand.

My body is breaking down!

Starved for too long of precious nourishment, her body was beginning the destructive process of feeding on itself. What next? Her skin was chapped, the inside of her mouth sore. Already she could only control her body's functions by controlling her diet. Would she lose her teeth? Her vision? Would she disintegrate like a slow-motion implosion, folding into herself, until her body, once a sturdy edifice, became rubble?

"Mommy!" Tori's cry pierced the barriers of Leila's consciousness. 'Mommy, come and get me!" Tori stood impatiently on the curb where the school bus had left her. The other mothers and children were walking away, leaving Tori alone on the corner.

Hurrying toward her daughter, Leila brushed her hands against the seat of her pants, discarding the telltale evidence of her hair loss. She held together the opening of her sweater, and with her head bent down against the rising wind, walked the last few yards with a run-hop gait that left her even more breathless.

"You're late," Tori accused, handing over her book bag.

"I'm sorry, baby."

"I thought you wasn't coming."

"*Weren't* coming," Leila corrected automatically. "But you saw me, honey, I was right across the street."

"But you wasn't, *weren't* walking. I called and called."

"Well, I'm here now. Tori, honey, let's slow down a bit, huh? Mommy's out of breath."

"Okay." As they adjusted their steps, Leila thought again about the loss of her hair. Things were moving along faster than she had anticipated. And although she felt much improved earlier in the day, exhaustion was now catching up with her.

"Know what? Jin Soo's having a birthday and I'm 'vited. It's in my book bag."

"What's in your book bag, honey?" Leila asked, distracted.

"The letter, you know, about Jin Soo's party."

"You mean the invitation."

"Yup. The in-ti-va-tion." Leila decided to let that one go. "We're gonna have cake and ice cream and I have to bring a present or I can't come in. Can we get her a Barbie?"

"We'll see, honey. Will you get the door, please?"

In the warm interior Tori quickly discarded her light jacket, but Leila, chilled and shivering, secured the buttons of her sweater before preparing a snack for the child.

"Read to me, Mommy."

As much as she wanted to grant her daughter's request, Leila felt incapable of reading a simple story, let alone enhancing each tale with dramatic voices and intonations for the various characters. Besides, the familiar headache was returning and with it would come a lassitude that would spread through her shoulders and limbs, leaving her weak, powerless, and without motivation.

And why was the room so cold!

"How about a movie instead?" Leila retrieved the favored *Little Mermaid* from the bookshelf and inserted it into the DVD player.

"On a school night? Okay, but Daddy said …"

"I know, honey. But just this once, 'cause Mommy's tired."

Tori's inquisitive eyes searched her mother's pinched face. She had seen that look before. She knew it well. It meant her mother would be in bed for a few days. She would sleep a lot, and cry sometimes. And tell Tori to be a good girl. Tori would be left to fend for herself, preparing her own crackers and milk or nibbling Cheerios straight from the box.

Of course, that was before we had Daddy. Maybe Daddy will take care of us. Maybe Daddy will make Mommy's headache go away.

"Lie down here, Mommy." Tori's tiny hand patted the couch several times. Without demurring, Leila did as she was told. "I'll get a pillow."

"And a blanket, please, honey."

By the time Tori returned to the living room, dragging a huge pillow and blanket on the floor behind her, Leila was asleep. Tori clumsily but gently spread the blanket across her mother's body, lowered herself to the floor next to her, and found security in the ever-available thumb that she promptly installed in her mouth.

Chapter 23

$\mathcal{J}$t was this somber picture that greeted David two hours later when he pushed open the front door. Tori's subdued welcome, a four-fingered wiggle while her thumb remained ensconced in her mouth, was all the warning he needed that things were not well at home.

David beckoned Tori to him with a toss of his head and his arms opened wide. As she came close, he set his briefcase aside, knelt to her level, and scooped her into his arms. She responded by removing her thumb and burrowing her forehead into his neck.

Neither spoke for several moments, but the father-daughter bond, tested daily by distance and time, was instantly renewed and reaffirmed.

"Daddy?" The whispered voice came from the juncture where shoulder and neck meet.

"Hmmm?"

"Mommy's sick."

David didn't respond but continued to hold her, running his large hand down her head and back with long, soothing strokes. He waited patiently for a signal that her self-confidence was restored.

Finally, she raised her head and with her eyes sparkling, announced, "We're having chicken for dinner. Mommy made it."

Echoing her upbeat tone, David replied, "Great. Let's check on Mommy and then we'll eat."

While Leila slept, David prepared a salad to go with their meal of roasted chicken and potatoes, which Leila had painstakingly prepared. Tori talked excitedly about the upcoming birthday party, and David promised to take her shopping for a gift for her classmate. After dinner, they returned to the living room to check on Leila, David making every effort to hide his growing concern about her deteriorating health.

Leila's eyelids fluttered open and met their anxious eyes gazing back at her, concern etched on their faces.

"So you're not as fine as you thought you were, huh?" David hunkered down to greet her at her level, his forearms resting lightly on his thighs.

Tori leaned her body against his, one arm thrown casually across his shoulders. "I had a good day, but I think I must have … overdone it a bit," Leila responded, her words wrapped around a wide-mouthed yawn. "What time is it? Did you guys have dinner?"

"Yes, and it was delicious. And since you brought it up, have *you* eaten anything today? You're beginning to waste away in front of us, woman."

"Don't scold, David. Yes, I had something to eat earlier." She crossed her fingers under the blanket. One more lie. "But since you brought it up, I could use a glass of milk."

"Okay, I'll get it." David pressed both hands down on his thighs and pushed himself upright. Tori, satisfied that her mother's responses indicated she was feeling better, reached for the remote control, pressed "play," and picked up the movie where she had left off.

"Isn't that movie finished yet?" David called after her as he left the room.

"Uh-uh! They didn't kiss yet."

"They didn't kiss yet; they didn't kiss yet," he mimicked her in a sing-song voice. Over his shoulder he added, "Okay, young lady, as soon as they kiss, it's bedtime."

"Bedtime; bedtime," Tori mimicked in return, swinging her head from right to left in time with her words.

Inside the kitchen, when David was secluded from the family's view, his cheerful demeanor faded. Leila had just lied to him! He was as sure of it as he was his own name. The guilt was visible in her eyes. The way they bored into his, trying to convince him of her honesty.

Years ago he had marveled at her audacity when she brazenly confronted her parents, indignantly denying their accusations until they recanted. He hadn't cared then about her willingness to stretch the truth. Now it maddened him that she would use the same tactics on him. What was she hiding? Why wasn't she sharing her concerns with him instead? After all he had done for her, couldn't she trust him? And if she readily lied about trivial matters, what else would she lie about? Where would the deceit end?

Forcing himself to exhibit restraint, David breathed deeply, wiped up a splash of spilled milk from the countertop, and returned to the living room carrying the glass of milk.

Leila had rearranged herself into a sitting position and reached eagerly for the glass. Was her enthusiastic response also meant to mollify him and deflect his queries? Well, he would let her think it worked. For now there would be no more questions. For now.

One thing was sure: there was more to this illness thing than she was letting on, and he intended to get to the bottom of her secrecy, with or without her assistance. She had placed her daughter and herself in his charge—granted, with some coercion on his part. He had willingly assumed that obligation. It was left to him to care for them the only way he knew how.

Identify the problem, apply the formula, solve the problem. That mantra, learned in college math classes, had served him well in his architectural career. Maybe he could apply it to real life as well. But who would help him identify the problem?

Tori interrupted David's introspection. She twirled around the room, animatedly waving her arms in free-spirited motion. Becoming aware that she held her parents' attention, she intensified her movements, accompanying them with squeals of delight. "Look, Daddy, I'm dancing just like Ariel."

"Not like that, honey, you'll hurt yourself." David caught her up in the middle of a spin. Catching her before she slammed into a reading lamp, he held her steady until her dizziness subsided.

"Dance with me, Daddy," she begged. "Please?"

"Okay. Let me take off my shoes." He kicked his loafers to one side. "Stand on my feet ... put your arm here ... that's it, now this hand out here. Good. And, one-two-three, one-two-three, see? Now we're dancing."

Father and daughter moved slowly around the room together. David took in his daughter's intensity as she watched every step their feet made. When the music ended, David picked up the melody. As he hummed, the little girl leaned her head way back and stared solemnly into his eyes. He found himself comparing her openness to her mother's guardedness. Where one exhibited honesty and trust, the other displayed doubt and deceit.

"I love you, Daddy."

Tori's voice interrupting David's musings. The words seeped into his chest and enveloped his heart in a cozy cocoon. He struggled to maintain his composure. He swallowed the rising lump in his throat and struggled to keep a semblance of rhythm in his feet. His humming ceased.

Leaning down he slipped his hands under her arms and lifted her to him. Tori's tiny arms immediately encircled his neck, and as before, she burrowed her head in the secret hollow between his neck and shoulder. David pressed a kiss in her hair and kept on dancing.

And when he finally felt sure he could control the wavering of his voice, he whispered, "I love you too, Tori."

And so they danced.

"Well, she's tucked in for the night," David announced some moments later when he returned to the living room. He threw himself down beside Leila, tossing an arm along the back of the couch. She winced in response to the sudden movement and he grimaced an apology.

"I had no idea little girls were such romantics. Can you believe she's so caught up in the happily-ever-after bit?"

"Of course I can. I was just like her, waiting for Prince Charming to come charging in on his white horse and sweep me off my feet, carrying me off to who-knows-where."

"At five years old?"

"Oh, yes! And at ten, and at seventeen. In fact, I'm still waiting."

With an exaggerated air of cockiness, David folded the fingers of one hand to touch his palm, opened his mouth wide, exhaled loudly across his fingernails, and polished them on the pocket of his shirt. "You've got *me*.

"*You?* I said 'Prince Charming,' not 'Prince Bully,'" Leila baited.

"Bully? When did I ever bully you, woman?"

"Well, there was the time when ..." She mumbled something indiscernible behind her fingers. "And then again you ..." She mumbled again, a faint glow of mischief shining in her eyes.

"See? Can't think of a single one, can you?"

"Sure I can. When I was in the hospital, you—"

"*Bullied you?*" David leaned into her, his eyes opened wide, his wrinkled brow almost touching his hairline.

"Well, maybe not bullied. But you sure twisted my arm."

"Okay, I twisted your arm." He relaxed against the sofa cushions. "Regrets?"

Leila's head shake was barely perceptible. "None."

A comfortable silence stretched between them.

"David, do you love me?"

Taken by surprise, David stalled for time. "You mean …"

"Romantically." Leila's bluntness prevented any vacillating. "Are you in love with me? You can tell me the truth."

"No."

"Were you ever?"

"Ah … I doubt it."

Was she hurt or disappointed by his answer? David had to know. "What about you?" he questioned. "Do you love me?"

"Nope, and I never did. No offense," she added quickly.

"None taken." David relaxed against the couch.

"Funny how we latched on to each other even when there was no real emotional attachment."

"Nothing funny about it. Stupid maybe."

"Yeah. Stupid."

"You should adopt Tori." Leila's voice was subdued.

The change in subject took David by surprise. He was still mulling over the mess they had made of their lives by marrying impulsively.

"Why?"

"She loves you. You love her."

He nodded. "Like my own flesh and blood. But she already has my name, so why …"

"Just to be safe—you know, in case your rights were ever challenged."

"You mean my rights as a parent?"

"Yes, your rights as her father."

"Who would challenge them? Not you? You orchestrated it."

"I know. But if I'm not around, you …"

"You planning on going somewhere?" He wasn't sure he liked the turn this conversation was taking.

"No … no, I'm not planning anything. I just think it would be a good idea."

Her hesitancy did not go unnoticed. The niggling questions about her truthfulness returned. What was she hiding? And why couldn't she come just clean with him?

"I'll think about it. Maybe I'll toss around the subject with the legal eagles at the office."

"Thank you. Can't hurt, you know?" The silence returned.

They spoke at the same time.

"David."

"Leila." David smiled. "You first."

"Have you had any contact with my parents?"

David shook his head.

"I called them once after I left," she continued. "Dad hung up the minute he recognized my voice. A few weeks after that I wrote them, but the letter came back stamped 'moved; no forwarding address.' I just wondered if you knew where they were."

David shook his head again but made a mental note to attempt to locate them for her. Maybe Cal could help as he had done before.

"What were *you* going to say?" she asked.

Their lighthearted banter had changed into something more serious. Leila had withdrawn again, rebuilding the wall around her that had been permeable some moments ago. He sensed that Leila was missing her parents, although she would deny such feelings. A fragile air of abandonment had become part of her demeanor. Why challenge her now? His questions would keep.

"Oh, nothing important." He adopted a nonchalant air. "We'll discuss it another time."

"Okay. Then if you'll excuse me, I'll say goodnight." The abrupt ending to their conversation left him puzzled. The evening had gone so well. She had opened up to him and he had loosened up. They had to find a way to bridge their strangeness with each other.

Leila slid her body to the edge of the couch, grasped the upholstered arm, and slowly raised herself upright. Watching her attempt to straighten her hunched body, David could barely stop himself from scooping her up and saving her the walk to her room.

"Need a hand?" he offered.

"No, I can manage. Thanks."

Accepting the gentle rebuff, David watched as she shuffled down the hallway, her body bending forward, her hand pressed against the wall for stability. With each step her breathing became more labored until, at the bedroom door, she paused, sucked in two deep breaths, and pushed open the door.

"By the way," he called after her, "Rhonda Gooden said to tell you she missed seeing you at church. She's going to stop by sometime this week. Said she'd bring you her mother's secret potion for curing what-ails-you. Her words, not mine." David quickly added the disclaimer and raised his hands in self-defense when Leila turned her head to dart a deprecating glance at him.

"And good luck to her," he muttered under his breath, frustrated at her reticence in sharing her real fears with him.

One thing he knew for sure: if they were going to build a life together, she had to learn to trust him with the truth, no matter how unpalatable it might be. If they couldn't share that, their marriage was definitely doomed for failure.

The coughing resumed at midnight. He'd been expecting it but hoped she'd have a good night. When it hadn't come he'd drifted into a fitful sleep, his body rigid, his mind unable to fully unwind in the soothing stillness of his surroundings.

At the next hack, David's lids flew open, his eyes piercing the darkness for an instant before his body sprang into action. Bursting into Leila's room, his open hand made circles on the wall until it encountered the light switch and the room flooded with brilliant incandescent light, causing both occupants to blink rapidly until their eyes adjusted.

As before, she sat slumped on the side of the bed, two pillows stacked on her lap. Another fit of coughing overtook her and she lowered her face into the pillows in an effort to smother the abrasive sound. David, feeling helpless but compelled to act, lowered himself next to her and gingerly stroked her back. When the spell died away, she turned piteous eyes to him.

"I've become a real burden, haven't I?"

"No you haven't." David was adamant, but Leila closed her eyes, effectively shutting out his protests.

"More than a burden, a pain. I'm a royal pain. That's what my father used to yell at me, you know. If I came home after my curfew, or if the cops called him to pick me up, or something, he'd yell, 'Leila, I'm sick of your crazy stunts. You're becoming a royal pain.' Just like that." She swallowed a couple times and continued. "He would emphasize 'royal,' stretch it out, and run it together until it had only one syllable. Like oil. A *roil* pain! Well, I guess if he could see me now, he'd know he was right. I *am* a royal pain."

"Leila, listen to me," David interrupted. "I don't think of you as a burden, or a pain. Definitely not a *royal* pain."

"Well, you should."

"I don't!"

"Even though I saddled you with my illegitimate child?"

"I don't!"

"Even though we've probably depleted your life savings?"

"I don't! And you haven't!"

"Even though I've lied to you left and right?"

"I *don't*! But pretty soon we're going to have a heart to heart about your penchant for lying. I'm not going to hurt you, you know. You don't have to lie to me. I'm on your side. I want what's best for both of us. For the three of us."

Leila might have expected to penetrate David's staunch defense with her self-deprecating comments, to goad him into admitting that her presence had brought undesirable changes to his lifestyle, but he refused to let her think so. He was determined to stand firm to his commitment. There would be no chink in his armor. Nothing would cause him to crumble. He was learning that in Leila's short life, all the people she depended on—the men she admired, revered, leaned on—had crumbled. Her father. Her child's father. Sly. All of them had deserted her. David would stand with her because he had made that pledge several times—to God, to her, and to himself. But in his heart he knew she didn't trust him, even now.

"Even though ... even though *I* am the reason you have no hope of a future with Rose?"

At any other time David's response might have been impulsive and self-seeking. But in the time he and Leila had spent together, he had come to understand her own insecurities, her own need for a rock in what had been a shifting life. She wouldn't look at him. Her fear of being rejected showed plainly on her face. The little pulse at her neck pumped so hard that she must surely be deafened by its intensity. He had to reassure her.

"Leila." His voice was close. His breath stirred her hair. "Leila, look at me." She slowly turned to face him. "Who do you see?"

Let her see a man of honor. Let her see a man worthy of her trust.

"I see David."

"David," he affirmed. "Not your father. Not Sly. David. No, don't turn away," he added when she let her head fall to her chest. "Look at me. I'm going to tell you something, and you need to know that I'm being straight up with you.

"I hated you for a long time. I hated you for five years." He knew that his words penetrated and held, for Leila winced. He hurried on.

"One morning I decided it was time to let go of the hate. The next day, I met Rose. Rose is the sweetest, most selfless, most unassuming woman I've ever met. She's engaging, funny, a hard worker, and a good friend. And, yes, I fell in love with her.

"Rose gave me a very precious gift. She shared her faith in Jesus Christ with me and pointed me in the right direction. It is that faith-gift that sustains me. It is that faith that keeps me from falling apart when circumstances threaten to overwhelm me. And it is because of that faith that you will never become a burden to me because I no longer carry my burdens alone."

He had her attention. "I don't claim to have all the answers. I don't know why God allowed us to marry and then go our separate ways for five years. I don't know why he brought us back together after all this time or how he plans to have us build a life together. I don't know. I wish I did, but I don't. What I do know is that he promised in his Word not to leave me or forsake me. I'm holding on to that. I have to believe that every step I take is one that he ordered. He told me to go after you and bring you home. You're not a royal pain, Leila, and I'm dead certain you never will be."

Leila sidestepped the references to his faith and zoomed in on Rose. "How can you stay married to me when you love her?"

Without hesitating, David responded, his gaze steadily holding hers. "I'm trusting God to make this marriage work, yes, even to have us fall in love with each other. I will learn to let go of my feelings for her. I will learn to love you." He'd made it sound easy. It would be the hardest thing he ever did, but he was determined to do right by Leila and her child. And he would not do it alone.

Before Leila could respond to his intention to love her, spasms of coughing engulfed her body again, starting deep within her and exploding. She folded herself into the stack of pillows on her lap; her fingers curled into a desperate grip of the thin cotton pillowcases, her body convulsing with each wrenching spasm.

In between each attack a soulful moan escaped unrestrained from her belly, providing a respite from the attacks. She struggled valiantly to remain alert, grappling with the desire to give up the fight and slide into the darkness of unconsciousness.

Soon the coughing diminished. As Leila's breathing slowed, she seemed to come to a decision. She picked up their conversation where they had left off. "Wait till I tell you about the pox I've brought upon your house."

"Pox?" David asked, amused at her choice of words. "Isn't that like a Shakespearean plague or something?"

"Or something."

"So tell me."

Now that Leila had decided to enlighten him, David hoped she would be honest even if it meant exposing them both to pain. She'd lied to him or left out portions of the truth every time they'd talked together. Maybe this time ...

"Oh, David. This is so difficult."

"Take your time. Take my hand." He laid his open palm in her lap. Hesitating only for a brief moment, she placed her hand in his and watched as his long fingers curled around her slender ones.

"I'm dying."

David's response was immediate. "C'mon, Leila, lighten up. We're all dying."

"You don't understand. Sly and I, well, we ... shared needles ... and now my liver ... well, I'm infected ... I'm dying."

Leila's words hovered above them like a storm cloud, heavy and gray and full of doom, waiting for the opportune moment to unleash its fury. David wasn't sure how to respond. What could he say? Was she merely being dramatic? Was this real?

"Your doctors—"

"They offered injections and pills, but they were very expensive."

"I can pay."

"No. It's too late. It's too late," she repeated more softly, as if to remind herself, not him. "I'm dying."

David held himself immobile except for a slight tremor in the hand that lay across his lap. He felt blood surge from his heart to his head, felt his muscles bulge and tense. His eyes burned. He closed them against the sight of the frightened woman beside him. She hadn't been specific, but she didn't need to say more. She had some life-threatening or major life-altering illness. What it was, she still refused say.

In retrospect the signs were all there—he should have noticed them before. Her lack of appetite, fatigue, yellowing eyes, blotchy skin, and that enlarged abdomen.

And he had assumed her problem was the result of poor nutrition. How naive could a man be!

Concern turned to pity. Where were her parents? Where was their influence when her character was being molded, when she cried out for correction, guidance, discipline?

And he cried out to God: *Hasn't she been through enough? I brought her back from the ghetto. Did she have to come bearing a death sentence? What more do you want of her? Of me?*

In his heart the answer burst forth: *If not you, who?*

"You should've said something earlier," he chastised gently. "You should've told me."

"Yes."

"We need to set you up with a doctor. Maybe even run you to the hospital for..."

"No," she interrupted, her words coming vehemently. "No doctors. No more hospitals."

"What about Tori? Does she ..."

"She's clean. When she was born she suffered through drug withdrawal, but she didn't inherit...this. The infection...she doesn't have an infection. The infection came after she was born."

"You should've told me," he said again, but there was no accusation in his voice. He'd not been aware of the tension within her, but now he felt her body relax.

It occurred to him that this was the real reason for her lies, her half-truths, her evasive responses. She had finally released the burden that had plagued her body and soul.

He wasn't sure what to feel. He was relieved at finally knowing the truth. He was sad for her, for the waste of a life. He was angry at her parents for placing their social standing above the care and nurturing of their daughter. Angry at Sly. At himself.

It was his nature to fix things. He'd spent his adult life restoring old buildings, old rejects. Could he help restore her too? Surely there was a way. He'd spare no expense. One thing was for sure. There would be no more accusations, no more recriminations, no more confessions, no acts of clemency.

What's done is done.

Chapter 24

Morning had barely dawned when David, bleary-eyed from lack of sleep, reached for his Blackberry and punched in the number of his good friend and a longstanding member of Bergen Community Church, Charlie Lennox. Charlie—Charles Lennox, M.D. to his colleagues—must have recognized the rising panic in David's voice, for he was standing on the doorstep of David's home almost before David ended his call.

After a short discussion about symptoms, David led the doctor into Leila's room. Standing quietly beside Leila's bed, David watched while his friend conducted a very brief but apparently revealing examination of Leila's eyes and abdomen. Then Charlie asked David to leave while he talked some more with Leila. Afterward, David met him in the hallway.

He was taking a prescription pad from his bag when David asked, "What can I do for her?"

"Pray. And try to make her comfortable."

"That's it?"

"I'm afraid so, David. She's a pretty sick woman. Leila has advanced liver disease progression brought on by hepatitis C. Probably contracted it from shared needles during her drug abusing days. Her liver is severely compromised, and if that weren't enough, she also has stomach cancer."

"Don't tell me you confirmed all this in a ten minute exam?" David asked, his voice indicating incredulity. He knew the doctor had a reputation of being ultra-efficient, but certainly some diagnoses had to be confirmed by lab work, blood tests and that kind of thing?

"A brief exam, yes, and her own report, and a review of her discharge medications." Charlie's eyes poured into David's disbelieving eyes. "I guess you didn't know she had a bag of discharge medications in her suitcase. Meds she hasn't been taking, I might add. No, I'm not blaming you," he interjected when David would respond. "Fact is, Leila's made her choice. She's refusing any interventions. She doesn't want to fight any more. She's accepted the end result of this illness."

David inhaled deeply and blew out a long, slow breath. Without a word he took the prescription Charlie Lennox held out to him, folded it in half and stuck it in the hip pocket of his jeans.

So it's true. Leila's dying.

David closed the front door behind the doctor and leaned his back against its wooden panels. Feelings of helplessness and loss threatened to overtake him. A sob broke through the back of his throat and was followed by another. He plugged his mouth with a fist, anxious to stop the unfamiliar sound.

He hugged himself hard, his hands wrapped solidly around his middle. Braced against the door, his body folded as it slid downward until he sat on the floor, his knees doubled into his chest.

Weariness seeped through him. From his folded-up position on the floor, he added up the losses that had punctuated their lives and thought of all that might have been. His body rocked back and forth, a terrible keening sound emanating from deep within him. He cried for Leila, for a life gone awry, for her loneliness, for the child she was leaving behind, and for the parents who had abandoned her emotionally long before she'd walked away from them. He didn't know at what point his tears turned to prayerful petitions. He only knew he eventually found himself pleading for Leila's salvation and for her to experience a sweet passage into eternity.

Emotionally exhausted, he crossed his arms on his knees and rested his head on them.

Some moments later, David became aware of a pink, flannel-encased body standing before him. No words came from the body, but a hand snaked out from the pink cloud and gently stroked his head. In response, David unfolded one arm and encircled the child, pulling her close. And so the roles were reversed, the child providing solace.

Two solid *thumps* sounded on the door behind him. He wondered who it could be. He was in no mood to be sociable. Pulling the door open, he was immediately greeted with an effusive hug.

"Rhonda."

"Hey, babe," she shot at him while handing over a large shopping bag. "Chicken soup. Good for what-ails-you, my momma used to say."

"I think we're gonna need more than chicken soup for this ailment," David responded, his somber demeanor indicating the depth of his concern for his wife. He placed the package in the refrigerator and turned to help Rhonda remove her light jacket. "You might not want to stay when you hear ..."

"Nothing's changed since the last time I was here, babe," Rhonda said. "I'm staying."

"But you don't know what—"

"I'm a nurse, David. I know. But *you* didn't know, and *Leila* had to be the one to tell you."

David nodded his understanding.

"Charlie called me from his car. Told me to get over here *stat*. He hasn't done that since we worked the public health circuit together. He said you—hey, Tori-love." Rhonda turned to Tori hiding behind her father's leg. "Got any sugar in that thumb of yours?" Rhonda knelt to receive a slobbery kiss and hug from the child. "Mmmm, good. Just the way I like them." Rhonda made a funny face and raised her shoulder to swipe at her offended cheek. "So what's new around here, kiddo?"

David watched as Rhonda lowered her voice and remained on her knees before the little girl.

"Daddy had a boo-boo."

"Daddy had a boo-boo?" David puzzled expression confirmed that he was as in the dark about this announcement as Rhonda.

"Uh-huh. He cried."

"Oh, I see. And how did that make you feel, sweetheart?"

"I was sad. But I kissed Daddy's hurt and now it's gonned away."

"I'm so glad, dear. And did your sadness go away too?"

"Uh huh, but now I'm gonna be late for school. Then I'll be sad again!" she announced with exasperation, planting both hands on her hips and impatiently tapping one foot.

"Well, we can't have that, can we?" Rhonda stood, trying to conceal her smile. "Tell you what. Why don't I help you get dressed for school while Daddy fixes breakfast?"

"Okay." The two adults shrugged in unison and set about their tasks.

Much later, over coffee, David shared the details of Leila's illness as the doctor had explained them to him. It felt good to be able to unburden on someone who understood the circumstances of his marriage and the commitment he had made to his wife. Rhonda had a knack for joining biblical teaching with a medical viewpoint. It always made her counsel acceptable. The familiar texts from scripture, her unique insight, and comforting words reminded him of his testimony to Leila during the night. He didn't carry his burden alone.

"I've gotta run." She broke into his thoughts. "I'll be back in time to sit with Leila while you pick up Tori. Is there anything I can do for you while I'm out?" she asked as she pulled her jacket over her shoulders. "Shopping? Cleaners? Errands?"

"Just one." David reached into his hip pocket and removed the folded prescription. "Drop this off at the pharmacy?"

"Sure thing." Rhonda reached for the paper, unfolded it, and read the prescription. Smiling, she handed it back to him. "I think you can fill this one yourself." Patting him on the shoulder, she added, "I'll see myself out."

Curious, David opened the slip of paper, certain he would be unable to read the doctor's scrawl let alone recognize the medications. The prescription was neatly written in bold, rounded letters: *Do not fear for I am with you; do not be dismayed, for I am your God.*

He folded the paper and tucked it back into his pocket.

Inside the darkened bedroom, Leila struggled to rouse herself from a deep sleep. *I'm going to be late for Tori.*

The thought, which normally would have propelled her into action, had no effect on her emaciated body. None, that is, except for an increased pounding of her heart and a slight separation of her eyelids, just enough for her to make out the shadowy outline of a woman seated in a chair at the foot of the bed.

The woman must have been reading from the book that lay open on her lap, for her lips moved slightly without emitting sound. *Or maybe she's praying?*

Leila attempted to swing her legs over the bed but only managed to rustle the sheet with her toes. Her efforts caught the attention of the woman in the chair. She closed the book, laid it aside, and came toward the bed. "Ah, you're awake."

"Rhonda. What are you doing here?" Leila's throat was parched, and the movement of warm air past her lips stung the open sores that had erupted all over the soft tissue inside her mouth. Ignoring the pain, she attempted to speak again. "I have to get Tori."

Rhonda recognized the beginning signs of agitation.

"Shhh-shhh. She's with David. He picked her up at school and took her out for ice cream. He's trying to prepare her for your, ah, going away."

"Oh. So he's finally coming to grips with it." Leila's body relaxed against the pillows. She closed her eyelids as she spoke. "Tori knows what's coming … I prepared her for it a while ago. In Miami. I expected her to be in foster care by now, but David … saved her … from that fate." Quick, shallow breaths punctuated her words. "David's the one who needs to be prepared for my, er, going away."

Rhonda digested this information without comment.

"Rhonda, talk to David." Leila's previously inert eyes became intense. She had to coercing the woman into joining her mission. "You … must … convince him. Adopt Tori legally. I tried to tell him before, but he …" Her voice dropped to a whisper. "It's not Tori's father I'm afraid of. It's my parents. They don't have an heir, you see. That's the kind of thing that's important to them. They'll try to take her away. That's why he has to adopt her."

Leila raised her hand in an imploring gesture, and for the first time noticed that her hand bore intravenous apparatus with a long tube connecting her to the familiar poly bag of clear solution. "What's this? Who did this? I told them I don't want—"

"It's okay, dear. The doctor ordered it when he was here this morning. Now don't worry, babe"—Rhonda held up a hand to ward off the impending protest—"there's nothing in the drip to, you know, prolong anything. It'll just make you more comfortable."

Rhonda adjusted the flow of the liquid and returned to the chair.

Leila's eyes followed her movements. "Rhonda, there's something else."

"Okay. Tell me."

Leila hesitated, appearing to gather her thoughts before speaking. "I took something very precious from David. I want to give it back."

"What did you take from David, hon?"

"Rose. I came between David and Rose. He loves her. I shouldn't have been part of David's life from the beginning. I tricked him into marrying me. I want to give him back to her.

"Honey, I'm sure they'll work things out when the time is right. You just concentrate on—"

"No. Please, Rhonda. I tried to find her number. I want to meet her. I want to let her know I'm okay with her loving David. I want to meet the woman who'll be raising my Tori. Please, Rhonda, you've got to help me. I know I don't have much time left. Please." Her final imploring plea had been barely audible.

"Whew! Talk about a last wish." Rhonda muttered, partly to herself. "Honey"—she stroked Leila's hand—"I can't arrange for Rose to come here without David's permission. Somehow I'll have to convince him that what you want is not so unreasonable. I'll try ... but it's gonna be a challenge."

"Thanks, Rhonda," Leila whispered. Her body relaxed, and she closed her eyes and fell asleep.

"How'd it go?" Rhonda greeted David as he entered the room. Tori walked ahead of him. The child was unusually subdued.

"I have no idea." David threw himself down on the sofa and stuck his legs out in front of him. Rhonda sat down again. "I did the talking, she did the listening. Halfway through her ice cream, she pushed the bowl away from her, folded her hands on the table, and rested her chin on them. That was it. No words, no tears, nothing."

"Leila told me she had prepared Tori for her death. Maybe she wasn't as prepared as she thought?"

"You got me!" He shrugged, looking defeated.

"How was she in the car?"

"Silent. No smile, no interest in anything outside. Just nothing. Reminded me of Leila when she was in the hospital."

"Would you mind if I tried talking with her?"

"Go right ahead, but don't mention Leila's ... you know ... except, of course, if Tori brings it up herself."

Rhonda nodded and went off to Tori's room. Moments later, Rhonda reentered the living room. "She's sleeping, and that little thumb is right back in her mouth."

"Well, at least she has that," he said, ignoring Rhonda's look of surprise. "It's not that I've given up on helping her break the habit," he explained. "It's just that the next few days are going to be difficult for her. She'll need all the comfort she can get, and if she gets it from sucking her thumb, so be it! I won't deny her that security. If it takes her until she's fifteen years old to willingly give up the habit, I'll wait until then." It was a ridiculous premise, he knew. But what else could he do? He blew out a breath.

"I remember when I first saw her, she was about as quiet as she is now. She just sat on that dirty old chair. The kids around her were playing, acting like kids. She just sat there, hanging on to that raggedy doll for dear life, sucking on her thumb." He massaged his forehead. The headache that started earlier that evening was now full blown. "She hasn't been like that since I brought her home from Florida.

He turned weary eyes to Rhonda. "When a child suddenly refuses to speak, there's something troubling going on inside. This thing about her mother ... we've come so far ... I don't want her to regress. Think I should talk to a therapist?"

"It's only been a few hours, sugar," Rhonda reassured him. "Don't you think you're jumping the gun a little?"

"C'mon, Rhonda. You're a mother and a nurse. You know there's always more going on inside their little heads than they let us see."

David eased himself from the sofa and strode across the room while he spoke. He pivoted on the ball of one foot, returned to his starting place, and repeated the motion. "It's too late for me to help her mother, but I *know* I can help Tori. I've got to!"

David threw himself down on the sofa again, stretched out his legs, and let his head fall onto the upholstered back. He stuffed both hands into the side pockets of his jeans. His shoulders slumped forward from the motion.

"Mary." The name crossed his lips before he realized it had entered his mind.

"What?"

"Mary Madsen. If anyone can get through to Tori, Mary Madsen can." A glimmer of hope spread through David and burst into his eyes, dispelling the gloom that had settled there.

"Rose's mother?" Rhonda cautiously mentioned the taboo name.

"Yes."

"Funny you should mention Mary," Rhonda began, feeling her way around, "because I need to talk to you about Rose."

David immediately gave her his full attention. "What about her?" His brow knit. His heart skipped a beat and picked up a wild rhythm. *Is she hurt, or ill? Has she found someone to replace me in her heart?* He jumped to his feet, nervous, like a skittish colt being approached by a stranger holding a saddle.

"What about Rose!"

"Leila wants to meet her."

David wasn't sure whether to laugh or cry. For a brief moment he'd experienced great fear when every wish, hope, fear, prayer, and desire he had for Rose surged through him and demanded a response. His hands felt clammy. He rubbed them together and then on the seat of his pants.

"Why?" He swallowed the lump in his throat. "Why?"

"Because she's curious about the woman who, in all likelihood, will replace her as Tori's mother." The words fell from Rhonda's lips and hung in the air between them.

Bring Rose here? Have her come face to face with Leila? David posed the questions to himself and answered them vehemently. "No."

"It's Leila's dying wish."

"No!" Mary would come. She'd be good for Tori. To see Rose again, meet her sparkling eyes, hear her laugh, smell her perfume—"No. No way."

"But David …"

"Absolutely not!"

With a sigh of acceptance, Rhonda left the room to check on her charge for a final time before ending her shift. As she walked away she raised one hand above her head, her open palm parallel to the ceiling. David watched her retreat and heard her mutter, "You take it, Lord. It's all yours."

David experienced an ounce of regret that his response had not been gentler. Rhonda and her husband had been souls of kindness to him, but he was still touchy about Rose. He couldn't bear to have her name mentioned. His loss was still too painful to share with anyone, even his closest friends. Rose was cherished and special, and he would not invite her sweetness to be sullied by this segment of his life.

David's body hunched over his drafting table, a pencil behind his ear and another held securely in his hand. It felt like years since he'd seen Rose. In fact it had been only a couple months. Yet their lives were now so far removed from each other that it might well have been years. He wondered how she was doing, if she had recovered from their anguished parting. He relived those moments, saw her tears, felt her sadness.

Lately he found he couldn't even mention her name in his prayers. He was being careful not to covet what was not his. But he wanted Rose. His love for her had not diminished. The desire to have her for his own still raged within him.

He had a wife who was slowly exiting this world, but she was still his wife. They had vowed to forsake all others, to cling to each other. She had broken her vow. No law on Earth would hold him guilty for turning his back on her. But he was at the mercy of the highest court, the Supreme Judge.

Who said it was better to have loved and lost? He would have preferred never to have loved. No, not true.

A faint rustle sounded behind him. He swiveled on the high stool. Tori was propped against the arm of the leather sofa clutching a blanket to her face. Behind the blanket her cheeks puckered and released in a slow, steady rhythm, and David knew her lips were closed firmly around her thumb.

"Want some dinner?" he asked but received no response. "Thirsty?" Nothing.

"How about a DVD? We could watch Ariel together?" Still nothing. "Oh, honey. I don't know how to help you." He got down from the stool, strolled over to the armchair close to her, and sat on the seat. He stared at her for long, silent moments but her face remained emotionless.

Then David tapped his knees twice, inviting her to climb up. She approached slowly, and as she got closer, she turned her back to him. He grasped her by the waist and lifted her onto his lap.

He smoothed her hair from her face.

She burrowed into his chest.

He kissed her forehead.

She sucked her thumb.

On this one level, the bonds they had formed weeks earlier still held.

Chapter 25

When Tori did not come bounding out of bed the next morning, David went into her room to wake her for breakfast and to get dressed for school. From within the folds of her warm blanket she raised sad but alert eyes to him. She didn't move. David decided to call Mary Madsen.

Mary arrived at noon.

She was accompanied by Zach and Buddy.

In the hallway David smothered the older woman with a bear hug and kiss on her cheek. "Mary, it's been a long time." She hugged him back, laughing in delight at his welcome. "Zach—" He continued greeting his guests. The men shook hands, hugged, and slapped each other's back.

"Rose." David was aware they were being watched by the others. He had been able to welcome her parents without self-consciousness. Not so Rose.

He was happy to see her.

He wished she hadn't come.

Ambivalent feelings played across his face. Anxiety churned within him. His breathing became shallow. Surely she must be experiencing similar emotions? And yet she had come.

He steeled himself against the pain. She extended her hand to him. He grasped it firmly, but only for a moment. She pulled back and he let go of her fingers. He finally released his pent-up breath, but the awkwardness remained.

Reluctantly, David turned away from Buddy and continued his introductions. "This is my daughter, Tori." David's hand cupped Tori's head as he made the introductions. Tori grasped a handful of his slacks and refused to let go.

"Your daddy told me he had a little girl," Mary said to Tori, coming closer to the little girl, "but he didn't tell me you were so pretty. Tori, would you hold my purse while I remove my coat?" Mary started to shrug out of her jacket while thrusting her purse toward Tori. Her quick movement caught the child off-guard, and Tori took the purse without hesitating. She let go of David's slacks, slung the strap of the purse over her forearm, and leaned again into her father, maintaining contact with him. Her cheeks pulled hard on her thumb.

"I brought something to show you." Mary handed her coat to Zach, keeping her eyes trained on the child, and retrieved her purse. "It's a picture album. Want to see?" Without waiting for a response the woman opened the album and started a running commentary.

"This is my granddaughter, Susan. She's about the same age as you. How old are you? Six? Five? Susan's six. I'll bring her to visit you some time. You'd be great friends. And these are her new baby brothers, David and Jonathan. They're twins, you know. They're zeros—not even one year old yet. Here, you take the album while I find a place to sit." She held out the open album to Tori.

Without blinking, Tori removed the thumb from her mouth, grasped the picture book with both hands, and followed Mary into the living room.

David shook his head in surprise and saluted Mary's back. What a woman. In fewer than five minutes of meeting her she had coaxed

Tori's thumb from her mouth and engaged her. He shook his head again and turned to the others, who stood watching his reaction.

"You can stuff your eyes back in their sockets now, David," Zach smiled. "She's a class act, isn't she?"

"You're telling me."

"I remember when our kids—"

"Dad," Buddy interrupted. She addressed her father but her eyes were fixed on David. "I'd like to meet Leila now."

David turned his attention to Buddy, recalling the other reason for their visit.

"Did Mary fill you in?"

"We talked of nothing else on the way here. You stay with Dad. I'll be fine."

David led Buddy to Leila's room, pushed open the door, and stepped aside to allow her to enter. He pulled the door partially closed behind her. As he walked away he felt concern that the sight of Leila might be upsetting to Rose. He recalled how shocked he had been at her appearance when he first met her again in the hospital. But, of course, Rose hadn't known the old Leila, so there was nothing to compare. Just as well.

For an instant David chastised himself over his concern for Buddy. It was Leila who needed him. From the beginning he had withheld his emotions, satisfied that he was doing all he could for her. It had been enough, hadn't it? It was all that was required of him, wasn't it?

"I need to stretch my legs after the long ride in the car," Zach said, distracting him. "You up for a walk?"

"You're on," David said. He reached for a light jacket from the closet in the hallway and followed Zach out the door.

Buddy placed her oversized Gap bag on the floor and used both hands to push the large, padded armchair closer to the side of the bed, but not so close that she was within touching distance of the dozing woman. Now that the others had left the room she could drop her show of bravery. Anything she knew about this disease—almost nothing—she'd learned from the TV, usually from skeptics sharing their fears.

Her eyes darted back and forth between the bed and the chair, measuring the distance between them. Hopefully she would be safe enough at this distance. Satisfied with the positioning of the chair, she lowered herself into its plumpness and waited for a sign that Leila was awake.

There was no movement from the bed except for the abrupt rise and fall of Leila's chest and shoulders. Her shallow breaths ending in raspy gurgles, and the quick inhale-exhale followed by a long period of stillness all added to Buddy's growing apprehension.

Not until they were well on their way to Bergen this morning had Mary revealed the true cause of Leila's illness. As Buddy recalled, Mary's convoluted retelling of David's phone call had mentioned pneumonia, dehydration, no appetite, and exhaustion.

Buddy rubbed her open palms against each other until the gathering moisture disappeared. The muscles in her neck tightened. She was keenly aware of the staleness of the air in the room and of inhaling the same air as the dying woman. Or worse. She might be inhaling the air Leila exhaled.

Steady, she chided herself. *Get a hold of yourself.*

Try as she might, Buddy found she couldn't stop the direction her thoughts were taking. *What if David has already been infected? And Tori. Have they both, unknowingly, been sentenced to a similar death? And where does that leave me? What about us?* The questions led her to admit for the first time that she still had lingering hopes of a future with David.

She realized her thoughts were not those of a woman of faith, but there was real fear rising within her. She had to get out of here.

Quickly. An unrestrained sob erupted from her throat. She balled her fist and stuffed it into her mouth before giving in to a full-blown panic attack. Her breaths came hard and fast for a time and then finally steadied as she gained control.

She took a slim, leather-bound Bible from her bag. She fanned the pages absently but did not open it. Instead she clasped it between her hands and began to pray for the woman who was passing away before her. When she realized she was whispering familiar phrases without her heart being in them, she stopped praying.

Buddy's eyes swept the room. It seemed functional but cold. No pictures on the walls or dresser, no candles, plants, doilies, or discarded clothes or toiletries. The room was masculine. Sterile.

"You came." The whispered words came from the bed.

Buddy smiled at the frail woman, but the smile did not reach her eyes. "I had to. You had a very unusual request."

"I wanted to ... meet you. You're ... very ... pretty." Leila punctuated her words with quick breaths, and Buddy held her response until she was sure the ailing woman had completed her sentence.

"Thank you. I wanted to meet you too. I've been curious about you, but I guess I don't have your courage."

"Courage? Not me. I just wanted to see who David ... who Tori would ... I just wanted to meet you. Say ... I'm sorry for taking David away. Try to set things right. I tricked him, you know. I didn't tell him about the baby. He never loved me. I loved Sly, but he didn't want me. Oh, I hurt so many."

Buddy attempted to calm Leila, who was becoming more agitated as she spoke, but she would have none of it.

"No, no, gotta tell you. David's a good man. Me, I'm no good. Nobody cares about me. Mom, Dad, Sly, David ... don't want me. Nobody, only Tori. Take care of my Tori. Please be good ... to my baby."

"Leila. Leila, listen. No." She held up her hand to stop Leila when she opened her mouth to speak. "It's my turn to talk. Are you listening? Good."

God, give me the words.

"First of all, you're wrong about David. David is not a good man. No—" She held up her hand again when Leila attempted to refute her statement. "My turn, remember?

"Do you know what this is?" She held out the Bible but continued without waiting for a response. "It's a Bible. It is God's written word. Now in here it says there is no good person on the face of this earth. That's right. Not me, not you, not David. The only difference between David and you is that David is *righteous*. That means he has acknowledged his sinfulness to God and accepted that Jesus died to pay the penalty for his sin. Now, when God looks at David, he sees Jesus. When David does good things, it's really Jesus working through David."

Buddy paused briefly. She hoped Leila was focused on her words. It was hard to know, but there was no more agitation.

"You say no one loves you? Well, you're really wrong on that point. Do you know the reason Jesus allowed himself to be crucified was because it was the only way for people like you and me to get to heaven? Do you think he would have done that for you if he didn't love you?"

"Why didn't he stop me from … from getting this?" The plaintive question held no arrogance.

"Oh, Leila." Buddy's eyes swept the ceiling in her search for a gentle answer. "I don't know why he's allowing you to go through this pain and suffering, but I do know he doesn't want you to face this alone. Look at all he's done. He sent David all the way to Miami to bring you back when you could have died alone. He gave Tori a father to love her and care for her. Who knows where she would have spent the rest of her life if David hadn't come along? He brought me here to talk with you and share his message of love. And I know that if you'll let him, he will be waiting for you in heaven with arms open wide."

Leila appeared to be wrestling with Buddy's words.

Lord, what more can I say? Give me the words.

"Let me read something to you." Leila flipped through the pages of her Bible. "It was written by a young shepherd boy. I like to think he had just rescued one of his sheep from falling into a pond or had just scared away a wolf, or something. I picture him sitting on a hillside watching his sheep grazing contentedly and comparing his care of the sheep to the way God takes care of him. It's a psalm, and by the way, the shepherd's name is David.

"'The Lord is my shepherd, I shall not want ...'" Buddy recited the familiar words, and as she repeated them, she gained reassurance for herself as well while she comforted David's wife. At the end of the passage, Buddy closed her eyes and allowed the comforting words of scripture to wash over them. She would not let her own words interfere.

"The 'valley of the shadow of death,'" Leila whispered. "I'm in the valley of the shadow of death. And I'm afraid. Help me, Rose; what do I do?" Leila's weakened voice intensified with each word and became mournful.

"You talk to him, Leila," Buddy continued, "just like you talked to me. Tell him what you're feeling. Tell him how sorry you are for what you've done. Ask for his forgiveness. Tell him you want to be with him in heaven."

Some hours later when David looked in on them, Buddy was reading another Psalm. Sensing another presence nearby, Buddy looked up and met David's eyes. From opposite sides of the room, their gazes locked. Time had not diminished their attraction for each other.

The emotions playing across his face released a flood of ambivalent feelings within Rose. She lowered her head and broke the contact.

David's heart contracted. He looked down at the pathetic, wan body of the woman who lay between them. For all he knew this was the only way she would have heard the message of Grace: flat on her back, without hope of recovery. This was probably her final opportunity to reserve a mansion in the kingdom. He could not deny her that.

"I was wondering if you needed anything," David said.

"No, we're fine," Buddy answered. "Well, maybe some music?" Although her face was turned toward him, her eyes evaded his. David inserted a CD into the player and left the room as the voice of a gospel singer filled the silence.

In the hallway he ran into Mary.

"You didn't forget about the party, did you?" she asked. "Tori's really looking forward to it. It'll be her first real party. And you haven't taken her shopping for a gift yet. You could do it this evening after supper. Zach and I will stay with Leila. Is Rhonda coming by? I don't know anything about changing an IV and that bag looks almost empty."

In her typical manner of speaking, Mary blurted out everything she wanted to say before pausing, expecting her listener to sort out the mass of information and respond.

It took David a few minutes. "I'd forgotten about the party." He stroked his brow with the tips of his fingers. Something didn't add up. How did Mary …? "How'd you find out about the party?"

"Tori told me."

"She told you? You mean she talked?" David's eyes opened in wonder. "What happened? Why did she stop talking to me?"

"Well, it seems that when things were at their bleakest in Miami, Leila told Tori they might not be able to stay together because she was ill and Children's Services would come for Tori and give her a nice home somewhere in the city with another family and lots of kids. So when you brought up the subject again she figured you'd be sending her away if her mother died. Did you say the angels would come to get her? Because, apparently, Leila used the same words, you know, the angels coming to get her, and the poor child connected both sets of angels, figured you'd send her back to Miami to lord knows what kind of foster family—you know how kids get things screwed up in their head." Mary took a quick breath and exhaled. "Anyway, we can talk about this later. Right now—"

"Right now I have to take her shopping before the mall closes. Gotcha." He leaned toward Mary and placed a kiss on the top of her hair. "I'll never be able to thank you enough. You're the best."

David felt a flutter of happiness for the first time in many days. It was a good time to take his daughter shopping.

Buddy was practically running out the door of David's home when his Jeep swung into its designated parking spot in the courtyard. The headlights swept across her and for a moment she hesitated, caught in its beams like a deer on the highway.

Turning away, she gathered the folds of her sweater around her, and with her head lowered against the rising wind, she deliberately ignored the occupants of the vehicle and rushed toward her father's car.

She couldn't bear to see David again. This day had already proven to be more difficult than she'd anticipated. Watching him in his own home living out the role of husband and father triggered a streak of jealousy within her that she thought had long been laid to rest. The care and attention he had directed toward his wife was exactly what she expected of him. It was no more than he owed the woman. It was no less than she deserved. Yet that very attention left Buddy feeling isolated and neglected.

To top it all, deep within her soul, she'd uncovered a fear of the illness that was slowly eating away at David's wife. As the odor of sickness and death permeated her senses, Buddy had found it difficult to quell the rising panic. Might the other members of the household succumb to the insidious disease? How could she be certain their health was intact? How could she feel sure that in spite of David's ministrations, in spite of Tori's hugs and kisses, that they would get away unscathed? How could she—

"Rose." David's voice reached her, but she ignored him. She dropped the bunch of keys and lost precious seconds when she stooped to retrieve them.

At least this trip to David's home had yielded one victory: she had helped Leila recognize her need for a Savior.

In the aftermath she had been confronted with her own reactions to this woman. Not just her physical condition, although she was aware that David might be susceptible to whatever was ending Leila's life. In her most secret, most despondent moments before Leila was found, she had hoped, even wished, for her death. So great was her love for David, so overpowering was her desire to be with him that in an unguarded moment, she had wished for Leila's death.

How could she have been so weak? It bothered her that she had so easily given in to her sinful desire. And so, while she prayed for Leila, she had also prayed for herself, and for the first time she completely gave over David's care and the outcome of their relationship to her Lord.

After the intensity of that purging, the last thing she needed was to be confronted again by the man she so dearly loved. In her emotionally drained state it would be too much to bear. She quickened her steps.

She was fumbling with the keys on the huge bunch when the insistent voice called out to her again.

"Rose! Wait." David opened the back door of his Jeep and unbuckled Tori's seatbelt without looking away from Buddy. "You're leaving? I thought you were staying through the weekend?"

"I was," Buddy tossed over her shoulder. "I changed my mind."

David slammed the door and hurried over to her.

"I'll be back Sunday to pick up Mom and Dad."

"Don't go." David's plaintive plea hung in the air.

Buddy slowed her steps and turned toward him, but her eyes remained downcast. "I can't stay. There's nothing here for me. There's no reason to stay."

David raised a hand as if to detain her and then let it fall it to his side. "I don't understand. We—"

"There's no 'we,' David, not now, and not in the future." Her voice became stern. Once and for all she had to make him understand. She could not be with him. "You have responsibilities here that don't include me. They can't include me! You're married. You have a daughter."

And you're probably harboring a time bomb inside your body!

The unspoken words threatened to burst from her lips, but she swallowed them. A picture of Leila's disease-ravaged body flashed before her. She turned, raising hurting, red-rimmed eyes to meet David's. She adored him, admired his devotion to his daughter and his loyalty to his dying wife. Why couldn't they have met at another time?

Despair threatened to choke her. Her fingers clenched and unclenched around the cold metal keys. She forced herself to swallow several times and followed the gulps with a deep, cleansing breath. With a tightening of her lips and an unyielding determination, she swiped the back of a hand across her brow.

"There can never be a 'we,' David," she whispered, her deliberate emphasis of each word masked her quivering voice. "I'm sorry."

Quickly, before she could change her mind, Buddy entered the car and turned over the engine. Steely determination guiding her every move, she drove away from the Bergen residence and out of David's life forever.

Chapter 26

David turned away from the sliver of autumn sunshine peeking through the bedroom window and tried to focus on the directions Rhonda was giving him. He had overheard her earlier conversation with the doctor and knew there had been no improvement in Leila's condition overnight. Not that they had expected any. Their only mission now was to make her as comfortable as they could and wait for the inevitable.

"Spencer will bring Tori home from Jin Soo's party when he picks up my Dana," Rhonda was explaining. The legs of her crisp, white uniform pants shirred against each other as she moved around the room, the sound contrasting with the deathly silence that engulfed them. "I'm going to hang out around here for the rest of the day," she added in a whisper, as if she was afraid of disturbing Leila's rest.

"Fine," David agreed. "She's awfully quiet?"

"Not as agitated as before, you mean?" Rhonda nodded as if she had some special insight. "She's one of the family now. She won't fight her passage into eternity. She'll have a peaceful passing, mark my words."

David wasn't paying much attention to Rhonda's analysis. He was feeling a bit uncomfortable sitting here, waiting for Leila to take her final breath. The whole episode was too much like his mother's passing: hushed voices, the nurse fidgeting with tubes and gadgets pretending to be helpful when, in fact, they both knew there was nothing more to be done.

A light tap sounded at the door. Before David could rise to see to the visitor, Charlie Lennox entered the room, closely followed by Mary and Zach. Each one glanced first at David, then at the heaving chest of the dying woman, and then back at David, their faces expressing concern, pity, and resignation.

David wanted them all gone. He wanted to leave too. The whole idea of death made him uneasy and this scene revived too many painful memories.

"Take my seat, Mary." David stuffed his hands in his pockets and propped himself against the dresser.

Rose should have been here. He missed her. He was angry with her. How could she walk away from him so casually when he needed her so desperately? "No *we*," she'd said. *Fine. If that's what she wants, so be it.* He would not allow himself to think of her again. Ever. Right now Leila needed him. He would do for her what Rose refused to do for him. He would stay with her. As uncomfortable as it was to be here, he would stay.

"David." Leila's feeble voice beckoned. He pushed himself away from the dresser and walked over to her. "Take care of Tori." Her voice was barely audible. Her unseeing eyes stared straight ahead.

"I will. I promise."

Leila was silent again. David felt the others expel their pent-up breaths and settle back into their former positions, waiting but not eager.

Rhonda was right. There was no sense of urgency in Leila. No agitation. She was at peace. Rose had done that for her. He had been with her all these months, but Rose had led her to the cross. He was grateful for that. Maybe it was the only reason she had come. *For Leila, not for me.*

"David?"

"I'm here."

"Tell my parents … tell them I'm sorry."

"I'll find them," David agreed without enthusiasm.

"Promise me. Promise me, David."

"I promise. I'll search for your parents and tell them … what you said."

"David?"

"I'm here, Leila."

"Tell them about Jesus. Make them listen."

Leila's plea made David immediately remorseful. He should have been more diligent in his efforts to find Leila's parents for her. As part of his renewed commitment to her he should have sought reconciliation with them. But he hadn't known she was dying, he argued with himself. He would do as she asked. He would find her parents, introduce them to their granddaughter, and tell them about Jesus.

"I promise," he whispered to Leila. And this time he meant it.

"Cold. So cold." Leila's whispered words quivered like her body.

David unfolded a light blanket and covered her. Then he climbed into bed beside her. Lying on top of the blanket, he aligned his body with hers and gently folded her in his arms, whispering soothing words of comfort as if to a child. Her shivering ceased.

Several moments later, surrounded by prayers for a peaceful end to a life fraught with adversity and affliction, Leila exhaled her final breath and was ushered into the arms of her Savior.

The Christmas season was yielding little joy for Buddy. For the first time since her teenage years, she did not go with the youth group when they dressed up in Dickens-type costumes and caroled throughout the streets of Cape May, and although she agreed to join them at a parent's home for hot chocolate and marshmallows afterward, by that time she was experiencing a raging headache and instead went to bed.

On Christmas morning Sam and Becky arrived at the Madsen home with their three squealing children and armfuls of presents. Buddy, dressed in a white, fleece sweat suit and a jaunty Santa Claus hat greeted them at the door with more enthusiasm than she was feeling. Her pounding headache had not let up during the night, and now her throat was beginning to hurt as well.

After breakfast, she joined the family for carol singing followed by Zach's reading of the Christmas Story. Then while the children were opening presents from their grandparents, Buddy served homemade eggnog to the adults. What she really wanted to do was climb into bed, cover her head with her pillow, and block out the sound of laughter, for as badly as her head and throat were hurting, her heart felt ten times worse. She missed David so much her heart would surely break. She couldn't go on like this. Their time apart had proved nothing except that she truly loved him. But he had not tried to contact her, and her one message to him, left with his secretary, had not been returned.

By dinnertime Buddy was ready to admit that her pain was caused by more than emotion. A fine coating of perspiration covered her forehead and upper lip, and her eyelids drooped. She was sporting a full-blown fever.

Mary ordered her to bed.

She went willingly.

At a show house three weeks later, Buddy peeled back the last bit of tape that secured the string of Christmas lights to the porch railing, rolled it between her fingers, and tossed the sticky ball into the snow-covered hedge below. She carefully lifted the long string of lights high above her head and backed away from the railing, taking extra care not to step on the tiny bulbs. Another Victorian Christmas season had ended, and, thankfully, there were no more chores but the undoing of the decorations.

She grasped the plug between thumb and forefinger and slowly wrapped the cord around her elbow. She carried the pile of tinsel, bulbs, and ornaments to their storage place. Her task completed, Buddy headed for her car. It was unusually cold for January, and she hugged her woolen sweater closer to her body, a spontaneous shiver setting her teeth chattering. She folded her lips between her teeth but the chattering continued, and her teeth nipped the edge of her bottom lip before she could move it out of the way.

Maybe it's just that my heart is frozen.

She grimaced at the maudlin thought and pushed it away before she succumbed to the sadness that lately was always close at hand.

She drove home.

Home. Her parents' home, not hers and David's. Never theirs, because she had sent him away and declared unequivocally that there was no future for them. How she wished she could retract the words, or at least temper them with a measure of kindness or understanding. But she had been angry, proud, and afraid. She had lashed out in fury and confusion, hurting him, but hurting herself more. And he hadn't called. Not once in the three months since his wife died had he contacted her or her family. His message was clear: he accepted her declaration.

It was over.

Stupid, stupid, stupid, she berated herself. Tears welled in her eyes but she blinked hard, determined to keep them at bay. It was too late for tears, too late for recriminations. She must make every effort to keep that stark reality in the forefront of her mind. It was over!

Chapter 27

When the harsh chill of winter gave way to the milder temperatures of spring, David made a pilgrimage to the home of his childhood. He had met with a realtor who agreed to place the property on the market as soon as David removed the furniture and memorabilia he wanted to keep for himself. It was a chore he did not relish, and he'd put it off for as long as he could.

Now, on this holiday weekend as he stood in the blacktop driveway, the house, left vacant since the death of his parents, seemed to call out to him to come home. He had paid a landscaping company to care for the lawn, hedges, and flowerbeds that had been his mother's pride and joy. Fresh mulch had been spread over the flowerbeds, and here and there purple and white hyacinths stood proudly against the backdrop of the fresh, brown mulch. It was still too early in the season to mow the lawn, and sprigs of onion grass, eager for a taste of the warming sun, interrupted the clean lines of the green-brown cushion of grass.

Still needing to delay his entry into the house, David decided to scope out the back of the property. On his way into the backyard he noticed that clumps of green and white Hostas had already begun to shoot through the shredded bark. He recalled how excited his mother used to be at the first sign of the leafy plants that lined the path to the backyard, and which grew thicker with each succeeding year. He closed his eyes, inhaled deeply, and savored the freshness of the unsullied morning air.

Through the stillness he picked out the chirping of newly hatched birds. In his mind's eye he saw his beloved mother taking down a wash-load of sheets and towels, closing her eyes as she sniffed each piece of laundry before folding them. He never did understand why she insisted on hanging out the sheets and towels while other items were thrown into the dryer.

Around the corner his eyes swept across the expanse of the yard. The landscapers had been thorough in their task. Broken concrete pavers had been removed and replaced. The wooden slats of the old garden swing were repaired and painted. Then he saw them: the pale pink, early blooming shrub roses with the delicate perfume that immediately reminded him of another Rose. Rose who he adored and who had become dearer to him even though they were apart. Rose who was sweet and unspoiled. Rose who understood love of family, and love of God, who walked away from him when her heart was breaking because it was the right thing to do.

As he circled around to the front of the home, he felt a desire to live there again. Although his last memories of living there were sad, he'd had many more pleasant experiences growing up in that home with two doting parents. He should bring Tori here. They would live here again and make it their home.

Could he restore its warmth and fill it with the laughter of children? His and Rose's? Would she have him? Would she reconsider?

God, give me one more chance to make things right between us and I promise I'll love her as she deserves to be loved.

Somehow he had to make her see that she had to take him back. Right now, before another day passed. Postponing his survey of the inside of the house and not allowing himself time to change his mind, he took Tori's hand, climbed into the car, and headed south.

He was maneuvering the Jeep down the off-ramp of the Cape May Bridge when new doubts built inside him. What if Rose turned him down? What if she had moved on with her life and found someone new? It had been five, no, six months since their last fateful conversation. He had spent six months rehashing that encounter, trying to remember her precise words and his response.

What had caused her to be so adamant? Could it be she really didn't love him? Had their separation enlightened her about her true feelings for him? What could have caused her to beat such a hasty retreat?

And now, here he was, gate-crashing the family gathering all because he couldn't forget her, couldn't erase the look of her, the scent of her, the taste of her. Without her, he was just downright lonely. He missed Rose something fierce. He missed her family, the children, their laughter, the caring.

Maybe he could just watch the family from across the street as they arrived for their annual reunion dinner. At least he assumed there would be a family reunion. Maybe he shouldn't …

He eased his foot from the gas pedal, and as the vehicle slowed, he turned the steering wheel hard and swung into the driveway of a deserted restaurant. What was he thinking!

"Are we there yet?" Tori's voice piped up from the backseat.

"Almost, honey. Just a few minutes more."

On the other hand, if he didn't make one last attempt to win her back he could consider her lost forever. And what better time to try to win her back than when the family was together and everyone was in a charitable mood? Besides, he'd already invested three hours in driving time, and Tori wouldn't be satisfied with watching from across the street.

His decision made, David slipped the Jeep into a forward gear and reentered the deserted highway.

Buddy stood on tiptoe and raised her arms to encircle Joe's neck. Grinning, her brother grasped her by the waist and spun her around before setting her back on her feet.

"So the last Madsen male is off the market," Buddy teased.

"I don't know if I would use those words exactly."

"Well, *I* would," Diandra, his fiancée, spoke up. She wiggled the fingers of her left hand where Joe had just placed a marquise-cut, solitaire diamond engagement ring. "You're taken, pal, and don't you forget it."

"Yes, ma'am." Joe chuckled and flashed a compliant salute at his future wife. He let go of Buddy to hug his fiancée.

As soon as she could graciously do so, Buddy excused herself from the jovial group. She felt the familiar, gloomy aura descending on her and wanted to escape before her mood cast a pall on the gathering. Lately, the bleakness was always close, ever since that fateful trip up north.

Ever since she'd walked away from David.

Retrieving a lightweight jacket from the hook by the back door, she slipped her arms into the sleeves and went outside where the air was as cold as her heart. The calendar said spring, but old man winter had returned for one last onslaught. Ignoring the deck chairs that had been brought out from their winter storage on the first warm day, Buddy lowered herself to the wooden steps and stuffed her hands into the pockets of her jacket, her shoulders hunched against the rising wind.

It should have been me!

The minute the mean-spirited thought seeped into her brain, she quickly repented of it. It wasn't that she envied Joe and Diandra their happiness. It was just that she wanted to share that same happiness with David. But she'd sent him away, and he'd stayed away. And she missed him.

The muted sounds of rising laughter mocked her self-imposed isolation. An indulgent tear slid from the corner of her eye and down her cheek. She impatiently dashed it away with one hand, but another quickly followed. This situation was of her own doing. She had to be the one to repair it or live with it forever.

Behind her, Buddy heard the door open and close. Padded footsteps drew closer. She'd anticipated her father's company. He was keenly aware of her frequent sad spells, and usually allowed her a few moments of solitude before coming over to cheer her up. She eased her body over to the far end of the step and made room for the man who lowered himself next to her.

He placed a hesitant arm around her shoulders and Buddy immediately leaned into his chest releasing her pent up tears.

David thought his heart would break all over again at the sound of Buddy's muffled sobs. It felt so good to hold her close. He hoped she was ready to accept him.

"I sincerely hope those tears are for me." David's warm breath disturbed Buddy's hair as he whispered the words. "No, please don't move away." His arm tightened around her, holding her fast. When she relaxed again, he gently lowered his chin to her head. "Just listen to what I have to say. Please.

"Six months ago, you told me we could never have a future together, and then you walked away. I wanted to come after you then, to make you see things my way. But I had another priority, one that wouldn't wait. After I'd taken care of that, I became very angry. Angry at you, angry at me, at the world, life, you name it.

"I'm not angry anymore, Rose. What I am, though, is in love with you. More in love with you than I was when you walked away.

"No, wait, let me finish," he said when Buddy struggled to speak. "I want to spend the rest of my life with you. I want us to be a family— you, me, and Tori. I love you. But if you tell me you still believe now as you did six months ago that there's no future for us, I promise to go away and never bother you again.

"I am satisfied that I did what God expected of me, and I did it in the spirit he expected. When I renounced you and went after Leila, I didn't know she was going to die. When she was discharged from the hospital, I expected her to completely recover. I brought her home with the intention of being her husband in the fullest sense. I knew it would be difficult, but I knew your dad was right. I had no choice. It was the honorable thing to do."

David lifted his chin from her hair and gently turned her face to his. "I love you, Rose, and as God is my witness, if you will have me, I will love you all my life. And if you tell me you cannot love me in the same way, I'll go back to where I came from and never bother you again."

He didn't have to wait long for her response. "Oh, David, if you go, I'll be so miserable. I realized a long time ago that I was wrong to say the things I did, and I wasn't sure you would forgive me. I love you, David, very, very much. And I want us to be together. Always."

"Does that mean you'll marry me?" He leaned away and stared into the eyes he loved. Her sadness had changed to the impish grin he remembered, though her eyes still glistened from her earlier bout of weeping.

"Are you asking?"

"I'm asking."

"Yes, David, I'll marry you. Just name the day." She leaned into him, and he folded his arms around her. Nothing and no one would come between them ever again.

Chapter 28

Two Weeks Later

As flattering to her athletic figure as the creamy-white suit was, Buddy Madsen wished propriety would have allowed her to dress in her favorite attire—jeans and a casual top—for the most meaningful event of her life. Well, maybe not jeans, but certainly something less confining than this tailored calf-length skirt, lilac shell, and Eton-style jacket.

Admittedly, she did cut a dashing figure in the Donna Karan outfit, but she was so happy that she wanted to shout and wave her arms in glee, and one just couldn't display such abandon while wearing a designer suit.

"Buddy, we have to leave now or we'll be late," her father shouted from the bottom of the stairs.

"Coming," she called back.

She performed a final twirl in front of the full-length mirror and then picked up the tiny Bible Mary had covered in white bridal satin and embellished with tiny white pearls and a posy of purple violets. She had chosen the violets over a white rosebud as a tribute to her absent sister. She traced the edges of a single petal of the silk flower with a newly manicured fingernail and lapsed into a pensive mood.

Violet, I wish you were here to share today with me. I miss you, little sister.

"Buddy, let's go!"

Buddy made a final sweeping glance around the room, her eyes resting briefly on the pieces of matching blue luggage that were packed and ready for their overnight stay in Philadelphia and early morning flight to Jamaica. A shiver of anticipation slid down her spine.

As she descended the stairs, Zach, Mary, and Tori gathered below to greet her. If Buddy harbored any lingering doubts about her attire, her family's stupefied gazes immediately put them to rest. She was a beautiful bride!

"Ready?" Zach asked.

"Am I ever," she replied, and she planted a kiss on his cheek. She immediately regretted giving in to her impulse when tears filled both their eyes. "Daddy, I love you so much." She lifted a tiny drop from the corner of her eye with a pinky. "But if we cry, I'll have to redo my makeup and then we'll *really* be late."

"Okay, honey." He smiled, blinking rapidly. "Still want to walk to church?"

"One last time? Wouldn't miss it, Dad."

As they had done most Sunday mornings since Buddy learned to walk, father and daughter strolled down Maple Drive on their way to Sunday services. The Cape May air was fresh and crisp, the salty taste of the Atlantic just barely discernible on the tips of the tongues of its residents. Clumps of yellow and white daffodils lined their path, their heads bobbing encouragement in the gentle spring breeze. Buddy's eyes drank in their beauty, her brain storing images that would not be readily available when she made her home with David away from this place. But, God willing, they would make many visits here, certainly at Easter for the Madsen family reunions.

Father and daughter entered the heavy paneled doors of the church, greeting familiar faces as they made their way to their usual seats. Zach and Buddy joined Mary, Tori, Sam, and his family in the second pew from the front. Behind them Roger, Anna Faye, and Susan, their eyes bright with excitement, leaned forward to whisper animated greetings.

"Where are the twins?" Buddy wanted to know.

"Downstairs in the nursery."

Mary whispered *shhh* and the visiting took on a quieter tone. Buddy searched the incoming faces for Joe, who had promised faithfully to have someone trade shifts with him at the firehouse. She offered up a quick petition that he would be able to join them and willingly left the outcome to her Lord.

At the stroke of eleven, the choir entered the loft followed by the music director and Pastor Miller. The invocation was given and the congregation was directed to join the choir in singing the chosen hymns and choruses, the words to which were projected on the wall. And so the regular Sunday morning worship service began.

As their voices swelled in song, Buddy felt a slight tug on the hem of her jacket. Looking down, she caught Tori crooking a finger at her. Buddy leaned closer.

"There's my daddy." Tori jabbed her finger in the direction of the pastor's study. Buddy glanced up at the same moment that David did. Their eyes met and held for the space of several heartbeats, and then he winked at her, and she looked away, for her own heart fluttered with such intensity that she was certain its cadence resounded around the room.

At the point in the service designated for the message, Pastor Miller moved to his place behind the podium.

"Friends," he began, "you're in for a treat today. We have a young man and a young woman who want to pledge their lives to each other today with all of you as their witnesses. David ... Rose ..." As he held out his hands to David and Buddy, they got up from their seats on either side of the aisle and came together before the pastor, Buddy nervously clutching the tiny Bible. Violet may not be at her side, but she would not be far from her heart on this special day.

The two met in the aisle and their hands reached toward each other for a touch of reassurance before they turned to face the pastor. A gleam of understanding swept through the congregation, accompanied by a ripple of *aaah* and excited tittering. Then all became quiet as the simple ceremony began.

"Dearly Beloved ..."

All eyes fastened on the handsome couple who stood erect, reciting their vows clearly and without hesitation. Joe Madsen arrived late and tiptoed past the ushers to an empty seat close to the back. In the row behind him, another latecomer slipped into an empty pew and adjusted her hat and sunglasses before settling down for the remainder of the ceremony.

"I now pronounce you husband and wife. You may kiss the bride."

The couple drew together and sealed their vows with a tender kiss as the congregation broke into applause. Starry eyed, they reluctantly pulled apart and turned to face their audience.

"Brothers and sisters, may I present Mr. and Mrs. David Willoughby," Pastor Miller said to the crowd. Again there was spontaneous applause, the loudest ovation emanating from the pews occupied by the Madsen family.

Buddy turned her head to whisper something to David. He responded to her words with an indulgent smile. He beckoned Tori with a toss of his head and the little girl quickly joined the couple at the front.

Now they were complete. In the eyes of God and man, two had become one and three had become a family. They had pledged their lives to each other forever. Till death do us part. Buddy knew it was a promise David would keep. She could be sure of that, because he had kept that same promise before, to another woman he had married, a woman he did not even love.

Her smiling eyes swept the crowd of familiar faces. Her gaze rested on Joe. He'd made it. Dear Joe, who meant so much to her, who had been her confidant and friend and defender in her teenage and early adult years. Joe, her champion and indulgent big brother.

Joe responded to the love in her eyes with a wide grin and a nod of approval and added his applause to that of the other guests. Holding her gaze as long as he could, he slid slowly along the pew until he was out of her sight. Buddy immediately transferred her gaze to the woman seated behind him who seemed vaguely familiar, although she couldn't quite recall where they might have met.

Buddy looked away. Then she looked back. As she did so, the woman reached up to her face and slowly lowered her sunglasses with one hand. She held out the other hand just under her chin, palm facing outward, her index and pinky fingers pointing straight up, her thumb stretching out at a right angle to her index finger.

Buddy recognized the sign: *I love you.*

And then she recognized the face: *Violet!*

She wanted desperately to move out of her husband's arm, run down the aisle, and fold her sister in her arms. She was back. The prodigal had returned to the fold and was here at her wedding. But how did she know? How could she?

Just as quickly as he had slid from her view, Joe slid back into his original seat, breaking the visual connection between Buddy and Violet. He held a silencing finger across his lips, another sign Buddy instantly recognized: don't tell.

The arm at her side nudged Buddy into awareness. David guided her to the seats Pastor Miller indicated. Buddy sat through the remainder of the service unaware of the proceedings. Someone made the announcements, the pastor gave the benediction, and the organist played the recessional. By the time Pastor Miller said the final amen, Violet had slipped out of the church and back into oblivion.

Where was she? Buddy kept her smile wide and her eyes bright, determined not to let her consternation show and put a damper on the day for David and her family. Inside she wept for her sister and for their loss. How she missed her!

Obviously Violet was not ready to face the family, but she had risked discovery for love of her sister. It was her gift to Buddy.

Turning to gaze at her husband, all the love she possessed making her face glow, she pledged her devotion anew. They would triumph over any trial that came their way because they had already withstood the tests of time and circumstances.

"Finally mine," David whispered.

"Truly, truly yours," she whispered back. "Very truly yours."

In the background the organist played the final hymn. Buddy laced her slender fingers through David's and felt his sturdy ones curl around hers. It was time to start their life together.

She could hardly wait.